Herbert Rosendorfer was born in 1934. He spent two years at the Academy of Fine Arts in Munich and then studied law. He became assistant judge to the public prosecutor in Bayreuth, an attorney and, since 1967, a judge at the district court of Munich.

He has contributed to numerous newspapers, magazines and anthologies and was responsible for music broadcasts on Radio Tyrol. He is the author of several works of fiction including *The Glass Bell*, *The Builder of the Ruins* and *The Shutdown Person*, and a collection of writing on art and politics, *Over the Kisses of the Earth.*

GERMAN SUITE

Herbert Rosendorfer

Translated by Arnold Pomerans

QUARTET BOOKS
LONDON MELBOURNE NEW YORK

First published in Great Britain by Quartet Books Limited 1979
A member of the Namara Group
27 Goodge Street, London W1P 1FD

First published as *Deutsche Suite* by Diogenes Verlag AG Zürich, 1972

ISBN 0 7043 2199 8

Printed in Great Britain by
Billing & Sons Limited, Guildford, London and Worcester

Typeset by Clerkenwell Graphics

Für Ellen

CONTENTS

FAMILY TREE I

LUDWIG I
d. 1868
King of Bavaria 1825-48

MAXIMILIAN II
d. 1864
King of Bavaria 1848-64
m. Princess Marie of Prussia

OTTO
d. 1867
King of the Hellenes
m. Princess Amalie of Oldenburg

LUITPOLD
d. 1912
Prince Regent of Bavaria from 1886
m. Archduchess Augusta
of Habsburg-Toscana

LUDWIG II
d. 1886
King of Bavaria 1864-86

OTTO I
d. 1886
so-called King of Bavaria
1886-1913

LUDWIG III
1845-1921
Prince Regent 1912-13
King of Bavaria from 1913
m. Archduchess Maria Theresia
of Habsburg-Este

RUPPRECHT I
1869-1955
King of Bavaria
m. (i) Duchess Gabriele from Bavaria
(ii) (morganatic) Frau Schumata

FRANZ
b. 1875
Prince of Bavaria

WOLFGANG
1879-1940
Prince of Bavaria
m. Princess Eudoxia
of Montenegro

HILDEGARD
1881-1958
Princess of Bavaria
m. Prince Moritz of Hesse-
Darmstadt (1847-1941)

JUDITH
b. 1909
Princesses of Hesse-Darmstadt
m.
(for the sake of form)
the painter
Stephan
Schneemoser

EMILIE
b. 1910
m. Crown Prince, later King,
later still
ex-King Luitpold

ECBERT
b. 1911
Prince of Hesse-
Darmstadt

Hermanfried
Schneemoser
b. 1931
cf. Family Tree II

LUITPOLD I
1901-58
King of Bavaria 1938-45
m. Princess Emilie of Hesse-Darmstadt

GARIBALD
b. 1904
Prince of Bavaria, 'the Counter'
m. Princess Laetitia Annunziata Murat

OTTO II
b. 1933
King of Bavaria from 1955

MAX ARNULPH
b. 1936
Prince of Bavaria

IGNAZ
b. 1932
Prince

HEZILO
b. 1936
Prince

LUDMAELIA
b. 1940
Princess

FAMILY TREE II

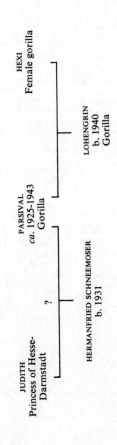

JUDITH
Princess of Hesse-
Darmstadt

?

HERMANFRIED SCHNEEMOSER
b. 1931

PARSIVAL
ca. 1925-1943
Gorilla

LOHENGRIN
b. 1940
Gorilla

HEXI
Female gorilla

Prelude

Though some people (and by no means the worst) still pas-
sionately blame Dr Schneemoser for all the misfortunes of the
Illustrious House, they are quite wrong. Passion has a
predilection for over-simplification. Part of the blame – and
one may argue just how much or how little – must certainly be
laid at Schneemoser's door. But things are much too en-
tangled to be unravelled by passion, let alone of the political
kind. Men may think they make history by the mere force of
their personalities, but often they do no more than spin
dreams while fate takes a hand and drops the odd grain of
mischief into the froth of their endeavours without bothering
about the misfortune she thus visits upon the innocent. Or
perhaps about the good fortune. Mankind has probably been
assigned a fixed quantum of happiness, which needless to say
does not stretch far enough. Were all of it shared evenly, too
little would fall to each to make any difference. That is why
man vies for happiness as he does for money. The more one
of us has of either, the less is left for the rest. For every man,
or capitalist of fortune, there is a whole army of unfortunates,
of out-of-luck proletarians so to speak. And the odd thing is
that the capitalists of fortune never weary of their lot. They
are either too short-sighted, or else shrug it off saying: 'Well,
that's life. It's impossible for all of us to be happy.'

But, and this brings us back to Dr Hermanfried Schneemoser, what precisely is happiness? Schneemoser himself

would have been the last person to ask. At most he would have said: 'Happiness is being Dr Hermanfried Schneemoser.' And not a few would have agreed with him.

On occasions, Mother Nature has been known to throw a spanner into the works of men's deepest strivings, and thus produced one or two very nasty pieces of work indeed. Fortunately, the vigilant mechanic of Normality is usually on hand to patch things up. But even the best of mechanics has been known to overlook things, whereupon Mother Nature quickly seizes her chance. Then woe betide mankind! Experts will tell you that such things happen far more often than is commonly believed.

The 1931 Munich *Fasching* was unusually gay. People could sense that the coming tide of national skulduggery was about to engulf them, not least because a growing number of nonentities dressed in diarrhoea-coloured uniforms were strutting about in the streets, yelling 'Germany awake!' and raising their arms in the fool's salute. By 1932, people would no longer dare to let themselves go; and the *Fasching* of 1933, as everyone knows, culminated in the blood-bath of 30 January. In 1931, however, people were still exuberant, and extraordinarily so.

It was during this *Fasching* that the lyrical poetess Lia Leander – dressed in black at the Ball and as Naked Truth in the 'Seerose' – recited patriotic speeches, and caused Ringelnatz to laugh so much that he reputedly swallowed a Virginia cigarette. The festivities took the form of a wake. The invitations were obituary notes, and the hall was draped with black crêpe and decorated with artificial skeletons and coffins. The coffins were genuine. An inventive photographer, one of Miss Leander's friends, had borrowed them from an honest coffin-maker, ostensibly for a series of deterrent advertisements on behalf of a firm of herbalists. When the coffins – twelve in all – were being unloaded outside the 'Seerose', a large crowd quickly gathered, wondering if an epidemic had started or a mass murderer had escaped. One of the coffins, containing an unclad girl bedecked with artificial flowers, was carried in at midnight by eight dwarfs dressed as hangmen. The girl rose out of the coffin and danced the 'Morning Gymnastics of a Dying Swan'. There was a legal sequel to this affair, for when the coffin-maker got wind of what had happened, he refused to take the offending coffin back and asked for compensation. He could not possibly resell the article, he claimed, because no decent corpse could be expected to rest in a coffin sullied by the very much alive presence of a naked young girl. In the end, the coffin-maker was awarded damages and agreed to repossess the (spiritually) impaired piece of woodwork.

Black was the official colour of the *Fasching* that year. An art student by the name of Gicki, fairly well known in Swabian circles, turned up in nothing but a broad black collar. Though Gicki had passed through a great many hands in her time, no one realized that she was a princess by birth.

Gicki was no beauty; perhaps she was not even good-looking. She was tall, had long dark hair, a slight double chin and the inturned nostrils of so many sexually athletic women. Gicki, it was said, made quantitative rather than qualitative demands of her lovers. She was, as many could have told you, not difficult to satisfy, provided it happened often enough. Quite a few of her partners confessed contritely that after their initial delight they had rushed out of her studio in Clements-Strasse, in fear of their lives. One who was able to give a particularly dramatic account of his encounter with Gicki was Iwan Hungertobler, later renowned as a painter of horses. Iwan, a Swiss despite his Christian name, had cast all the warnings of his friends to the wind, and, worse still, had grossly overestimated his staying powers. Although he came from a good family in Winterthur, Iwan had had no moral or aesthetic objections to Gicki's erotic demands. However, after two or three hours, he was suddenly alarmed by the terrifying thought that Gicki's frenzy might assume bestial proportions, that once fully satisfied she might bite off his head in the manner of certain locusts. Saying that he had a sudden call of nature he

3

jumped out of Gicki's bed at about 2 a.m. and took to his heels, even though Gicki, obviously forewarned by experience, had previously taken the precaution of hiding his shoes. When Gicki realized that despite the season (it all happened in March), Iwan had decamped in his bare feet, she ran after him, as was her wont. At the corner of Clements-Strasse and Viktoria-Strasse, Iwan chanced upon a policeman, who looked properly embarrassed when the fugitive asked to be protected from his relentless pursuer. The policeman could only turn helplessly to Gicki and ask: 'Have you any means of identification?' Iwan, who at once took advantage of this official interlude to seek safety in darkest Viktoria-Strasse, was still able to hear Gicki reply with great dignity: 'Don't be an ass. I am the Princess Judith.'

It was generally believed — and there were good reasons for trusting the accuracy of Hungertobler's account — that Gicki had simply tried to confound the policeman with her spurious claim to a title. Gicki herself, when asked about the incident, would laugh uproariously. She had no intention of revealing to all and sundry that she was, in fact, the Princess Judith of Hesse-Darmstadt, and as such a niece of the King of Bavaria.

Princess Gicki put in an appearance at the Black Festival in the 'Seerose', and loudly applauded the 'Morning Gymnastics of the Dying Swan' (envy was not in her nature) but as far as she was concerned the real fun did not start until a few hours later when she and several students left for the nearby Veterinary Institute, where the *Fasching* was being celebrated with even greater gusto. The happy mood of the veterinarians was unmistakable, and by the time Gicki arrived, a number of the younger students were already in an advanced state of drunken stupor. The Professor was asleep in an empty cage normally reserved for large dogs. Gicki and a lecturer disguised as a cockchafer withdrew to a couch in the Professor's rooms. They forgot to lock the door, and worse still the couch had castors. They were soon discovered, and several exultant students wheeled couch *cum* loving couple into the lecture theatre, amidst loud cries of humorous approbation. Once inside, a student choir formed a circle round the couch and accompanied the inadequate efforts of the (highly unpopular) lecturer with loud calls of 'Heave-ho!' The lecturer gave up in a fit of fury. The happy mood was now rapidly reaching a climax. Gicki remained on the couch for the rest of the festivities. The students worked out a points system for evaluating their efforts on Gicki's behalf. Two totally impartial referees handed out marks and noted the results on the blackboard. (Next day, the Professor stared foolishly at the complicated calculations.) There was, however, no clear victory; no one could be declared champion of the night since towards the end of the proceedings someone had the bright idea of fetching Parsival. Parsival was a tubercular gorilla from Hellabrunn Zoo, who had been admitted to the Veterinary Institute for observation. For experts, and even for the younger students, it was mere child's play to work the gorilla into, let us say, the right mood. Gicki was enthusiastic, even though Parsival did no more than was expected of him.

Later, the Princess Judith of Hesse zu Darmstadt und Bei Rhein, declared solemnly that she had mistaken Parsival for a veterinarian in fancy dress. It proved impossible to get to the bottom of the affair, as all concerned explained — with more or less justification — that they had been stoned out of their minds, and Parsival wisely kept his own counsel.

In November 1931, when Gicki gave birth to a son, Hermanfried by name, the child's looks were not such as to suggest that Parsival or any other ape had been the child's sole father. As we have said, Mother Nature is quite capable of producing the odd nasty piece of work all of her own accord. No one can say why; perhaps it is just a sign of her high spirits. This may explain why people speak of the 'tricks of nature'.

By the time Hermanfried was born, the waves of panic that had lapped round the House of Hesse-Darmstadt had barely receded. In the summer of 1931, the first clear signs of Gicki's pregnancy had laid the entire family low with mortal terror. Gicki's father, Moritz, Prince of Hesse-

Darmstadt and brother of the last Grand Duke deposed in 1918, heard the news while taking a glass of Heddesheimer Honigberg and reading the *Müncher Neueste Nachrichten* on the veranda of his villa in Bogenhausen one mild summer's day (it had been raining until noon, and the sun had not broken through until 4 p.m.). When he had taken it all in, the paper dropped from his hands, and for four and a half days he was totally unable to read on. In fact, he stopped moving altogether. At night he had to be carried to his bed where, as far as others could tell, he lay perfectly still but with his eyes open, and uttered not a word. There were grave fears for his sanity.

Gicki's mother, the Princess Hildegard, bore the news with greater composure. Only when Gicki, after an embarrassing inquisition into the identity of the child's father, had confessed her affair with the ape, did the normally sedate rooms of the villa resound with the old lady's piercing wails. In vain the servants attempted to convey their mistress to bed wrapped up in wet sheets — she kept rushing out of the house and knocking her head against various trees in the park. The locals — and old Bogenhausers remember it to this day — crowded round the gate following the strange and mysterious goings-on with much solemn head-shaking. In the end, Princess Hildegard had to be tied to her bed, whence her wails continued unabated.

The father stared gloomily at his daughter's burgeoning belly, slowly wagging his head. 'No!' he exclaimed, softly. 'No!'

But this untoward event — did I say untoward? how frightfully inadequate is the expression: this diabolic, unspeakable, soul-shattering event — refused to be argued away. At last, Prince Moritz decided that the only solution was mass suicide by the entire family. However, out of respect for his strict Catholic wife — Princess Hildegard was a sister of King Rupprecht, the reigning monarch of Bavaria —he asked for a Papal dispensation before taking this drastic step. In the event, Cardinal Faulhaber demurred, and advised an abortion. Unfortunately it was much too late.

And so — with time pressing hard — the family was forced to face things squarely. The head of the House of Hesse-Darmstadt, Prince Moritz's brother, the ex-Grand-Duke Ernst Ludwig, was summoned to Munich. The Prince's brother-in-law, King Rupprecht, also turned up in Bogenhausen, as did the court lawyer, Counsellor Dr von Scheuchenzuber.

All present were agreed that Princess Judith should disappear from Munich until after the birth. Their choice fell on Switzerland, which had always proved accommodating in cases of this kind. Unfortunately, the birth of the more than ill-bred scion of the Grand-Ducal House in Vevey or Locarno would do nothing to alter the unpalatable legal fact — laid down in a recent decision by the Reich Supreme Court as conveyed by Dr von Scheuchenzuber — that the bastard would bear the name of a Prince or Princess of Hess.

'A nephew of the victor of Fehrbellin,' sighed the ex-Grand-Duke, 'and a half-a . . .'

'Shush!' said Prince Moritz, and pointed to his wife, who was still in need of special care and consideration.

'Ever since 1919,' Counsellor Scheuchenzuber went on to explain, 'nobiliary predicates have been treated as part of the surname. Even here in Bavaria, the only federal state to have remained a monarchy, the legal position is identical. Since, moreover, an illegitimate child . . .'

'But,' said the ex-Grand-Duke, 'if he happens to be a half-a . . .'

'Shush,' Prince Moritz said again.

'What was the point of my coming to Munich, if I'm not allowed to open my mouth,' muttered the ex-Grand-Duke.

'. . . since, moreover, an illegitimate child bears the name of its mother, it is legally certain this child will be known as a Prince or Princess of Hesse zu Darmstadt und Bei Rhein etc. etc.'

'May I,' said the ex-Grand-Duke Ernst Ludwig, now deeply offended, 'may I at least point out that I, for my part, find this prospect altogether revolting?'

'Prince or Princess, indeed,' wheezed King Rupprecht.

7

'What if she has twins?'

Princess Hildegard gave a whistling sound and swooned.

'There you are,' shouted Prince Moritz, now red with anger and rattling his goitre, 'that's what comes of your stupid jokes!' And he rang for the servants.

'What jokes?' said the King indignantly, as soon as Princess Hildegard had been carried out and things had quietened down a bit.

'Pshaw!' hissed Prince Moritz, and licked the sweat from his upper lip. 'Pshaw!'

'May I say half-ape at long last?' ex-Grand-Duke Ludwig asked huffily.

Dr von Scheuchenzuber saw that it was up to him to prevent undignified scenes in this assembly of exalted personages, and quickly delivered himself of a pointedly dry lecture: 'I do not say that there is absolutely no legal way out. To begin with, you can have the child adopted. Or, if it should displease you to have it bear the noble title of a Prince or Princess respectively of Hesse-Darmstadt and Bei Rhein etc. etc., even during the possibly very brief interval before the adoption (which could be arranged within just a few hours of birth), you might consider having the child's mother adopted. In that case, of course, the child's mother would have ceased to be a member of the noble and venerable House of Hesse etc. etc. . . . .'

'Aha!' King Rupprecht of Bavaria wheezed through his nose.

'What precisely do you mean by that, Scheuchenzuber?' the ex-Grand-Duke and Prince Moritz asked simultaneously.

'Aha!' repeated King Rupprecht, 'Prince or Princess respectively!'

'Half-ape,' said the ex-Grand-Duke.

The Counsellor continued quickly and loudly: ' . . . would have ceased to be a member of the most Illustrious House and have lost all the civil, and also . . .' he raised his index finger and nimbly rotated his pince-nez through the air, ' . . . and also all the hereditary rights consequent thereupon!'

'Out of the question,' said Prince Moritz, drawing his now

wet handkerchief across his face and goitre. 'Gicki is my daughter, come what may. If anyone has to be adopted, it will have to be the child.'

'Not on your life,' said the ex-Grand-Duke cuttingly. 'No half-ape must be allowed to remain a Prince of Hesse for even one second. I repeat, not for one second . . .'

'Aha!' snuffled King Rupprecht, 'or Princess respectively.'

'I am not given to quibbling,' the ex-Grand-Duke continued, 'but I am a stickler for principles. No chimpanzee must befoul the noble name of the Lion of Hesse. Not for one second!'

'Gorilla,' said King Rupprecht, 'not chimpanzee.'

'The most fitting solution,' said Dr von Scheuchenzuber, catching his pince-nez in orbit with a practised hand and glancing at the legal memorandum spread out in front of him, 'is to find the Princess a husband. In that case, the child, regardless of its factual, that is its biological father, will, in law, be born as the legitimate offspring of the Princess's legal husband. Even if the marriage were dissolved soon afterwards, the child would – legally speaking – remain the undisputed offspring of the husband, and would have no claims whatsoever to the name of Hesse, let alone to the throne.'

'I should hope not,' said the ex-Grand-Duke. 'Just fancy, a half-ape on the throne of Philip the Magnanimous!'

'If I hear you say half-ape once more,' roared Prince Moritz, springing to his feet, 'just once more . . .'

'Chimpanzee,' said the ex-Grand-Duke Ernst Ludwig. 'Half-chimpanzee! On the throne of Philip the Magnanimous!'

'That would be an extraordinarily improbable and purely hypothetical event,' Dr von Scheuchenzuber put in soothingly.

'I don't give a damn,' said the ex-Grand-Duke. 'I am concerned with the principle of the thing.'

'Gorilla,' wheezed King Rupprecht. 'Not chimpanzee. I've told you before.'

At this point, Prince Moritz could contain his feelings no longer. The tears poured down over the yellowish bags under his eyes and mingled with the drops of sweat on his cheeks and chin. 'Do what you like,' he sobbed, 'do what you like.' He pushed his now dripping handkerchief into his collar, which was of an inordinately large size to accommodate his goitre, and ran it round his neck. He opened and shut his mouth a few times but only managed a groan, and then rushed out of the room.

King Rupprecht and the ex-Grand-Duke at once agreed to adopt the plan Counsellor von Scheuchenzuber had called the most fitting, namely to give Princess Judith away in marriage as quickly and secretly as possible.

'All that's left, then, is to select a husband,' said von Scheuchenzuber and closed his file.

'Look here, Scheuchenzuber,' said the King. 'You are a bachelor, aren't you?'

The Counsellor turned pale. 'Your Majesty! My Scheuchenzuber forebears would turn in their graves!'

'Don't take on so, Scheuchenzuber,' said the King, 'I was only having a little joke.'

The Counsellor did his best to pull his lips apart so as to produce a dutiful laugh. In this he failed miserably.

'Some domestic, then,' said the ex-Grand-Duke.

'Better not,' wheezed the King. 'If the father hadn't been a gorilla, I'd have agreed. But in the circumstances, you never can tell. Do you follow me? Far better the whole business is conducted as far away from home as possible. Far better, in every respect.'

'We shall find someone, Your Majesty, never you fear,' said Dr von Scheuchenzuber, who felt he was not yet out of the wood, 'I shall see to it myself.'

'Good chap, Scheuchenzuber,' said King Rupprecht.

'A half-ape,' said the ex-Grand-Duke, and blinked thoughtfully at the heraldic tapestry which showed the Lion of Hesse, though debruised by ten bars, standing proud and inordinately rampant.

'At least,' said Dr von Scheuchenzuber, showing that he had read the signs of the times, 'at least, he is not a Jew,'

During the following weeks Scheuchenzuber searched high and low for a suitable husband, inspired in his endeavours by the King's occasional jocular remarks that he was still not at all sure it would be a bad idea if Scheuchenzuber filled the part himself.

'But, Your Majesty! . . .' Scheuchenzuber would exclaim, aghast.

The King invariably replied: 'Good chap, Scheuchenzuber. Good chap. I was only joking.' But Scheuchenzuber knew his Wittelsbachs and had observed far too often what strange effects royal jokes can have, even in the twentieth century.

'Absolutism is far from finished,' he would muse to himself, as was his philosophical wont. 'At best it's glossed over with constitutional oils. And the same oils also blot out what few larks have joined in the dawn chorus of freedom.'

He was close to saving his skin by marrying his housekeeper — in his old age and with a heavy heart — when the name of Schneemoser was first mooted.

Stephan Schneemoser, who had adopted the nom-de-plume of Ysthvan Mardochai, came from Lengries and was a singularly untalented painter. Since he was lazy as well — which is strikingly uncharacteristic of untalented artists — and completely feckless, he was more than willing to accept the offered monthly remittance (offered in lieu of the other benefits and privileges which might normally have been expected to accompany such a marriage contract) and marry the Princess, whom it so happened he already knew — though not as such.

Things went off almost without a hitch. Even before the civil ceremony, the bridegroom was completely inebriated. Dr von Scheuchenzuber had seen to that, 'just in case'. A particularly reliable and loyal town clerk (member of the Yodelling Club 'Alpine Garland' and himself the illegitimate son of Prince Arnulph of Bavaria) betook himself to Bogenhausen, dressed with deliberate informality, to officiate as registrar. The bridegroom, too, had been instructed to turn up in a simple lounge suit, so as not to draw attention to himself. (Prince Moritz had even suggested that, for better disguise, Schneemoser should appear in overalls and ask loudly about the faulty wires outside the main door.

However, Dr von Scheuchenzuber thought this was going too far, and might cause unnecessary complications. In the end, it was left at the lounge suit.

Partly so as to avoid a further sensation — the villa seemed besieged by reporters — and partly to demonstrate their general displeasure, members of the Royal House of Wittelsbach and also of the bride's paternal House of Hesse, stayed away from the ceremony, thus ensuring that no dynastic significance would be attached to it. The witnesses were recruited from among the household staff, who were told about it just before the registrar arrived. Needless to say, the bridegroom had been enjoined to leave all family and friends behind.

The church ceremony was conducted by Princess Hildegard's confessor, Father Polycarp Queri, in the sacristy of the Theatine Church. News of it must somehow have leaked out, for when the party arrived, they found a reporter and a photographer lurking outside. Dr von Scheuchenzuber spotted the danger, but too late. Before the wedding party could beat a hasty retreat into the church — the inebriated bridegroom proved a great obstacle to this manoeuvre — and file out again through the back of the Theatine Cloisters, the photographer had managed to get in a few good shots, and next day a moving story about the romance of the art-loving princess and the poor artist graced the paper's front page.

The King thereupon informed the hapless Scheuchenzuber that if there were any further encroachments by nosy reporters, he would receive, not the expected decoration, but a public trouncing.

Scheuchenzuber responded to these unexpected difficulties with great aplomb. Instead of issuing a denial, which, as he well knew, would only encourage the reporters to redouble their efforts, he had the Chamberlain's Office issue a press release confirming the story of the love match. Since the Princess was despatched to Switzerland post haste, and as even the most persistent reporter could get nothing out of Ysthvan Mardochai for several weeks (thanks to a generous gratuity he had received on his wedding day, Yshthvan was revelling in a permanent state of total intoxication), the whole affair was quickly forgotten. Schneemoser-Mardochai nevertheless had a further windfall in the sale of a few of his canvases — he was never too drunk to keep his eye on the main chance. One painting, Schneemoser insisted, had to be sent to Prince Moritz's villa as a special gift to the bride. 'I, too, am not devoid of honour,' he wrote on the accompanying card, 'albeit of an artistic kind.'

The painting was entitled 'Three Concert Grands in an Arcadian Landscape with Crocodiles'. Prince Moritz, filled with grudging respect for his — Lord help us — son-in-law, on whom, incidentally, he had never set eyes, had the picture framed and hung in the conservatory.

'You never can tell,' said Prince Moritz, 'believe me, you never can tell.'

'A Michelangelo,' said King Rupprecht when he saw the picture during one of his visits, 'a Michelangelo, he certainly is not.'

Stephan Schneemoser alias Ysthvan Mardochai never saw his wife again. He drew his monthly cheque with great punctuality and, if alive, must be drawing it to this day — despite the fact that the marriage was dissolved soon after the birth of little Hermanfried Schneemoser.

Many, many years later, long after the war, when Stephan Schneemoser was approaching his fiftieth birthday, the Gicki affair was to cause him a great deal of heartbreak. Schneemoser, who was spending some time in Venice, met a young, beautiful and well-born nun under unusually adventurous circumstances. The nun fell desperately in love with him, and they planned to elope. Schneemoser planned to steal into the nunnery disguised as a hermit, but at the last moment he had second thoughts. Needless to say he had not told the beautiful and pious nun that, though legally divorced, he had been married in church and was therefore not free to lead her to the altar. Perhaps Schneemoser took an exaggerated view of the girl's piety: she might very well have brushed aside such minor canonical and moral

13

scruples. But Schneemoser was genuinely afraid that, one day, he would have to confess to her that they could never make a faithful Christain couple enjoying the blessings of Mother Church. He feared a catastrophic reaction, and was also concerned not to jeopardize his regular allowance. Let it be said in Schneemoser's defence, however, that the pecuniary consideration was not the main cause of his qualms and final act of renunciation. He was caught in a terrible dilemma; and, on the night of the elopement that never was, summoned up all his remaining strength and flung himself aboard the *Gondoliere* express. While the poor novice sat anxiously counting the minutes, the express thundered through the Inn Valley. Schneemoser felt the clatter of the wheels was not nearly loud enough to drown the clamour of his breaking heart. Back in Munich, he began to age quickly, and then fell seriously ill. He tossed about in the grip of feverish fantasies, though in his more lucid moments he tried to persuade himself, time and again, that his decision had been the only right and proper one. But that, as they say, is quite another story — one, incidentally, that unfolded at a time when Schneemoser junior, Stephan's putative son, was preparing to take the limelight.

Allemande

On 2 April 1933 a greetings telegram from the Reich President carried the following message:

PATRIOTIC FELICITATIONS ON WONDERFUL NEWS OF
ROYAL GIRTH STOP MAY THE PRINCE'S GERMAN
SENTIMENTS LEAD THE BAVARIAN PEOPLE INTO THE
THIRD MILLENNIUM STOP HEIL AND BLESSINGS UPON
HIS CRADLE STOP HINDENBURG

The Pope sent apostolic blessings, and the Nymphenburg visitor's book was signed by Karl Valentin and Karl Ludwig Troost, among many others. The 'girth' in the telegram was, by the way, a spelling error. It was never discovered whether the mistake was made in Munich during the dictation of the telegram or in Berlin when it was handed in at the post office, or whether it had crept into the President's own draft. In any case, at the time no one could have had the least inkling of the distressing implications.

Biologically speaking, the Prince was an ordinary, healthy child weighing some thirteen pounds. There were signs that he would be fair, and as far as anyone could tell, he had blue eyes, but then all babies do. For the rest, the boy born on 2 April 1933 in the Crown Prince's suite at Nymphenburg Castle was anything but ordinary or normal. He was the first-born son of the then thirty-two-year-old Crown Prince Luitpold of Bavaria and his spouse, Crown-Princess Emilie, née Emilie, Princess of Hesse-Darmstadt, and hence the oldest grandson of His Majesty, King Rupprecht I, who had reigned happily over Bavaria since 1921. As the Bavarian monarchy had weathered the autumn tempest of 1918, which had swept away all other German crowns like so many dry leaves, it was generally believed that nothing was likely to upset the *status quo* in the foreseeable future and the new-born prince would one day wield the sceptre over blessed Bavaria and the equally blessed Palatinate.

Alas, the kind of sceptre-wielding that fell to King Rupprecht in 1933, had ceased to be a simple affair. Even in the nineteenth century, though many Bavarian kings had waved their sceptres about with might and main, Parliament had done as it pleased. King Ludwig I had bandied his sceptre so violently that, in the end, the crown had dropped from his head. Ludwig II, for his part, had done so much sceptre-waving that he ended up in one of Dr Gudden's favourite straitjackets. It may well be that it was the much more subtle form of monarchism practised with such skill by Luitpold, the beloved Prince Regent (who refused the title of King even though he was the *de facto* ruler of Bavaria), that ensured the survival of the crown during the revolution of 1918-19 . . . King Ludwig III, the Prince Regent's son, was something of a bourgeois, not to say petit-bourgeois, prince. An ineffectual person of considerable girth (was it this hereditary taint that would have such baleful effects on the Prince born in 1933?), he left Munich for several weeks during the 1918 troubles but only left Bavaria for a mere four days. People still tell you that the Bavarian revolutionaries made their revolution purely out of respect for the ancestral House. Toller and Eisner, they say, felt good King Ludwig III would have been deeply offended had his country alone been left without a revolution, thus falling behind the rest of Germany. Maybe and maybe not — as Ludwig Thoma put it so succinctly. At any rate, the King returned to his capital and, under the Schrobenhauser Treaty with the Reich Government of 12 December 1919, was appointed Reichskommissar for Bavaria and the Palatinate. By this

Treaty, the King was constitutionally invested with the prerogative of a Prince Regent — a title that filled every true Bavarian revolutionary with a rush of patriotic fervour — and with all the personal privileges of the former King. Ludwig III was therefore King and commoner all at once — an extremely delicate state of disequilibrium that was almost beyond human comprehension, and at any rate proof against every revolutionary assault.

When Ludwig III died in 1921, his eldest son Rupprecht became his official 'successor'. A decree signed by Reich President Ebert on 22 April 1923 granted Rupprecht the *personal* right to bear the title of King of Bavaria, Duke of Franconis, Count Palatinate of Bei Rhein etc. etc., the wider constitutional question being left wide open. The gap was never closed, and advisedly so, though a handwritten document issued by a later Reich President (none other than von Hindenburg) on 1 January 1929 contained the telling phrase that the 'rights currently vested in the King of Bavaria in no way encroach upon the Constitution of the Reich'. For the rest, Bavaria could do as she pleased. Since the King enjoyed more or less the same privileges as his predecessor, this document was greeted by loyal Bavarians — and which Bavarian is not loyal to his King — as a *de facto* recognition by the Reich of monarchic rule. The Bavarian Prime Minister, Heinrich Held, and the Archbishop of Munich and Freising, Cardinal von Faulhaber, declared jointly on 18 May 1929 at a banquet on King Rupprecht's sixtieth birthday — hence not so much officially as explicitly — that there was no reason to 'assume that any constitutional changes had occurred in 1918 or 1919'.

When Crown Prince Luitpold soon afterward married Emilie, the daughter of Prince Moritz of Hesse-Darmstadt, then resident in Munich, the nation celebrated the great event with much patriotic pomp and circumstance. The conversion, in 1930, of the new Crown Princess to the Catholic faith ('in all sincerity' as a Court Bulletin put it) took place on *Wiesensonntag*, the Sunday marking the beginning of the *Oktober Fest*, with the joyful participation of the people, joyful not least because twenty oxen — the number corresponding to His Royal Highness's age — were roasted and shared out amongst the jubilant masses, who washed it all down with some 450 gallons of free beer.

On 2 April 1933, the day on which Prince Otto was born, the jubilation of the Bavarians and the nation's protestations of love for the ancestral House were no less noisy, though the King's position had by then become extremely delicate thanks to Hitler's so-called accession to power. Barely had the 'Coalition Government of National Unity' been sworn in — it included no more than four Nazis: Hitler, Frick, Göring and Goebbels, all the rest being non-party men, except for Hugenberg of the Nationalist Party and Seldte of the 'Stahlhelm' — than the Nazis reeled off so many new laws and decrees that the whole country began to feel giddy. 'I would never have believed that typewriters could work at such speed,' exclaimed King Rupprecht. 'For somehow or other these arsewipers must all have been typed out, unless of course Hitler secretes them like snot.'

On 4 February 1933, a week or so after the 'accession to power', came the 'Decree for the Protection of the German People', by which every basic democratic right was trampled underfoot. Just over two weeks later, on 27 February, the Reichstag caught fire. Next day came the 'Decree for the Protection of the People and State' and martial law. That state of affairs was to last for twelve long years. On 9 March, a Reichskommissar was appointed over Bavaria.

Reichskommissars, so they said, were meant to carry out 'such definite, and generally temporary, duties as could not be performed by the existing authorities'. The reader may remember that the sole constitutional rights vested in Rupprecht were those bestowed upon his father when the latter was made a Reichskommissar. It had always been an open question whether the late Ludwig III had been a *de facto* Reichskommissar or whether he was one *de jure*, by virtue of his royal prerogatives. In March 1933, however, Rupprecht saw fit to conclude from the appointment of a new Reichs-kommissar that the Nazis had decided to recognize the

Kingdom of Bavaria, not only *de facto* but also *de jure*.

'There is no doubt at all,' said our friend, Counsellor-at-Law Dr von Scheuchenzuber, 'that Your Majesty has been acting in the capacity of a Reichskommissar all along. In the view of the Reich Government, I hasten to add. In terms of the Bavarian Constitution, Your Majesty governs solely by virtue of Your Majesty's hereditary office. Well then, if a new Reichskommissar is appointed and Your Majesty — I hope Your Majesty will forgive the expression — has not been forced to abdicate, we must take it that Your Majesty is not a Reichskommissar, but has merely performed a Reichskommissar's duties. Hence the new appointment in no way restricts Your Majesty's powers. On the contrary it shows that the Reich has officially recognized Your Majesty's royal prerogatives.'

'May the Lord lend a kindly ear to your fine speech,' murmured the King.

'Incidentally, the new Reichskommissar is none other than my old friend von Epp,' the Counsellor-at-Law added. 'Your Majesty may remember Franz, Baron von Epp. He commanded Your Majesty's Own Infantry Regiment during the war, and in 1919 led the Volunteer Corps bearing his name against the Communists in Munich. Epp is a Munich man born and bred.'

'Quite so, quite so,' grunted the King, 'an absolute shithouse of a man.'

On 10 March, Baron von Epp came down from Berlin and at once paid his humble respects to the King. The Baron was a pensionable blockhead pushing seventy. That Hitler had appointed him of all people was a merciful blunder. But though Epp posed no real threat to Bavaria's independence, court circles took a rather gloomy view of the impending encounter. In the event, the audience lasted for more than an hour, though a mere twenty minutes had originally been set aside for the purpose. His Majesty and the Reichskommissar had an animated discussion about a problem that affected both of them most profoundly: the problem of their several haemmorrhoids.

'The Nazis,' the King later confided to his Chamberlain, Count Arco-Valley, 'the Nazis aren't so bad after all.'

Many others were saying the same thing at the time. In any case, the Royal piles had clearly saved the Wittelsbach throne, at least for the time being. For although the ensuing 'Second Unification of the Länder with the Reich' of 7 April 1933 set severe limits to Bavaria's independence, it nevertheless glossed over the problem of the Bavarian constitution. After their hectic activities in the spring of 1933, the Nazis left the inhabitants of Bavaria in relative peace, while they busily accumulated private fortunes by robbing alien and inferior races, and devoted what little time they had left to internal intrigues. The hope, however, that they would finish each other off in the process was never fulfilled — there were clearly too many of them for that.

The birth of the prince on 2 April 1933 had been perfectly normal. The first danger signals did not appear until a few years later, although during the christening both god-fathers, the Princes Wolfgang and Georg of Bavaria (deputizing for Pope Pius XI, Hitler, Hindenburg and the Archduke Otto of Habsburg) had to take rather quick turns at holding the unusually ponderous infant. Cardinal Faulhaber, who had received the child and the noble company at the door of the royal chapel in Nymphenburg with a smart 'Heil Hitler!' (he was then writing his *Judaism, Christianity and Germanism*) christened the boy: Otto Ferdinand Maria Rupprecht Moritz Pius Achilles Paul Adolf Wolfgang Georg Tassilo Ludwig Deodatus Valentin.

The choice of Christian names, and particularly of the first, was of the greatest importance, seeing that the boy, as the oldest son of the Crown Prince, was destined to wear the Bavarian crown. Now, as everyone knows, the more recent Wittelsbachs had atrocious bad luck with the name of their founding father. Prince Otto of Bavaria, the second son of Ludwig I, cut a very poor figure as the elected King of the Hellenes — and was in the end unceremoniously thrown out.

His nephew — unhappy Prince Otto, as people called him — and the younger brother and successor of Bavaria's fabled Ludwig II, proved so debilitated by his alleged 'melancholy' that he was forced to abdicate in favour of his uncle Luitpold, the extremely popular Prince Regent. King Otto himself was kept like a caged animal in Fürstenried Castle near Munich, and over the years that he spent in a straitjacket, did actually fall victim to melancholy — in the beginning, people said in whispers, he had not been all that fatuous, certainly no more so than other princes. There had been fears, however, that he might follow in the footsteps of his brother Ludwig, building an even larger number of castles and running up still greater debts. This was the real reason why Luitpold had handed the otherwise delightful King over to a set of brutal mental nurses, men who with the Prince Regent's tacit consent did their worst to the hapless King. For more than thirty years, King Otto was kept under lock and key, a form of treatment which has been known to destroy far less sensitive souls. Finally the poor man, forbidden to speak to anybody, even lost the power of speech. From time to time, he would beg for permission to be let out into the park. This he did by scratching against the locked doors of his prison with a walking stick. His jailers demurred, and the scratches on the door can still be seen by any visitor to Fürstenried Castle, and are perhaps the most moving monument to the House of Wittelsbach. In 1916, death released King Otto I from his misery, and no Bavarian prince had borne the name of Otto ever since — be it out of supersitition or bad conscience. It was no doubt in order to break the evil spell that Crown Prince Luitpold chose that name for his son.

'I see no reason why not,' was the King's only comment.

'No, my dear,' protested Crown Princess Emilie gently from her childbed. 'Better not.'

But the Crown Prince stuck to his choice, the more so as his friend and cousin, Archduke Otto of Austria, was one of the godfathers. Alas, it was soon to become superabundantly clear that his attempt to break the evil spell by headlong assault was doomed to failure.

Besides the spelling error that had crept into the President's telegram — a symbolic lapse at worst — no other danger signals appeared until about 1937, when Prince Otto was four years old. Even in 1936, when the Crown Prince's second son — Prince Maximilian Maria Arnulph Wilheim — was born, and the two boys could be compared, nothing untoward was noticed. It was only on Boxing Day 1937, in Tutzing, that something almost imperceptible but all the more alarming took place. It was half-raining and half-snowing that day.

'The fellow has caused us nothing but trouble of late,' Göring said to Crown Prince Luitpold.

'The trouble he is causing us today will, as far as it is humanly possible to tell, also be his swan song,' the Crown Prince replied.

They were both speaking of the former Quartermaster-General, Erich Ludendorff, who was being buried that day. Ludendorff, one of the great heroes of World War I, had been so patriotic and anti-semitic that even the purest of Nazis could have taken a page from his book. (One day, Putzi Hanfstaengel, the foppish boss of the Nazi Foreign Press Office, was heard to say: 'Compared with Ludendorff, Hitler is a Zionist.') On the other hand, under the influence of his wife Mathilde and after the miserable collapse of his presidential campaign in 1925, Ludendorff had also become the High Priest of Germanic Spiritualism, a creed whose loudly proclaimed philosophical idiocies were too much even for Hitler. Unfortunately, the great hero could not be liquidated like that upstart Captain Röhm, or other awkward party comrades.

The Nazi overlords had for years given the old general a wide berth, not least in 1937 when Hitler had his hands full with his trial war in Spain. Time and again some throw-away ideological remark by Ludendorff would arouse the Party top brass to impotent fury. (This was particularly true of Ludendorff's spiritual contacts with Bismarck, whose

22

mediumistically-transmitted political advice regularly gave Hitler fits.) But all they could do was to ostracize this sacred national cow or to smother it with silence. No wonder all of them sighed with relief when Ludendorff finally gave up the ghost. All those Nazis who had cut him for years, now assembled to watch his last rites with ill-concealed satisfaction. Hitler himself stayed away, but detailed Göring to deputize for him on this 'sad occasion'. King Rupprecht, too, did not appear in person, and was represented by his son.

It was a chilly wet day, and the blustery wind seemed to wipe an invisible dishcloth over Tutzing cemetery. Mathilde Ludendorff — who normally championed nudism and loved to wear transparent chiffon dresses — stood robed in funereal black at the edge of the grave. By her side was Ludendorff's former adjutant, Hans Streck, who had become a tenor after the war and for a time had tutored Hitler's alleged mistress, Geli Raubal. Streck now burst into Handel's *Largo*, accompanied by the Tutzing fire brigade band. While he sang, the wind kept blowing large wet snowflakes into his wide-open mouth.

Crown Princess Emilie stood a little way back from the crowd, just behind Crown Prince Otto who was dressed in *loden*. He had taken up position on an unmarked grave by the side of his cousin, Prince Ignaz of Bavaria, who was one year older.

Crown Princess Emilie was bored and looked idly at the two children. The five-year-old was half a head shorter and a good third thinner than her four-year-old son — not that Prince Ignaz was backward or stunted, far from it, it was just that Otto was inordinately big. Crown Princess Emilie shook her head. 'Strange,' she said to herself, and decided to consult a doctor some day soon.

'The last?' said Göring. 'Don't make me laugh, Your Majesty. As sure as she stands before us, that Mathilde is bound to keep in occult touch with the deceased, and it won't be three weeks before all that dirty old linen . . .'

'Why should that bother you, Herr General?' asked the Crown Prince.

'It doesn't bother me personally. But the Führer! — if only you knew . . .'

'Does he believe in that sort of thing?'

Göring gave a deep sigh. 'And as for Hess! Spinoza' spirit has told him to wear a black tie with his Party uniform. That's against all the regulations. And, what's more, Spinoza was a Jew, or wasn't he?'

'So rumour has it,' said the Crown Prince, though nobody could tell what he meant by that remark.

As Göring and the Crown Prince were about to return to their cars, they were approached by a man in a Homburg. He appeared haggard, and his sickle-shaped chin lent him a permanently sour expression. He was the banker and multimillionaire, Dagobert, Baron von Speckh, and as he shook hands with Göring and the Crown Prince, he whispered something to them in obvious excitement. Göring turned red, and then drew his plump whey face into a girlish pout. The Crown Prince's face, too, grew visibly longer and finally became as sour as Baron von Speckh's.

The Baron and Göring saw the Crown Prince to his car, and then walked on to Göring's. Göring patted the Baron's shoulder. The Baron then proceeded to his own limousine, climbed in, and immediately climbed out again: he had noticed that he was without one of his galoshes — the left one. It had obviously become stuck in the soft ground near the grave.

Baron von Speckh whistled to his chauffeur. 'We have to go back to look for one of my galoshes,' he explained. 'Let's just hope nobody has buried it by mistake.'

The cemetery lay deserted. It was raining now in a steady downpour, and the gravediggers had retired to their hut beside the chapel. Baron von Speckh and his chauffeur searched everywhere, even lifting the wreaths one by one, but all in vain. The Baron himself then extended his search far beyond the vicinity of Ludendorff's grave, and when his chauffeur pointed this out most respectfully, the Baron rounded on him ferociously. 'I don't need your damn stupid advice,' he roared, 'See, I've found the very thing!'

He held up an object that, though by no means the lost article, was serviceable enough. It was the right of a pair and one size too large. 'Better than too small,' said the Baron as he returned happily to his car. By delicately alluding to the imminent nightfall, the chauffeur had been able to dissuade him from what, in the circumstances, was a hopeless search for further galoshes.

Baron von Speckh's whispered remarks to Göring and the Crown Prince were to bear fruit some two years later.

By then, the King's dislike of the Nazis could no longer be concealed. His own obstinacy, his liason with Georgette Schumata, and Hitler's growing arrogance after the annexation of Austria in March 1939, confronted the Bavarian monarchy with a far graver threat than that posed by the revolution of 1919 or the 'seizure of power' of 1933. Luckily, the King's son, Crown Prince Luitpold, was considered a staunch nationalist and even a pro-Nazi. Counsellor-at-Law Scheuchenzuber accordingly proposed, at a secret Wittelsbach family council meeting that lasted deep into the night, that King Rupprecht abdicate in his son's favour. That, according to him, was the only chance of saving the Bavarian crown.

His advice was taken in April. Rupprecht's son — now King Luitpold — was duly sworn in on 1 May 1939, in the presence of Göring (a born Rosenheimer). Göring paid the new king homage on Hitler's behalf and was able to take back the King's own oath of loyalty to the Führer. At the same time, the new king proclaimed Göring — and this had been the substance of Baron von Speckh's whispered remarks — Duke of Rosenheim.

Baron von Speckh himself graced the ceremony in the mantle of a Knight of St. George. He wore it over his storm trooper's uniform and boots — this time he had left his galoshes behind.

Earlier, on 30 April, ex-King Rupprecht — as a private citizen and accompanied by Frau Schumata and the ever inconspicuous Dr von Scheuchenzuber — had boarded the scheduled express train to Florence. They had, of course, reserved a first-class compartment.

'. . . no hereditary monarchy,' wheezed ex-King Rupprecht at Counsellor-at-Law von Scheuchenzuber. 'And if what I've heard of that bristle-lipped crab-louse is true . . .'

'Your Majesty!' said the Counsellor-at-Law, and looked quickly outside the compartment. The corridor was quite empty.

'We must be careful,' groaned Scheuchenzuber, 'we are not yet across the border.'

'That bristle-lipped crab-louse is single. They say he has an illegitimate child in Obersalzberg. But he can't possibly hand over to him. Just for his own glory . . . never. Hitler will never proclaim a monarchy or have himself crowned Kaiser just for the hell of it. What sort of Kaiser would he be, anyway? A German Kaiser like Willy, that raving wood-chopper in Doorn? If he does, he can say good-bye to all his Prussian nationalist hangers-on. Or Holy Roman Emperor? That lot used to have an Adolf, didn't they, sometime in the thirteenth century wasn't it? In that case old Schickelgruber would have to answer to the name of Adolf II.'

'Only if he became a German King,' Herr von Scheuchenzuber hastened to explain. 'Adolf of Nassau was a German king, not a Holy Roman Emperor. In other words Hitler would only be Adolf II as a German king and Adolf I as a Roman Emperor . . .'

'I wouldn't put it past him, either. What with the old imperial crown in Vienna — now after the Austrian *Anschluss* all he has to do is to send for the damn thing . . . But still, I bet you he won't. He doesn't like anything quite so cut and dried. Those Nazis simply don't know what they want. True each one of these gangsters on his own . . . Just take that slimy corner-boy Göring, or that limping dwarf Goebbels — each one of them knows perfectly well what he wants: to grab whatever he can and to wax fat. They are like paupers at a church fête. But what they want as a gang, not one of them can tell you. Haven't you noticed?'

'Perhaps Your Majesty is putting it all too bluntly,' said Counsellor-at-Law von Scheuchenzuber, looking out at the broad Inn Valley basking in the sunshine of a radiant spring morning, 'at least while we are still this side of the border.'

'Have you read this bumph? These would-be philosophical rantings of Schickelgruber's? No? Well, I have. I sometimes think the printer and I are the only ones who have. Well I have, anyway. *Mein Kampf.* Most interesting. They simply don't know what the hell they want. And because they don't know, they can't possibly be *for* anything. They stand for absolutely nothing, so they simply have to be against something. In the event, they've hit on the Jews.'

The former King gently touched the shoulder of the woman in her forties who was sitting beside him. She was slender and dark, and had leant her sleeping head against a fur coat hanging from a hook in the corner of the compartment. The King's gentle touch did not disturb her.

'They don't so much govern as protect themselves,' Rupprecht continued. 'From one another — or perhaps I should say against one another. That's why that bristle-lipped gypsy half breed . . .'

'Your Majesty!' Scheuchenzuber pointed to the station board that was gliding past. FRITZENS-WATTENS it proclaimed in bold Gothic letters.

'. . . has to make sure that he is everything and nothing all at once. For the first few years he was Chancellor. And when that blatherer Hindenburg kicked the bucket, he quickly proclaimed himself President. But he does everything by halves. Führer — that's everything and nothing. If he were Kaiser, he might be dethroned, assassinated, banished, and a successor would take his place . . . All that's much too cut and dried for him. People who don't know their minds, like this jack-pudding from Obersalzberg, have to leave everything vague, for fear they might flush themselves down the drain. Do you get me? People whose hands are empty usually show their fists.'

'I get you only too well,' said Counsellor-at-Law Scheuchenzuber. 'Let's just hope nobody else does.' He groaned, bent down and looked under the seat.

'Take it from me, you won't find any damn Gestapo under that seat, I should have smelled one long ago.'

'But what about microphones, Your Majesty?' said the Counsellor-at-Law, getting back on to his feet, out of breath and moaning.

'Forget it,' said the King irritably. 'They don't care what I say. They've written me off as an old fool.'

'Where are we?' asked the dark-haired woman in a soft, very gentle voice, stretching a little with closed eyes.

'Coming up to Innsbruck, *ma chère*,' said Rupprecht.

'We've just passed Fritzens-Wattens, Madame,' said Scheuchenzuber, but the lady was fast asleep again.

'When we are married,' said the King, 'my son will have to grant her some sort of a title — or perhaps, since we'll be living in Florence, that ludicrous Vittorio Emanuele will have to make her a Duchess. Principessa d'Empoli for example. If there isn't one already. Empoli is a very beautiful place. Or maybe Duchess of Colle di Val d'Elsa. That's almost prettier still — Colle di Val d'Elsa. Do you know the place?'

'No, Your Majesty,' said Scheuchenzuber.

'We'll take a drive there one day. We'll have the time, quite a lot of time, in fact. You shall see: each week I'll be spending half a day in the Uffizi. Or in the Accademia with all the ancient Florentines — Lorenzo di Credi, Fra Bartolommeo, Lorenzo Monaco . . . the Trecento, the pick of Florentine painting . . .'

'I very much regret, but . . .' said Scheuchenzuber, still panting, yet obviously delighted that the King had begun to speak of less dangerous subjects.

'I know,' said the King, 'you have no breeding, more's the pity.'

While the train stood in Innsbruck station, the King stepped into the corridor and watched the to-ings and fro-ings on the platform. No one paid the least attention to the tall and lanky old gentleman. Still fighting for breath Scheuchenzuber got off the train to buy two helpings of sausage and two mugs of beer. On the station, above the entrances to the public lavatories, hung a portrait of Hitler wreathed in pine branches. Beneath it, a banner proclaimed: '*Ein Volk, ein Reich, ein Führer*'.

'Just look at him, that measly snot-picker,' the King said, when the breathless Scheuchenzuber had returned with the sausages and the beer. 'Adolf I — Holy Roman Emperor. There have been quite a few misfits amongst my ancestors, I do admit, but that kind of face . . . How can the man bear to look at himself in a mirror, I wonder? Just imagine if the Pope had to crown him — in Rome of all places . . .' The King bit into a sausage. 'I think even that bald-headed clown Benito might raise an objection or two. That Nero without a fiddle.'

An incoming train obscured the Hitler portrait and the lavatories. It had come from Zurich. A precocious eight-year-old boy dressed in a sailor suit and, incongruously, a green Bavarian hat, looked out of one of the compartments. The boy paid no more attention to the King than the King paid to him.

The child travelled on to Wörgl, and changed for Munich, where he was met at the Central Station by an inconspicuous gentleman in a grey *lodenmantel*, and taken to a villa in Bogenhausen. The boy's name was Hermanfried Schneemoser.

Courante

Young Schneemoser had been living in Bogenhausen for about a year. The reader will remember the villa and its park as Prince Moritz's residence, and the cries of pain and lamentations with which it had once resounded. The pain had been eased following the conveyance of Princess Judith to a discreet clinic in Geneva, but when her time drew near in November, those back in Bogenhausen had held their breaths once again.

Prince Moritz had spent the whole day by the telephone. When the call finally came at 4 o'clock, he did not bother to enquire about his daughter's health, but asked at once only about the nature of the child.

'A boy,' the doctor told him.

'You don't seem to get me,' Prince Moritz screamed down the instrument, 'is he an ape or a human being?'

For quite some time the other end of the line remained perfectly silent.

'A human being,' the doctor said in the end, 'to judge by first appearances.'

To make doubly sure, Hermanfried Schneemoser was left in the clinic, pending further observations. Princess Judith was packed off to South America before she could set eyes on the child. In 1937, when Hermanfried was sent to boarding school, Prince Moritz and his wife travelled to Geneva to look at their grandchild from a safe distance.

'I must say,' said Prince Moritz, 'he looks just like a normal child.'

'Perhaps it was a student after all,' said Princess Hildegard.

'God grant it be so!' muttered Prince Moritz with a genuinely pious sigh.

Hermanfried remained in Geneva for a further two years. Then three professors — a physician, an anthropologist and a zoologist — signed an affidavit to the effect that there was nothing simian about the scion of Hesse, whereupon his grandparents decided to have him brought home. Needless to say, the boy himself was not told why. When he arrived in Bogenhausen, he was taken in charge by a loyal servant. The man's name was Xaver Bohrlein and he had been told the bare facts in the strictest confidence. It was given out that he was the boy's uncle, and Schneemoser moved in with him in the servants' quarters below. Bohrlein was thought particularly reliable, not least because a hereditary dislocation of the jaw rendered his speech as good as incomprehensible. It was only by painfully jerking his head sideways that he could utter brief words — so that he never spoke more than was absolutely necessary.

Thus, a measure of peace returned to Bogenhausen — so much so, in fact, that Prince Moritz even began to take pleasure in his 'Arcadian Landscape' with three pianos, his artistic gift from Hermanfried's deputy father.

'Not at all bad,' he would say from time to time.

'A load of rubbish, if you ask me' said Princess Hildegard.

'You're nothing but a Philistine,' the Prince would retort. 'Perhaps we ought to order a companion piece. . .'

'Don't even think of it!' said the Princess.

'To go on that wall over there,' said the Prince, measuring the spot through his hollow fist. 'Perhaps "German Forest with Crocodiles".'

'Let's drop the subject,' hissed the Princess. 'I don't want anyone to mention the Gestapo in my house.'

The Prince's villa had not only turned peaceful but had fallen silent as well. Princess Judith was in South America, and for obvious reasons son-in-law Schneemoser never called. Prince Moritz's second daughter, Princess Emilie, was Queen now, and away in the Palace. Her brother, Prince Ecbert of Hesse, had married an Englishwoman, Lady Nettlecrop-Hicks, in 1935, and the couple spent all their summers in England. The outbreak of war had caught them in Nettlecrop Abbey. Prince Moritz used all his influence to get news of them. One day he was told that his son had been interned; another time someone reported that, being a great-grandchild of Queen Victoria, the Prince had been allowed to enlist in the British Army. In any case he was far away. The only child now living at home was the spurious grandson Hermanfried, the half-gorilla.

One day, having finished his *Münchner Neueste Nachrichten* and having thrown the *Völkische Beobachter* into the waste paper basket unread, Prince Moritz summoned Bohrlein and asked him to fetch his 'nephew' upstairs. Coffee and cakes were served. Princess Hildegard left the conservatory with a haughty look. Bohrlein showed that he had as much difficulty with swallowing food as he had with his speech, and he was plainly mortified by the great honour his master had shown him in inviting him to take coffee, when normally his ugly head-jerking and garbled speech kept him from even serving coffee at table.

Prince Moritz was rather at a loss with Hermanfried. Hermanfried, for his part, was embarrassed by the old gentleman in the enormous great collar, who kept appraising him with such keen interest. At long last, the Prince hit upon what he thought was a safe subject: he asked about Hermanfried's progress at school. Unfortunately, it seemed there was none. The boy knew everything better than his teachers. (In all fairness, we should add that in 1941 most good teachers were away at the front and the education of children was entrusted to retired old men and faithful party hacks rewarded for their loyalty with exemptions from military service.) Young Hermanfried entertained the Prince — whom he was soon afterwards allowed to address as 'Uncle Moritz' — with a whole chain of caustic remarks about his teachers' patent lack of knowledge.

These coffee afternoons soon became an institution. Bohrlein was no longer expected to be present; all he had to do now was to bring the boy — dressed in his Sunday best — up to the conservatory, and help the agile young Inge serve the coffee. Thanks to his family connection with South America, Prince Moritz could drink real coffee, not the usual ersatz. Prince Moritz spoke so enthusiastically of the child's entertaining manner that eventually Princess Hildegard too occasionally took to attending their coffee afternoons, though with strong private reservations. Though it must be said that her attendance never became a habit, and in her presence Hermanfried was expected to drop the 'Uncle Moritz' and to revert to 'Your Royal Highness'.

On 15 June 1941, the young Schneemoser was once again present in the conservatory. But on this occasion the boy said nothing at all, for this time there was another visitor, whose presence had even encouraged Princess Hildegard to put in an appearance.

Hermanfried Schneemoser had been born in November 1931, which meant that he was to be celebrating his tenth birthday in a few months' time. Now, by a special decree issued in 1936, every German boy was obliged to join the Hitler Youth — or more precisely the *Jungvolk* — at the age of ten. The decree applied to all except non-Aryans, i.e. Jews, Gypsies and Australian aborigines. No doubt, half-apes would have been exempted as well. The Hitler Youth Decree posed a grave threat not only to Prince Moritz's immediate family but also to the Illustrious House at large. Consequently after long discussions it was agreed to call in an expert on race problems under some pretext or other — who would be told the absolute minimum about the actual Wittelsbach-Hesse-Darmstadt circumstances, that is about the assumed gorillistic descent of the boy — and to ask him, just by the way, to inspect Hermanfried and perhaps to sign an affidavit.

'The best thing that could happen,' said King Luitpold to Prince Moritz, 'would be if the chap that Göring sends us were to state that the boy is human but unfit for the Hitler

Youth.' And he added: 'Why not ask him along to one of your coffee afternoons, and let him hear the boy poke fun at his teachers?'

And Prince Moritz did just that.

The 'chap that Göring sends us' turned out to be Professor Dr (*honoris causa*) Paul Schultze-Naumburg. He called at the villa dressed in checked knickerbockers, whose waistband seemed to ride up to his chin whenever he sat down. He was a tiny man, totally bald, and had the disconcerting habit of pouring himself vast quantities of sugar before stirring it with a never-ending succession of biscuits. Just before the biscuit completely dissolved, he would slobber it up with an agile tongue, and help himself to another improvised coffee-stirrer. Hermanfried seemed fascinated. Princess Hildegard, with decent emphasis, placed a teaspoon by the Professor's side several times, but Professor Schultze-Naumburg took no notice.

As his last name indicated, Professor Dr (*honoris causa*) Schultze-Naumburg came from the Province of Saxony. He had originally been an architect and had built a whole series of public conveniences in Berlin during the twenties, where-upon his colleagues had re-named him Shitze-Naumburg. That was something he hoped to forget — he was most anxious to change the memory of these malodorous brown stains on his past for a bright new brown shirt in the present. Even before the war, Schultze-Naumburg had submitted a magnificent plan for a new Party Hall in Nuremburg, but Hitler, who had an excellent memory, would have nothing to do with it. 'It looks just like an oversize water closet,' he said. And that put an end to Schultze-Naumburg's archi-tectural career. But not to his other profession: for many years now, Schultze-Naumburg had been one of the pillars of the 'Militant League for German Culture'. In that capacity he had written several books on 'Architecture and Race', 'Art and Race', 'Music and Race', drawing attention to the a-nordic cadences in Mendelssohn's music and the nordic faces in Dürer's paintings, and had been about to dismiss Michelangelo as a non-Aryan dabbler when he learned that he was Hitler's favourite painter. Schultze-Naumburg immediately changed tack to prove by an extremely shrewd analysis that, in the 'Last Judgement', all the damned had typically Jewish physionomical and physical characteristics, while all the blessed had genuine Aryan features. "The Last Judgement" by the Nordic Master Michelangelo — whose ancestors probably came from one of the twelve German settlements in the Province of Trent, colonized by German settlers, as his typically German name of Michel plainly suggests — is an honest profession of Ayran faith. ' "Master Michel" has stood up quite unequivocally for the cause of nordic photology.' However, this labour of Schultze-Naumburg's also did not meet with wholehearted approval in Nazi circles. Alfred Rosenberg's only comment was that as a true Aryan he would much rather dispense with a Heaven run by that half-Jew, or worse, Jesus Christ. It was then that Schultze-Naumburg decided to devote himself exclusively to the development of race theory. His latest great works had been an album with portraits of great Germans, accompanied by pithy racial glosses, and another book entitled *Nordic Beauty*.

'I can't say that I altogether follow you, Herr Professor,' said Prince Moritz. 'Mendelssohn came from Berlin and Michelangelo from Florence, and yet you tell me that the Italian is the more Nordic of the two.'

'Nordic is not the same as northern,' said the Professor.

'I see,' said Prince Moritz. 'You mean Mendelssohn may have been from the north, but was in fact a sordic.'

'There is no such thing as "sordic", Your Royal Highness. Mendelssohn was a Jew. And that makes things perfectly simple. A Jew is totally incapable of creating anything of lasting cultural value. Whatever a Jew produces is bound to be inferior and will decay in no time at all.'

'Well, what about igloos then?' said Prince Moritz.

'I beg Your Royal Highness's pardon?'

'I mean the Eskimos. After all, they must be quite exceptionally nordic, and yet their igloos melt away as soon as the sun shines on them.'

'As I said earlier, Your Royal Highness, nordic is not synonymous with northern. The Eskimos are, of course, a northern race, but they are anything but nordic.'

'And why ever not?' asked Princess Hildegard, vainly trying to edge the biscuits out of the Professor's reach.

'There is a strict race law, which helps us to tell with absolute certainty whether a man is a member of inferior West Indian or the even more inferior East Baltic races, or whether we must count him among the Nordic races.'

'Tall, fair and blue-eyed . . .' said Prince Moritz.

'Those are only the most superficial characteristics. The real criteria are much more subtle and differentiated.'

'I can well imagine they must be,' said Prince Moritz. 'Or else a Hottentot would be more Nordic than our Führer and Chancellor . . .'

'Moritz!' said Princess Hildegard.

'It's quite true that the Führer has a slight Dinaric touch, like so many Austrians. But the typically Germanic form of his ears bears clear witness to his Aryan descent.'

'And no doubt his typically Germanic moustache as well,' said the Prince.

'Moritz!' repeated Princess Hildegard.

'Your Royal Highness may have gathered,' said Professor Schultze-Naumburg, clearly determined to brush the Prince's acid interjections aside, 'that I myself — as I realize perfectly well — am not exactly a picture of what *some* old fo. . . that is, I mean. . .'

'Some old fogey,' the Prince added briskly.

'. . . of what people commonly believe a Germanic hero must look like. But! I have a pair of feet, let me tell you, a pair of feet, the likes of which you don't often meet. My feet — but perhaps you had better see for yourself.'

'No, thank you. Thank you very much,' said Prince Moritz, but Professor Schultze-Naumburg had already placed his soggy biscuit down on his saucer, ripped off his boots and was starting to roll down his moss-green socks.

'Just look!' he said, stretching his feet sideways across the arm of the sofa. 'Are these Germanic feet, or aren't they?'

'I should have thought all good Germans developed flat feet during the Barbarian Invasion.'

'With respect, Your Royal Highness, that remark was in rather poor taste,' said Professor Schultze-Naumburg. 'Just look at my toes! The thing to remember is that the second toe, the index toe as it were, must protrude beyond the big toe. If the index toe were shorter . . .'

There was a terrible crash. Inge, the maid, stood in the doorway, crossing herself repeatedly. The tray and all the china on it had dropped from her hands.

'Inge,' said Princess Hildegard. 'Whatever is the matter with you?'

'Jesus, Mary and Joseph!' cried Inge, pointing to the Professor's bare Aryan feet. They were sticking out from under his check knickerbockers and were draped ominously over the arm of the sofa. 'I thought something terrible had happened!'

Inge was eighteen and fetchingly buxom. Her thick black plaits were pinned up to form a solid 'Gretchen' bun at the back of her head. She came from the Bavarian Forest, Munich's traditional reservoir of domestics.

'There's nothing to be afraid of, dear child,' said Professor Schultze-Naumburg, opening his eyes wide as Inge bent down to pick up the broken pieces. She was wearing a pinafore with a most revealing neckline. 'These are Nordic feet you see before you . . .'

'It's a bit odd, all the same, Herr Professor,' said Prince Moritz. 'Especially for a country girl. To see you sipping coffee in your bare feet. . .'

'I can't for the life of me tell what you have against bare feet. Why are feet supposed to be so funny?'

'Not at all, I assure you, Herr Professor, but. . .'

Professor Schultze-Naumburg was turning purple in the face. 'That girl, let me tell you, is an inferior Dinaric — East Baltic hybrid. . .'

'What am I?' said Inge.

'Let's forget it, shall we,' said Princess Hildegard.

'Let's see your right foot!' screamed the Professor. 'I bet

your big toe is longer than. . .'

'Herr Professor!' said Princess Hildegard.

'Inferior, my foot!' hissed Inge.

Young Schneemoser, we might add in parentheses, was following the discussion with bated breath.

'Take off your shoes, will you now!' roared Professor Schultze-Naumburg, stamping round Inge in his Germanic feet. 'Would Your Royal Highness kindly instruct the girl to take off her shoes and stockings, I'd like to inspect her. . .'

Princess Hildegard put in a soothing word. 'You see, Inge,' she said, 'it's almost a science. Have you washed your feet? Well, then do the Professor the kindness of removing your shoes. . .'

With obvious reluctance, Inge sat down and did as she was bid.

'Didn't I tell you!' shouted Schultze-Naumburg triumphantly. 'Dinaric hybrids of toes, that's what she's got!' Inge looked down at her feet in consternation. 'And now,' said Schultze-Naumburg, 'your bust!'

'Her what?' said Princess Hildegard.

'Her bust,' said the Professor. 'Her breasts or bosom. Tell her to get undressed.'

'That's going too far, don't you think, Herr Professor? She's only a child.'

'Going too far, indeed! It's pure race science. The nipple is one of the most important features. I have photographed thousands of breasts of perfectly decent members of the German Maiden's Association who were only too happy to help me in my work. I am certain that this Dinaric hybrid has a black nipple. . .'

Inge, trembling all over now, put on her stockings and shoes.

'Off with your rags,' screamed Professor Schultze-Naumburg, 'I want to see your nipples. . .'

At this point, the telephone rang. Princess Hildegard was torn between fear of the Gestapo, personified by Schultze-Naumburg, and grave moral scruples, as Inge defended herself from the skilled racial clutches of the bare-footed

Professor, who was by now tearing away at her blouse. Hermanfried Schneemoser reached for a biscuit — in view of the exceptional circumstances he felt there was no need to ask for permission.

Bohrlein now appeared at the door, jerking his head violently and uttering primitive grunts. The Princess translated: 'Herr Professor, you are wanted on the telephone.' Schultze-Naumburg hurried out, fired a few words into the receiver and returned. Princess Hildegard had by then managed to push Inge out through a side door.

'Most dreadfully sorry, Your Royal Highness, but I simply must leave your hospitable home,' said Schultze-Naumburg. 'I've just learned' — and he lowered his voice — 'that Paris has fallen. Where are my socks?'

'Heaven help us!' said Princess Hildegard.

'What do you mean by "Heaven help us"?'

'I mean the French will never forgive us,' whispered the Princess.

'I should hope not. Ha ha!' roared Schultze-Naumburg, waving his moss-green woollen socks in the air. 'I shall immediately leave on a journey of racial exploration.' He put on his socks, and hummed what sounded very much like the great Nordic hit 'We're off to the Folies'.

'Pappy,' said Princess Hildegard to Prince Moritz, 'Just look at you! Didn't you hear? Paris has fallen.'

'. . . Once over there, I shall make a very intimate. . .' Schultze-Naumburg bent down and as did so the top of his knickerbockers rode up to his chin again.

'Pappy, don't just sit there! Won't you at least close your mouth. . .' Princess Hildegard gave Prince Moritz a slight nudge. He slid down sideways and rolled on to the floor.

Thus died Prince Moritz of Hesse-Darmstadt und Bei Rhein, Count of Hanau zu Lichtenburg und Von Katzenelnbogen, Lieutenant-General (ret.), Knight of the Garter and of the Order of St Hubert, etc. etc. While Princess Hildegard had a sobbing fit, Professor Schultze-Naumburg beat a hasty retreat, and Inge screamed, Bohrlein kept a calm head and rang for a doctor. Hermanfried Schneemoser was left to his own devices, and sat miserably on the sofa beneath the 'Arcadian Landscape' with three pianos. Incidentally, he was forced to join the Hitler Youth after all, on 20 April 1942. But for the moment he took another biscuit, dipped it into the coffee and munched it very slowly. As he did so, he moved his head in a manner that might equally well have been a nod as a shake.

Prince Moritz's remains were taken to Darmstadt for burial in the archducal vault. Princess Hildegard donned the widow's veil and joined her daughter, the Queen, in Nymphenburg Castle. Bogenhausen was abandoned by all except for Bohrlein and Hermanfried Schneemoser. One day, perhaps a year or some eighteen months after Prince Moritz's death, Bohrlein took the boy upstairs into the now permanently locked rooms and showed him the 'Three Concert Grands in an Arcadian Landscape with Crocodiles'. Then, twitching spasmodically, he addressed the boy at what was for him inordinate length. How much Bohrlein actually knew of the family secret, and how much he knew he proceeded to repeat in his garbled fashion — or how much of it young Hermanfried was able to interpret — remains a matter of conjecture. Prince Moritz had, by the way, left Hermanfried a legacy: the painting above the sofa and a sum of money to pay for his theological training, for the Prince had decided that Hermanfried was cut out for the cloth. The heir never had the chance of taking possession of the first part of the legacy.

At the time Nymphenburg Castle itself and, more generally, the Royal capital, had been drastically depleted of Royal Highnesses — by the summer of 1942, Schneemoser was the only, if illegitimate, member of the Royal Family still in Munich. ('Your Secret Royal Highness' Prince Moritz had sometimes called him behind his back. 'None of your silly jokes, if you please,' had been Princess Hildegard's constant retort.) In the summer of 1941, when Princess Hildegard had moved to Nymphenburg, the King — Luitpold I — had still been in residence, and so had the Queen, the two sons of the royal couple — Crown Prince Otto and Prince Max Arnulph — the old Prince Franz (the King's uncle) and Prince Garibald the Counter (the King's cousin) and his family. Prince Garibald was the oldest son of Prince Wolfgang, the youngest brother of King Rupprecht. He was an extremely dogmatic person, and for that very reason had, at a relatively young age, adopted a vocation that was bound to provide the right answers with complete certainty — or so the Prince believed. He had taken to counting. His wife, the Princess Laetitia Annunziata Murat, was a rather dull and, with the years, a rather malicious person. The Murats, as the reader may like to know, were not only no ancient family, but if the truth be told, no nobility at all. True, Joachim Murat, an innkeeper's son from Cahors, had been proclaimed Grand-Duke of Berg, and for a few years had even reigned as king over Naples but, after his abortive attempt to recapture the city with twenty-six brave men in October 1815, the victors had treated him no better than they would have treated any other innkeeper's son. His own sons fled to America, where one of them married a distant niece of George Washington — which may have counted for something in the United States, but counted for absolutely nothing in Europe, where Washington was just another upstart revolutionary. The Murats had a hard time of it. Having been Neapolitan royalty, they could not possibly revert to the innkeeper's trade. Worse still, the aristocracy and the politicians never took them very seriously. In the circumstances, all they could do was to cement their spurious nobility by marriages and by manufacturing ancestors. In this, they were only doing what the Bonapartes, the Bernadottes, the Beauharnais, the Neys and all the other Napoleonic parvenus had done before them. However, the Murats were rather slow: it was not until the 1930s that they finally made good with Prince Pierre Murat's marriage to Isabella of Bourbon, the oldest daughter of the Count of Paris, and with Princess Laetitia Annunziata's betrothal to Prince Garibald of Bavaria.

This apparently made Princess Laetitia Annunziata, in respect of family tradition, much more aristocratic than all the Wittelsbachs put together. Prince Garibald owned a hunting lodge in Jachenau, where he would spend his leave from counting, though he occasionally continued his great work for two or three weeks even there. One day a high tide flooded the cellars and the ground floor of the lodge. Princess Laetitia, braving great dangers, took the 200 volumes of the *Almanach de Gotha* to safety on the top floor. This labour of love left her no time to rescue anything else. (The three children, the Princes Ignaz and Hezilo and the Princess Ludaemilia, were saved by their father who reluctantly interrupted his counting for that purpose.) Princess Laetitia Annunziata was not only extraordinarily noble but also uncommonly pious — or more precisely, uncommonly Catholic. With her own fair hands she had knitted a surplice for the Nymphenburg family chaplain — one Monsignor Theodorich Zach. Unfortunately she had measured him very cursorily, so that the surplice looked all askew and much too long on him. Monsignor Zach was forced to tie the garment up with several pieces of string, and looked like a poor infant in swaddling clothes whenever he wore it. All his protests were of no avail: he simply had to don the beastly thing or run the risk of mortally offending Princess Laetitia.

These royal presences in Nymphenburg Castle, who, as we have said, were joined by the Queen Mother in 1941, had all been forced to behave with great circumspection since the outbreak of war. The Royal Family, in particular, never appeared in public, and this for several good reasons. The King would occasionally take the salute dressed in simple field grey, but the Crown Prince, who had celebrated his eighth birthday in 1941 and had already been proclaimed an honorary SS–Untersturmführer, was never seen at any public functions — neither at the May Day celebrations in Königsplatz, nor at the Corpus Christi Day procession. He was not allowed to attend church outside the Castle, nor even to visit his grandparents in Bogenhausen. Since Princess

Hildegard, too, had left her Bogenhausen abode as little as was humanly possible, she had not seen her oldest (legitimate) nephew for a good two years.

On her first day back in Nymphenburg, there was not only coffee and biscuits but even a tart, which the court confectioner — in genteel recognition of the family's recent bereavement — had decorated with black icing and the joint Bavarian-Hessian coats of arms. Coffee was served in the Princess's own suite. Those present — apart, that is, from Monsignor Zach — were all ladies: the Queen, the Queen Mother and Princess Laetitia Annunziata. Princess Hildegard was cloaked in an immeasurable quantity of black material, together with a black veil. For at least the fourth time that afternoon she was relating to the assembled company how she had said 'Pappy, don't just sit there. Won't you at least close your mouth', before nudging him, whereupon the poor man had dropped dead from the sofa.

'Do you mean to tell us,' asked Monsignor Zach, 'that your nudging him was the cause of his death? Whatever was the matter with him that a mere nudge . . .'

'He was quite dead by then,' stated the Queen.

'In that case,' said Monsignor Zach, 'I can see what happened.'

'The children will pay their respects to you later,' said the Queen to her mother.

Princess Laetitia Annunziata turned up her nose, whereupon the Queen gave her a scathing look. 'It has to be done sooner or later,' she hissed.

'Little Otto,' said the Queen Mother, 'I haven't seen Little Otto for two years.'

'Little Otto!' Princess Laetitia Annunziata muttered softly.

'Why *little* Otto?' asked Monsignor Zach loudly.

'Oh, do hold your tongue,' said the Queen.

'I fail to see . . .' said the Monsignor, still speaking loudly.

'That's always been your trouble,' said the Queen. 'Do bless the tart, won't you. If you don't, it might stick in my dear cousin's throat.'

Monsignor Zach blessed the black tart, but insisted — he was a pedantic man, and especially so when it came to questions of heraldry — that there were three bars too many in the Hessian coat-of-arms. 'What's more the Bavarian lion looks more like a pig than . . .'

'. . . the children!' exclaimed Princess Laetitia Annunziata.

The door opened and in came:

A five-year-old, fair-haired boy with a rather serious, pinched face that looked like a caricature of his great-great-grandfather, Prince Regent Luitpold. He was Prince Max Arnulph. After him came a creature measuring just under five feet, pale, corpulent and with thighs as large as tree trunks. Everything is relative: five feet is next to nothing in an adult, but in an eight-year-old boy it looks wildly exaggerated. However, it was not Prince Otto's height that startled — we cannot say many people, for few people were allowed to see him, and some did not even notice his unusual height at first sight — but a far more inharmonious, one might even say obscene, aspect of his appearance. The child was horribly fat, as if suffering from glandular deficiency. He looked like a freak who, unable to grow more skin than the normal person, had been forced to distribute his epidermis most sparingly over his bulging flesh so as to make a very little go a very long way. His blood vessels, tendons and muscles, and whatever other unappetizing bits meander through the human body, seemed to burst through his parsimonious skin. On closer inspection, this impression proved quite erroneous, but at first sight the boy undoubtedly looked a terrible fright.

'For Heaven's sake!' said his grandmother. 'Why on earth did you have to put him in a sailor's suit? He looks like a whale!'

Princess Laetitia Annunziata had a fit of the giggles, and quickly hid them behind her hand. Crown Prince Otto began to sob. The Queen jumped up and pushed the two children out of the room. 'Now you know the worst, Mama,' she said, having first shut the door firmly.

'Is that why you didn't call on us these past two years?'

The Queen nodded. 'We never allow him out of the house,

44

except at night when the front gate has been locked, and we take him into the park. He has private tutors, all of them sworn to silence . . .'

'But is he normal in other respects?'

'Of course he is. He only cried because you called him a whale.'

'But honestly, you shouldn't dress him in that sailor's suit!'

'What else do you suggest? An SS uniform? So that the Nazis can say we are holding them up to ridicule?'

'A tunic,' the Queen Mother said with cool deliberation. 'Some sort of tunic or toga, or some Indian garment, something more flowing and billowing. The very thing, if you ask me . . .'

'A Franciscan habit,' said Prince Laetitia Annunziata, 'that's what I've been saying all along.'

'But he is a Crown Prince,' protested the Queen. 'He is born to be a king, not a monk!'

'Perhaps there's no alternative,' said the Princess Laetitia Annunziata.

'You should never have christened him "Otto",' moaned the Queen Mother.

The Queen now told her that various doctors had examined the Crown Prince. Each of them had advanced some theory or other about the boy's strange affliction, but not one of them had been able to state categorically whether or not he would ever stop growing. Most of them had taken the pessimistic view. The boy, they said, had all the physical characteristics of the normal eight-year-old though on a superdimensional scale. What made matters still worse, he invariably grew by sudden bursts: sometimes he would remain static for several weeks, only to shoot up and out so much within the space of a few hours that you could watch it all happening with the naked eye. That was why Cardinal Faulhaber — who had been familiarized with the situation — had raised strong objections (for aesthetic rather than theological motives) when the family proposed to take the Crown Prince, under strict isolation from all other pilgrims, to the Holy Shrine in Altötting. The Prince of the Church was afraid that the Prince of Bavaria might have a sudden burst of growth in the chapel, and get stuck inside. In that case, it might be that the precious building would have to be pulled down. In the end, therefore, it was decided to bring the miracle-working image out of the chapel.

But all to no avail.

Entrée and Rondeau

There are a great many theories about Hitler. According to some, he was nothing short of a demon; others still regard him as a genius. Not the least unsympathetic are those according to whom he was simply just the bragging and tawdry Adolf Schickelgruber. All alike, however, have failed to explain his end, and this despite the most extensive probings. True, there are many accounts of his last few days in the Chancellery. Everyone has heard about Hitler's desperate pig-headedness, his false optimism, his marriage to Eva Braun, the burning of the two corpses and an Alsatian dog in the Chancellery gardens . . . but there is no one who actually *saw* Hitler being shot or poisoned. All this has, of course, assisted in the creation of a legend. From soon after the end of the war until the late fifties there was rumour after rumour: Hitler had been spotted in a remote Tyrolean hut, or in the Paraguayan jungle; some claimed that he had escaped to Oceania in a submarine; others that he was being kept locked up in a private zoo by Stalin.

The most interesting theory — but let me anticipate: it is as misleading as the rest; the only correct one is the one that will be advanced in this book — came from the pen of the Scottish journalist, Angus MacDowell. According to Mac-Dowell, Hitler was able to disappear so mysteriously and completely because he never existed. The figure, or rather the fiction 'Adolf Hitler', was dreamed up early on in the history of the Nazi movement. Max Amman, one of the founders of the National-Socialist Party, had been the proud owner of a dog named Hüttler (so-called because he was normally confined to a hut in Amman's garden). In 1919 or 1920, during a Party dinner in the 'Schelling Saloon', one of the Party founders who suffered from flatulence did what was only human in the circumstances. With great presence of mind, he explained away the resulting malodour by exclaiming 'Bad Hüttler!' From then on, Party circles adopted the habit of blaming anything untoward or unpleasant — all debts, all transparent lies, and finally all responsibility — on 'bad Hüttler' (which later became 'Hitler'). Thus Hüttler — who became known affectionately as Adolf in about the middle of 1922 — gradually turned into a fictitious but almighty Party scarecrow, one in whose name every Party notable could do as he liked. MacDowell admits that numerous people claimed actually to have seen Hitler, but contends that they merely thought they had done so. They were all suffering from the kind of mass delusion normally found in people watching the Indian rope trick.

When the Russians entered Berlin and occupied the Chancellery, they asked the handful of terrified Nazis left behind where Hitler had got to. The Nazis looked under tables and beds and even in the lavatory, with cries of 'Wherever can he be?' Alas, he could not be found.

This explains why, at the Nuremburg trials, most of the accused (except for a few who were so afraid that they cracked up and confessed) shifted the blame for everything onto poor Hitler. By that time, Max Amman's 'Hüttler' had long been dead.

Most of the Royal Family — the Queen, the Queen Mother and the two Princes — spent the last two years of the war in Eichkatzlried. King Luitpold remained in Nymphenburg until the end of 1944, when the Allies stepped up their air raids and forced him to take shelter in Berg Castle on Lake Starnberg. (Nymphenburg Castle had been camouflaged with paint — people would call it pop art today.) Eichkatzlried lay in the neighbouring province of Tirol-Voralberg, in the so-called 'Reich Air-Raid-Shelter' which was deemed proof against all enemy aircraft. In the thirties, when skiing was the latest craze, a Jewish actor had bought an old farmhouse here, and fitted it out with all mod cons. In 1938, the place was taken over by the Custodian of Jewish Property, and for a time served as a winter resort for Nazi thugs of the second and third rank. Next, it was handed over to his Excellency, Count Oshima, the Imperial Japanese Envoy, and it was from him that the Royal Bavarian Chancellor's Office had purchased the farm in 1943.

The Queen had decided — as a precaution — to take up residence incognito. ('People will prattle about us soon enough.') She had accordingly adopted the alias of Duchess of Bogen. The only adult male in the household was the Queen's Chamberlain, Lieutenant-Colonel Count Seybothenreuth, who found time hanging heavily on his hands in this sleepy backwater. Crown Prince Otto grew taller and taller and fatter and fatter all the time. Even conveying him from Munich to Eichkatzlried had posed a serious logistic problem. He had been given a mild sleeping powder before being driven to Pasinger station in a convoy of several limousines at the dead of night. Waiting for him, stood not the Royal train but an inconspicuous express which carried the illustrious party to Eichkatzlried within two hours. Once there, the train did not stop in the station but was brought to a halt several miles beyond, at Birkensee, whence the farmhouse was only a few minutes' drive by car.

The locals took it all in their stride. The old name of 'Hungerbichl' fell into desuetude soon after the Jewish actor had disappeared from the scene — he had always walked about in exaggerated Alpine costume, and been known locally as the 'gentleman farmer'. As soon as the Japanese Ambassador and his retinue moved in, Hungerbichl became known for miles around as the 'Chinese Place', a name that stuck even when Hungerbichl was acquired by the Most Illustrious Royal Family, or — as the locals called them —

the 'Chinese baroness and her children'. As a result, the Queen was able to keep her real identity hidden for much longer than she had ever anticipated.

When Crown Prince Otto woke up from his protective sleep, he found himself in a large farm bed — at the time he was ten years old, five feet seven inches tall and 207 pounds in weight — from which, to his astonishment, he could look across a still, dark lake mirroring tall mountains and reeds that had just turned a glorious red.

Hungerbichl Farm, or 'the Chinese Place', was built on a lush, gentle slope, with its portly flank running towards Lake Birken, which lay some two to three hundred yards away as if in a large, shallow basin. The farmhouse was dominated by a sturdy, very old beech. Beyond the lake rose a dense pine forest; the nearest shore was marshy, with a few gleaming birch trees and the odd cembra-pine. Quite often buzzards would nest in the pines, and at noon when everything was still and the smoke rose vertically from the chimney stacks of neighbouring farms hidden by the forest, the buzzards would ascend into the sky, circle above the fen uttering their piercing 'Yeeees', and suddenly fold their wings to plummet down upon some totally helpless rat or mouse. There were a few hawks as well. They nested among the higher branches, and whenever one of them — the locals called them 'chicken-robbers' — circled the valley, the hens would grow nervous for miles around, squawking, laying their eggs in a panic, and fluttering about in terrible confusion. The cocks and the more intelligent of the hens would duck their heads down and race straight for the chicken coop. Then the hawk, still circling majestically, would pick out one from among the rest, gradually close his circles, and dive down on the poor fowl with such force that the victim disappeared in a cloud of white feathers, from which the hawk, his lifeless prey in his talons, would rise up with a few powerful beats of his wings and disappear into the forest. A peasant woman screeching and ululating like one of her hens would generally come running up with a pitchfork, but only in the rarest of cases would she succeed in driving off the hawk, and never in saving the life of her hen.

Beside the lake, a wooded ridge ran towards the north, where the jagged silhouette of a chain of tall rocks closed the valley. The small hamlet of Eichkatzlried — a sinister old place on a hill, with solid yellowy-gold towers, walls and with sombre gates — could not be seen from Hungerbichl: to reach it, you had first to cross the ridge flanking the farm, and that took a good half-hour. The Crown Prince, who was not allowed to leave the immediate vicinity of the farm, never so much as caught a glimpse of Eichkatzlried; only Lieutenant-Colonel Count Seybothenreuth made his way there on a bicycle whenever he could — which meant every single day. On the outskirts of the town a large and inordinately ugly hotel had been converted into a convalescent home for Luftwaffe officers, and, as such, it boasted a fashionable officers' club. It was to this place that the Lieutenant-Colonel invariably steered his bicycle to change one kind of boredom for another. But bored though he invariably was, he was never so bored as to volunteer for front-line duty.

'Don't even think of reporting for active service, Seybothenreuth,' the Queen would admonish him now and again. 'We have much greater need of you here. Just look what is happening out there: Stalingrad, the retreat in Africa. And any day the Americans will be landing in France. Not even you can help them now.'

'Emilie!' hissed the Queen Mother, 'for God's sake, think of the Gestapo!'

'There's no Gestapo round here, Mama.'

'You never can tell,' said the Queen Mother.

And in fact, you never could tell, not even in Royal establishments. For the rest there was no sign of the Nazi Government, or of the war, in Hungerbichl. Only the buzzards circled high up in the sky and the hawks higher still, and above them all, metal hawks and buzzards would appear from time to time — in 1944, they began appearing every second or third day with almost monotonous regularity. Imperturbable, and deceptively slow, they set up a dull roar that set the earth trembling below. 'Dear God in Heaven,' whispered the Queen Mother. In Eichkatzlried itself there was no worthwhile target for these metal birds of prey, but everyone knew where they were going, and why. And when the squadron returned no less imperturbably and noisily a few hours later, the Queen Mother, her face a shade paler, would utter another 'Dear God in Heaven!'

Like the farmyard hens, Nationalist Socialist heroes in other parts of the Reich kept rushing to and fro, not knowing whether they were coming or going. The least asinine of them had long ago raced full pelt for the 'Reich Air-Raid-Shelter' in Tyrol-Voralberg. Much earlier, His Excellency, Hermann the Glorious, Duke of Rosenheim, had proclaimed: 'If a single enemy aircraft succeeds in entering German airspace, you can call me Meier,' and now people everywhere were saying that Reich Marshal Hermann Göring had been promoted to the rank of Obermeier for his splendid services to Germany's air defences.

Hence, it would not be true to say that the two Princes felt nothing at all of the war. True, they went short of very little — even the gigantic helpings which the Crown Prince needed to satisfy his outsize hunger whenever he had one of his sporadic bursts of growth, were always found. But whenever the bombers thundered across the mountains, even the children recognized the ominous threat, sensed the hell of blood and flesh these iron hawks would open up with deadly certainty, within the hour, not so far away. Now and then the Crown Prince was allowed to visit an isolated spot on the lake and sail a model boat. Whenever he was surprised by the bombers — which could be heard from far away, their thunder roaring across the narrow valley long before they came into sight — the Prince would haul in his little boat and rush back home, where the Lieutenant-Colonel would already have switched on Radio Laibach, which always gave the flight path of enemy aircraft in a few ominous words. Between the messages — to inform listeners that they were tuned to the right wave-length — an unpleasantly muffled pulse would keep piercing the silence.

'Obermeier's bad conscience', people called it, which showed that they overrated him still.

But though the children knew perfectly well what was happening, they forgot all about it again during the quiet days. And indeed, they had no inkling of why two visitors should have appeared quite unexpectedly on 1 August 1944 — a few days after Hitler had unhappily escaped Stauffenberg's bomb. The visitors came from two directions. Herr von Scheuchenzuber arrived by train from Innsbruck, while Monsignor Theodorich Zach appeared on a small motorcycle, covered with dust and completely famished. He was dressed in a grey rubberized coat that reached down to his heels and was fastened to his wrists and ankles by special straps. Despite the heat he had also pulled a sou'wester over his round clerical hat.

Scheuchenzuber and Monsignor Zach conferred with Lieutenant-Colonel Seybothenreuth in great secrecy and in a great hurry. Then they had an audience of the Queen. Counsellor-at-Law Scheuchenzuber departed the very next day, having first drawn up several weighty documents.

'Off so soon?' asked the Queen Mother.

'Alas yes, Your Royal Highness.'

'Why don't you stay on for a few days?'

'Out of the question, Your Royal Highness, quite out of the question.'

All this happened during luncheon on 2 August. The meal was taken earlier than usual, since an army car was waiting to take the Counsellor-at-Law to the station at 12.30 p.m.

Two days later, the radio proudly proclaimed that German troops had evacuated Florence 'according to plan'.

'So, that's why Scheuchenzuber was in such a hurry,' said the Queen.

'Dear God in Heaven,' moaned the Queen Mother. 'Did he manage to see Rupprecht, I wonder?'

'He probably got there on the very last train, Your Royal Highness,' said Lieutenant-Colonel Count Seybothenreuth.

'Dear God in Heaven,' said the Queen Mother. 'I only hope and pray nothing untoward has happened to them!'

'On the contrary,' said Monsignor Zach, who had not been in nearly so great a hurry as Counsellor-at-Law Scheuchenzuber, and had stayed on for a few extra days in peaceful Hungerbichl, before roaring off towards Munich wrapped in his rubbers and sou' wester.

Ever since she had moved to Nymphenburg, the Queen Mother had barely given a thought to the villa in Bogenhausen, and none at all since she had gone on to Eichkatzlried. She preferred to put young Hermanfried Schneemoser out of her mind.

All the servants had run off, one by one, soon after Prince Moritz's death. Only old Bohrlein had stayed behind. No one knows what would have become of Schneemoser without his 'uncle'. Bohrlein cooked for him, washed his clothes, darned his socks, and admired his amazing scholastic progress. In the autumn of 1941, Schneemoser had entered the High School — the renowned Ferdinand-Maria Gymnasium in Wiedenmeyerstrasse, which had just been rechristened Albert-Leo-Schlageter High School and was run by a headmistress qualified for the post not so much by her pedagogic attainments as by her correct Germanic sentiments. This lady, Frau Dr Ingrid Gerch, or rather Fräulein Dr Gerch, was a student of folk-lore by profession, and the teachers whispered amongst themselves that she had earned her doctorate for a thesis entitled 'The formal history of Bavarian homespun'. She was fairly tall and skinny, wore her hair piled up on the top of her head in a slovenly bun, had large feet and a predilection for grey skirts, grey knitted jackets and dun-coloured woollen shawls. She could be quite venomous if put out in any way by one of the teachers, but posed no threat to the pupils, simply because she did not actually do any teaching. At first sight, people took her to be much older than she really was; however, she had given clear proof of her youthfulness soon after the outbreak of war. Though unmarried, she had decided that she too must do her bit for the racial recovery of the nation and had accordingly presented the Führer with a child. Fräulein Dr Gerch kept the father's identity strictly to herself. The male staff were certain that, in view of her onion-shaped bun and her woolly jackets, the man must have been an erotic desperado. 'The black-out, you know,' said Dr Zwirnsteiner, the senior master.

One thing, however, soon became certain: Fräulein Dr Gerch could not have been particularly choosy in picking her Führer-child's father, at least not from the racial point of view. The child had black hair, was stunted and bow-legged, and by the age of only two had developed a pro-nounced hook nose together with a pair of piercing black eyes. 'He's sure to grow out of it,' said Fräulein Dr Gerch, stung by the many insinuations. Alas, the boy never did.

The child had been named Rudolf Sigurd. Sigurd was a tribute to the Nordic ideal. The first name, however, ought to have been Adolf, not Rudolf, for if Fräulein Dr Gerch had had her way, the Führer would have received this wonderful present in person. Unfortunately, Fräulein Dr Gerch was fobbed off — and that only thanks to her connections in the NS Women's League — with Rudolf Hess, who though not actually present at the NS name-giving ceremony (which stood in for baptism among Party faithfuls), did convey his NS blessings by letter. These blessings proved of rather doubtful value, since on 10 May 1941 when little Rudolf Gerch was just one year old, Hess decided to make off to Britain and entered the annals of Nazi history as a traitor.

Schneemoser, who was a terribly precocious child, could give an excellent imitation of the coy manners of Fräulein Dr Gerch, who liked to refer to herself as 'just a great big girl'. Xaver Bohrlein always had a good laugh, though he did not fully grasp what the boy was trying to do. He was as slow of understanding as he was hard of hearing.

Princess Hildegard, the Queen Mother, had not only forgotten her villa in Bogenhausen, let alone Xaver Bohrlein, but had, as we said, completely repressed the existence of

Hermanfried Schneemoser. Bohrlein did the best he could in the circumstances, and Schneemoser made no complaint either: he was only too grateful that someone was there to tend to his physical needs. As for his spiritual needs, he had long since learned to satisfy them by himself. He found his existence in the villa with its large park, both of which he was free to roam at will, altogether idyllic. Nor was he overly worried by the bombs that had been raining down ever since 1943, and still more insistently since the beginning of 1944. The villa was never hit, a fact Xaver Bohrlein attributed to his own physical strength. (He had been a wrestler and a weight lifter in a circus.) Whenever there was an alert, he would swear for all he was worth, jerking his head violently up at the sky, and as he uttered his convulsive and incomprehensible curses, his bald pate would develop the most ominous of creases and his eyes would pop out of his head. No doubt all this was intended to warn the enemy bombers off. They destroyed schools, churches, the Royal Palace, the Pinakothek, the Court Theatre, but they kept well clear of the villa in Bogenhausen.

But what the enemy bombers failed to do was nearly brought about by the Führer's 'last muster' in the spring of 1945. Despite his physical strength, which resembled the dumb persistence of the planarian rather than the agile skill of the trapeze artist, Bohrlein had been rejected by every possible Army medical board. He had felt terribly hurt, the more so as he had a deep love for march-pasts, parades, banners and particularly for brass bands. But now, at the beginning of 1945, when Hitler was summoning even the lame and the halt to the colours, Bohrlein too was at last called up. He nearly burst with pride.

'You see, my boy,' he tried to say, his words rendered more jerkily incomprehensible than ever by his excitement, 'when they're in real trouble they know whom to send for.'

Schneemoser read the call-up papers. 'And what will happen to me?'

'Never you worry. I shall take you along,' Bohrlein stuttered. 'Just let them try to harm a single hair on your

56

head.' He had been chopping wood when the call-up papers arrived. He now picked up the chopping-block with one hand and flung it against the wall of the cellar with such force that the whole house shook. 'Just let them try!'

But the authorities, though desperate for cannon-fodder, thought better of it as soon as they set eyes on poor Bohrlein and heard him speak. Completely shattered, and mortally offended, Bohrlein came back home. He had never been interested in politics, but from that day on he was eaten up by hatred of the Nazis.

On 30 April 1945, the Americans entered Munich. They met with little if any resistance — even the ingenious tank-traps built by specially exempted labour and placed across Reichenbach Bridge on the Gauleiter's personal orders, had proved no match for them.

Central Munich was one great heap of rubble; the Palace lay in ruins. Nymphenburg Castle, by contrast, was almost undamaged. After the arrest of all the Nazis or suspected Nazis the Americans could lay their hands on by the afternoon of 30 April, their commander, General Howard S. Taylor, decided to call on the King at Nymphenburg Castle. No one ever knew whether he intended to arrest the King as well, or to pay his respects; all we do know is that Nymphenburg was ready for him with a cleverly planned charade.

Next morning the General drove up before the main steps. He came in a jeep escorted by two further jeeps carrying soldiers armed to the teeth. The men remained below — the General, obviously not expecting to find dispersed SS units in the castle, was accompanied by just one adjutant. He had no need of an interpreter since both of them spoke German. He was received by an emaciated equerry and then by the Grand Master of the Royal Horse, Count von Seebach-Wurzau. The Master of the Royal Horse saluted the General and begged permission to present him to His Majesty. That was precisely why he had come, General Taylor explained.

'This other gentleman, as well?' enquired the Count,

glancing at the adjutant.

The General reflected for a moment and then said: 'Yes, this other gentleman as well, if His Majesty would not mind.'

Preceded by the Master of the Royal Horse, the small party passed through four empty rooms. In the fifth room they were met by Counsellor-at-Law Dr von Scheuchenzuber and also by Monsignor Zach, who had been nervously pacing up and down and making animated remarks to the Counsellor-at-Law, only to fall silent the moment the Americans entered. Count von Seebach-Wurzau introduced the two gentlemen to the General who, though impatient, was still perfectly courteous.

Zach and Scheuchenzuber joined the procession to the next room.

General Taylor had been fully briefed by Intelligence, who had given him a concise but telling account — with photographs — of the life of King Luitpold I, and the General had looked them over once again at breakfast that morning.

The man who now stood straight as a ramrod in the middle of the room was not the King he had seen in the photographs, but an ancient old giant of a man with a bushy white moustache.

The General was taken aback.

'Your Majesty,' said the Grand Master of the Horse, 'may I present General Taylor. General — His Majesty King Rupprecht I, King of Bavaria, Duke of Franconia, Palegrave of Rhein.'

'Oh . . .' said the General. 'My papers say the King's name is Luitpold.'

Rupprecht gave the Counsellor-at-Law a brief wave, whereupon the latter pulled a piece of paper out of his pocket, unfolded it, and read out a Proclamation to the effect that King Luitpold I, having offended against the will of the Bavarian people, against the House of Wittelsbach and against the Holy Church by conspiring with the Nazis, had been stripped of all his royal prerogatives. His Majesty, King Rupprecht, was accordingly the sole legitimate ruler of Bavaria. The document also explained the significance of the Roman suffix 'I': though His Majesty was King of Bavaria for the second time, he was nevertheless the first Rupprecht to occupy the Bavarian throne — now as before. Prince Luitpold — the deposed King — had also been excluded from the succession (in respect of his own person, though not of his line). The new successor to the Crown, accordingly, was Prince Otto, the King's grandson.

Whatever instructions General Taylor may or may not have received from his superiors, one thing was certain: they had made no provisions for this singular turn of events. The General saluted, vaguely wished the King good luck, and left.

Outside, he enquired of Counsellor-at-Law von Scheuchenzuber — for purposes of his report — what type of government the old-new King was likely to adopt.

'No problem at all,' said the Counsellor-at-Law, 'a constitutional monarchy.'

'And what about democratic freedom and basic human rights?'

'They will all be guaranteed in the Constitution.'

'Well, well!' The General turned to Scheuchenzuber once more and asked, almost diffidently now, what had happened to ex-King Luitpold.

Scheuchenzuber merely shrugged his shoulders.

Old King Rupprecht had been brought home by a circuitous route from Florence via Switzerland in late April. Counsellor-at-Law von Scheuchenzuber no less than Frau Schumata (whose cousin held an important office in the State Department) had used all their contacts to make the journey possible.

The Crown Prince — and that had been the true import of the call paid by Scheuchenzuber and Monsignor Zach to Count Seybothenreuth — should also have reached Munich by 1 May. But unfortunately his journey had been more in the nature of an obstacle race.

To begin with, Crown Prince Otto was expected to manifest a new burst of growth at the end of April. 'We had best leave Mama in Eichkatzlried,' the Queen had decided. She would also have liked to leave her younger son, Prince Max Arnulph, behind in the safety of Hungerbichl, but when he heard of the plan, the boy set up such a caterwauling that she quickly agreed to take him along after all.

The 30 April 1945 was a Monday. In Eichkatzlried it was not just snowing; there was a veritable blizzard.

'We could ask for nothing better,' said Lieutenant-Colonel Count Seybothenreuth.

The Count had managed to procure a car. It was an ancient Opel Kadett, requisitioned from its owner at the outbreak of war and now painted in camouflage green. Unfortunately that colour, and also the fact that it had a petrol instead of a charcoal-driven engine, set it off plainly as a German Army vehicle. The car had recently belonged to the Eichkatzlried garrison commander, and Lieutenant-Colonel Seybothenreuth had taken possession of it by virtue of a special order, signed by the Supreme Commander South-West, General von Vietinghoff, in person. The order was undated, and had been handed to Seybothenreuth by Counsellor-at-Law Scheuchenzuber during his visit in August 1944 so that all the Lieutenant-Colonel had to do was to add the date: 28.4.1945. The garrison commander had seemed a bit taken aback, but though the Tyrol was still in German hands at the time, and though all sorts of Nazi rabble were still abroad, the time for asking questions had passed.

'There's the problem of what to wear,' Lieutenant-Colonel Count Seybothenreuth said to the Queen.

'Why?' asked the Queen.

'Well, because we are travelling in an Army car.'

'You have a permit, haven't you?'

'Indeed, I have. But it says nothing about a lady and her two children!'

'Why shouldn't an officer carry a lady and two children . . . after all they might be . . . in any case I still have a blank pass . . .'

60

'Do you really want to draw attention to our party, Your Majesty? Do you want every blessed military police patrol to check our papers, even if they have to let us go in the end?'

'No one must catch sight of the Crown Prince, whatever happens,' the Queen said quickly.

'And what do you suggest, Your Majesty? How do you think we can slip through to Munich undetected?'

'But that's your responsibility, Seybothenreuth. It's you who have to get us to Munich, not I,' the Queen said indignantly.

'Then may I humbly propose that Your Majesty dress up as a man?'

'As a man? And where do you suggest I find the clothes?'

'I have brought one of my suits with me, Your Majesty. Perhaps the legs and the arms need some alteration, but for the rest I'm sure it will do.'

'And the Crown Prince . . . ?'

'The Crown Prince . . .'

' . . . is much too fat to fit into one of your suits.'

'We'll find some way. The most important thing is not to arouse their suspicions with a woman. As for the younger Prince, we can push him down whenever necessary and hide him under some blankets.'

And so the Lieutenant-Colonel lent the Queen — who, as luck would have it, was rather flat-chested — his pepper-and-salt tweeds and a shirt and tie. The Queen put up her hair and hid it under a check cap. Otto was told to pull a black rubber waterproof over his sailor suit. A hat, left behind by the 'gentleman farmer' in the old stables and dug up by the children (it was a worn-out, shapeless old pork-pie with a thin and faded plume in its band), also came into its own: the Crown Prince who had to leave all his own toys behind — 'we are carrying more than enough as it is, and you'll get everything back in due course,' his Grandmother had told him — insisted on being allowed to take the dirty old hat along at the very least.

'Will you throw that beastly thing away this instant,' the Queen shouted, for she was growing increasingly nervous.

'But no!' said the Lieutenant-Colonel. 'It's a brilliant idea. Let him wear it and pull it well down over his face. And I'll paint on a moustache . . .' He was about to tell an anecdote about two peasants who had dressed up a pig so as to smuggle it into town during the black-market days of the 1920s, but thought better of it just in time.

The party set off at nightfall, the Lieutenant-Colonel — in uniform — at the wheel. He had drummed up three cans of petrol and had stowed them away in the boot, leaving room for just a small suitcase with the Queen's things and a bag with his own. Next to the driver sat the disguised Crown Prince — he would never have fitted into the back, which the Queen now shared with nine-year-old Prince Max Arnulph.

It was snowing hard, and the roads were covered in slush and mud. For days, the remnants of the Führer's Italian Army had been pulling back in increasing disarray. Not one of them could have told you where the front line was — all they knew was what the radio had told them: that Hitler was dead and that, as one of his last acts on earth, he had ordered Göring to be strung up as a traitor. Here and there, odd copies of the *Völkischer Beobachter* still kept circulating with news of Hitler's heroic end in Berlin. Little was known of the whereabouts of Dönitz, the new Führer. In Eichkatzlried, the Royal party had still been able to listen to a commentary by Hans Fritsche, that popular humorist-despite-himself; he had told them in anguished tones that the Americans had foisted a Jewish Burgomaster on Cologne.

Lieutenant-Colonel von Seybothenreuth had decided to take the Kufstein-Thiersee-Bäckeralm road across to Bayrischzell. It was poor and unfrequented, but had the advantage that it was more or less impassable to the massive convoys fleeing north.

'How long before we get to Munich?' asked the Queen, when the Lieutenant-Colonel turned off the Hungerbichl road on to the main road at Lake Birken in the direction of the Tschurtschen Valley.

'Normally it would take us four hours,' said the Lieutenant-Colonel. 'But, as things are, we will have to reckon on at least double that time, and then only if every-thing goes according to plan.'

Alas, nothing at all seemed to be going to plan. To begin with, a group of stragglers had taken the wrong turning at the Eichkatzlried crossroads, and were descending into the Tschurtschen Valley in complete disorder. The road is fairly wide here and easily mistaken for the main road, at least by strangers. But just past Lake Birken it begins to twist and turn, grows narrow and winds through huddled villages and across a mountain pass at Ulrichsmühle. Here the stragglers had abandoned their field guns, their ammunition and every-thing else they could do without. Some of it lay about in the ditches; the rest blocked the road. Just outside Ulrichsmühle stood a long file of abandoned lorries.

'Like rats,' said the Lieutenant-Colonel. For as the Royal car approached, a pack of shadows could be seen flitting away from the lorries: the peasants had come to loot. They were being stupid, of course, for the soldiers had taken any-thing edible or valuable with them on their headlong flight into the woods. Still, the peasants did not leave altogether empty-handed: they carried off maps, a box of rubber erasers, and a stack of apparently useless conical cardboard tubes . . . Old Mother Stallwanger, notorious for her rapacity, cleared out the divisional duplicating van, and removed some 100,000 blue stencils, just in case — paper is always needed, even in the Stallwangers' backyard. Five years later, when the old woman died, the district surgeon scratched his head as he looked at the corpse's ink-blue posterior.

The Lieutenant-Colonel had to drive with exceptional care. Needless to say, all the army vehicles had been dumped with their lights switched off. To make things worse, the snowstorm grew fiercer the further they pressed into the Tschurtschen Valley, and the darkened headlights — tiny slits in the black-out covers — were next to useless under such conditions. By the time they had cleared the pass and were going down again, this time into the Inn Valley, it was well past ten o'clock.

'Are you asleep, Your Majesty?' asked the Lieutenant-Colonel.

'The child is asleep,' said the Queen.

'Splendid,' said the Lieutenant-Colonel.

'Do you think we will ever make it?' asked the Queen. The Colonel said nothing at all.

'No one, but absolutely no one must catch sight of the Crown Prince,' said the Queen.

'That's no special problem, Your Majesty, because no one must catch sight of any of us.'

The drive through the broad Inn Valley did not take all that long: the road was luckily completely deserted. True, even here abandoned field guns and even armoured cars cluttered the road, but quite obviously most of the fleeing troops had decided to give the exposed valley a wide berth. A wrecked train just outside Wörgl showed that during the last few days of the war the American bombers had been able to do as they pleased, even in the 'Reich Air Raid Shelter'.

Count Seybothenreuth drove as fast as he dared. From the mountains came the sound of sporadic gunfire.

'Are they still fighting around here?' the Queen enquired anxiously.

'Not at all,' said the Lieutenant-Colonel. 'Probably our own men, potting at deer for their dinner — that's if we are in luck.'

'And if not?'

'SS firing at deserters.'

'For God's sake, I should have thought they had their hands full with the enemy.'

'They have probably put two and two together and decided that it's much safer to fire at Germans than at Americans . . .'

The car reached the turnoff near Lake Thier without further trouble. Here the road was, if anything, worse than the road through the Tschurtschen Valley had been, and Lieutenant-Colonel Count Seybothenreuth had to slow down once again. It was getting on for midnight when Prince Otto began to groan.

'Whatever is wrong with him, Your Majesty?' asked the Colonel without turning round. The Queen kept silent.

'What's the matter with him, Your Majesty? Why these groans? Or are you asleep?'

The Queen burst into sobs. Count Seybothenreuth stepped on the brake pedal so hard that the car skidded to a sideways halt.

'Your Majesty?'

'I'm starving,' yelled the Crown Prince. 'I've got to have some food . . .'

'Dear God in Heaven!' wailed the Queen. 'It would happen now of all times. Do drive on, Count, please drive on as fast as you can.'

The Count straightened the car and started up again. The road was very steep now and the car made very slow progress. The Crown Prince was groaning for all he was worth.

'Here, Ottito,' said the Queen handing him a biscuit. Her son nearly devoured her hand in the process.

'We didn't bring enough food,' wailed the Queen, 'not nearly enough.'

'Whatever is the matter with the Prince, Your Majesty? Is he ill?'

'A sudden burst of growth. Another one. And now of all times! Each time that happens, he grows up to four inches at a stroke. And then he eats anything he can lay his hands on.'

Just then, the Crown Prince set up a great bellow. His little brother woke up and joined in.

'I can't possibly concentrate on the road with all that noise, Your Majesty!'

'I'm afraid there's absolutely nothing I can do about it, Colonel.'

'Oh . . . owwwww . . . my feet, my feet,' wailed the Crown Prince.

'He's outgrown his shoes,' gasped the Queen. 'Please, dear Count, won't you drive a little faster!'

Prince Otto's shoelaces had burst. He took off his shoes,

and felt slightly better. But when his waterproof exploded with a loud report and the buttons shot through the car like so many bullets, the Colonel brought the car to another halt.

'I can't possibly drive on like this. Let him finish his growth. How long does it usually take?'

'It differs from time to time. Once it took two days and two nights.'

'Charming,' said the Count.

'Dear God in Heaven, and the whole forest teeming with SS!'

'When that lot sees the Crown Prince growing, they'll run for their lives.'

The Crown Prince picked up a hamper and dug into it with both hands, liberally shovelling biscuits, fruit, sausages, cakes and chocolates down his throat.

'Charming,' said the Count.

The Crown Prince's head was growing as well, and suddenly the old pork-pie he was wearing shot off like a discus and rolled away across the road.

'Leave it alone,' screamed the Queen, as the Prince — despite the discomfort he was suffering — jumped out of the car, obviously determined to rescue his beloved hat from the ditch. 'Please, let's drive on, Count Seybothenreuth!' urged the Queen.

Count Seybothenreuth had climbed out as well. Though he had refused to sacrifice his life for the Führer throughout the war, he was still an officer and a gentleman, the last of a long line in fact, and as such fully trained to look danger straight in the face. And it must be said in all fairness to him that if those now under his care and protection had been threatened by the least danger, he would have stood up for them like a man. Count Seybothenreuth was no coward. But as he now peered at the Prince, while clutching the open door of the car, his whole body began to tremble.

'I have never seen the likes of it,' he whispered at least ten times. 'He is bursting out of his skin, right out of his skin, that's all you can call it . . .'

By then, the Queen, more familiar with this strange

spectacle, had pulled herself together. She consoled and stroked the younger Prince and replaced him on the back seat. 'It's all done now, he has produced his four inches; the worst is over,' she said. 'Please get back into the car, Ottito.'

Count Seybothenreuth was still trembling, as he stood rooted to the spot. When one is over five foot ten inches, every new inch seems to make one a whole head taller. And actually to watch it happening, four times over, must have been a most terrifying experience. In the dark, Count Seybothenreuth had the distinct impression that the Prince had doubled his original size, and that he had expanded like rising dough. The Count's face betrayed his fear that the Prince would keep swelling until he filled the entire universe. Only when another few shots rang out from the mountains did he more or less regain his composure.

'Please let's drive on,' the Queen urged again.

Without another word, the Colonel jumped back into the car. The Crown Prince squashed back in by his side, hatless now, with his shoes hanging from his toes like a pair of slippers. The waterproof had burst all its seams, and a four-inch gap between Prince Otto's sailor blouse and pants revealed an expanse of naked belly. For the rest, the material of the sailor suit was elastic, though not enough to allow of any further growth whatsoever. The suit was stretched like a high-tension cable.

They did not get very far. Though Lake Thier itself was perfectly dark and still, the small village of Landl, on the border between the All-Germanic Provinces of Munich-Upper Bavaria and Tyrol-Vorarlberg (formerly Austria), was full of life. Armed with burning flares and electric torches, three to four dozen men were rushing noisily through the streets despite the late hour — it was close on midnight now. The tocsin was pealing from the church steeple, and the red-white-and-red Austrian flag had been hoisted up on a pole in front of the Gasthaus Post. Right across the main street, two empty haycarts, their shafts bound firmly together, blocked all traffic. Several men were trying to set fire to a pile of something or other in the middle of the road.

67

A man wearing a red-and-white armband, his rifle slung and the corners of his mouth drawn downward in good partisan style, stopped the Royal car and shone a torch at its occupants.

'We've got a prisoner of war,' he yelled to the rest of his gang. Then he roared 'Hands up!' at the Colonel. 'Surrender!'

Landl had learned a few hours earlier that Dr Karl Renner had proclaimed Austria a republic the previous Friday, and that he had demanded the restoration of the 1938 borders, at the very least. The Landlers immediately decided not just to sit by until the Americans moved in, but took up arms and deposed the Nazi major at 9.30 p.m. The priest at once intoned a Te Deum. Two Nazi flags, from which the white circle with the swastika had been ripped out, and a sheet which a peasant woman had been glad to sacrifice (and at the time this was a real sacrifice on her part) were improvised into an Austrian banner. The remaining Nazi flags, Hitler portraits, and all the many volumes of *Mein Kampf* (which every good peasant had received as a wedding present from the Party), the motherhood crosses, and the Party membership cards, were all piled up outside the 'Post'. 'Long live the Austrian Republic! Long live Free Tyrol!' yelled the tenant of Stimpfriegl Farm. He had been mayor of Landl before the *Anschluss* and was now back in office.

As the Royal car had turned into the main street, the locals were just dragging one Anton Joseph Kofler, the local Nazi boss, from the chicken coop in which he had sought refuge. At first he had refused their orders to don the Party uniform he had worn with such pride until that day, but it had taken only the fewest kicks to his posterior before he had done as he was told. His wife, Watty, had stood sobbing by his side while handing him a brown shirt from the depths of the chest into which his uniform had been hurriedly flung.

Anton Kofler in full uniform, with Party insignia and swastika armband, was then ducked several times in the Stimpfriegl cesspool. As a result of this, he did not look a very colourful or edifying spectacle, although the original colour of his uniform had suffered little change. The NS leader, dripping dung, was then locked up in the mortuary, where he sat shivering and cursing on a trestle normally reserved for the coffins. At this point old Mother Janner had appeared upon the scene. She was an ancient and very poor woman who lived in a tiny hut just outside the town, where she kept a few goats and earned her living by weaving baskets. She had had three sons, all of whom had died in the war: the first in Carelia, the second in Africa and the third in Italy.

No one had heard the old woman. Suddenly, there she stood right in front of the mortuary.

'Let me in,' she said very quietly.

The guards hesitated. Kofler set up another howl.

'Let me in,' repeated old Mother Janner, not very much louder.

Then the guards did as they were bid, and Mother Janner stepped into the mortuary. The gibbering Nazi boss retired at once to the furthermost recess.

'Three boys,' said Mother Janner. 'Three strapping lads. Just one good clout for each one!' And she was as good as her word — three times her bony hand landed on Kofler's cheek. Three tremendous, earthy Tyrolean slaps. Then Mother Janner turned on her heel, not wasting another glance on Kofler or the guards.

A German Colonel in an army vehicle was just what the Landl freedom fighters had needed to make their day. But Count Seybothenreuth, who knew nothing of the events we have just related, though he had a fair idea of what was going on, instinctively put his foot down hard on the accelerator. The Austrian freedom fighters screamed, and the Colonel threw the gear lever into reverse, so quickly that some of the good countryfolk behind had to leap out of the way. He then did a three-point turn at the corner and raced recklessly back into the valley, with bullets whistling past the windscreen. He must have covered a good three miles by the time he reached a small track into the forest. He drove the car a few hundred yards along it and switched off the engine.

'For the moment we are safe,' he said.

'What do we do now? asked the Queen.

'We shall have to proceed on foot.'

From the behaviour of the locals, Count Seybothenreuth had been quick — but quite wrong — to conclude that the Americans must have occupied Bayrischzell across the border, and perhaps even the Bäcker Pass.

'We can't make it by car. They've blocked the only road out of Landl,' he explained.

'But how are we to get across, with you in full German uniform?'

'I can't possibly proceed in — saving Your Majesty's presence — my underpants!'

'Well, why not change into a suit?'

'Because Your Majesty is wearing it.'

'Here,' said the Queen, and pointed to the car.

'Here, what, Your Majesty?'

'There's a two-piece costume in my case.'

Count Seybothenreuth demurred. The Queen said he was behaving like a prude. The Count then fell back on his officer's honour, pointing with affronted dignity to the absurd fox collar of the Queen's jacket.

'How dare you mock your Queen's wardrobe!'

Count Seybothenreuth twisted and turned and brought up a hundred excuses, but all to no avail. The Queen stood her ground: in any case, Seybothenreuth had to admit that his uniform endangered them all.

He accordingly divested himself of the Führer's field-grey tunic and trousers behind a large tree, and changed into a dark-grey 'classic' two-piece tailored suit, with silver stitching, over a cream-coloured, frilly silk blouse, and finally pulled a pair of silk stockings over his hairy legs. As the Queen's shoes did not fit him, he retained his black army half-boots hoping that no one would notice. The worst was not so much the fur collar as the Queen's hat: a slanted beret with a silver pin in the shape of a laurel-leaf and a long black feather that rose up impressively if somewhat asymmetrically.

Not until he had finished did it strike Seybothenreuth that it would have been far better for the Queen to have worn her own clothes while he changed back into his suit.

70

'You surely don't expect me to strip in front of you and the children, do you? In any case, it's done now.'

Count Seybothenreuth threw his field-greys into the car with a grunt. All he retained of his uniform was the belt and holster.

'What ever do you want with those?' asked the Queen.

'You never can tell, Your Majesty.'

The Queen reached into her suitcase and handed the Count a patent-leather handbag that went extremely well with the costume. Seybothenreuth dropped his pistol into the bag and flung the belt and holster after the uniform.

Their march was slow and laborious. The forest was pitch-black and when they eventually emerged, most of the tracks were covered in slush. Count Seybothenreuth walked ahead, his skirt hitched up, stumbling over twigs and roots, often hitting his head against low-hanging branches. The Queen had taken little Prince Max Arnulph by the hand; he was sobbing quietly with fatigue. Whenever possible — when the going was not too rough — the Colonel would carry him and the Queen as well for short stretches. The Crown Prince, meanwhile, stomped through the undergrowth like a boar. He was the least put out by their plight. Now and then he would even carry his little brother. By the time their eyes had grown used to the darkness, the four of them, or at least the two grown-ups, had the feeling that they were making fairly good progress. All the same, they would never have reached Bavaria had Count Seybothenreuth not been a soldier and a hunter, one who had learned to take his bearings under even the most difficult of circumstances. After some two hours — already the grey dawn had begun to lighten the eastern sky — they reached a wider lane, and soon afterwards a cross-roads with a signpost. The signpost said 'Bayrischzell – 1¼ hours'.

'The worst is behind us,' exclaimed the Count. He led the Queen and the children to a bench under a large tree, and was considering the next move, when a torch flashed on nearby. Two huge figures leapt out from the dark, and one of them fell upon the person of the Queen. Count Seybothenreuth rushed to the rescue, was dealt a tremendous blow to his chin and fell to the ground. By the time he could get back on to his feet and retrieve his pistol from its unaccustomed container, the two figures had jumped away and were racing up the road for all they were worth.

'Don't shoot,' whispered the Queen, 'or you might give us away. Those two were in a terrible panic themselves.'

The Royal party moved on. The lane was much drier now and quite broad, and Count Seybothenreuth could cool his aching chin at several wells by the wayside. At 4.30 a.m. — it was now the morning of Tuesday, 1 May 1945, and black-birds were singing as if the world was one great haven of peace — Bayrischzell lay before them.

Once there, the Colonel, dressed in the Queen's classic tailored two-piece costume, realized his mistake. The Americans had not yet arrived, though no German troops were about either. The locals had adopted a wait-and-see policy — that is, all of them were peacefully asleep.

Count Seybothenreuth rang the priest's door bell, and was met at first in a rather unfriendly fashion. But as soon as the priest realized the identity of his callers, he warmed to them at once and said he felt deeply honoured. He was made privy to everything — the Queen felt that in the circumstances it was only right to tell him all about the Crown Prince's strange complaint — swore solemnly on the sacrament to keep this terrible secret, and promised to help in any way he could. As far as he knew, the Americans had come as far as Rosenheim. He would, he said, try to contact Munich by telephone.

In separate rooms, the Queen and Count Seybothenreuth then changed clothes, realizing as they did that no one in his right mind would ever have taken the unshaven Count, even in the tailored costume, for a woman. The priest's servant produced what was, for the times, a sumptuous breakfast, and the Princes were put to bed for a couple of hours.

As luck would have it, the priest actually managed to get through to Munich. And why ever not, he explained, electricity is indifferent to military reverses; it flows happily so long as the line is not cut, which evidently it was not.

'Strategically speaking,' the Count speculated, 'this is something that will have to be taken into greater account than it has been in the past. Behind the enemy lines . . . no need for reconnaissance aircraft, no need to drop intelligence agents by parachute . . . all you need is to pick up a receiver . . .'

'It's a bit too late for that, I'm afraid,' said the priest. 'I don't think even telephones will help us to win the war at this stage.'

The priest got through to the diocesan court, which transferred the call to Monsignor Zach. The Monsignor confirmed that the Americans had taken Rosenheim, and Tölz as well. Count Seybothenreuth and his illustrious company were advised to make for the latter, where a car would be waiting for them outside the presbytery.

But how were they to get to Tölz? The poor priest in Bayrischzell had no car. True, the village doctor did own one, but it had run out of petrol. In the end, the Count managed to drum up a landaulet and a horse — a peasant handed both over to the priest against the two gold ducats which the Queen had been prudent enough to take along against just such eventualities.

'Can you handle the reins?' the priest asked the Count.

'I expect I shall manage,' said the Count, whose chin was still painful, but who, now he was back in male clothes, felt capable of handling anything at all.

The priest even managed to solve the Crown Prince's problem. Since the boy, now measuring six foot, two inches, could not possibly travel in his belly-exposing sailor suit and exploded waterproof, the priest lent him a cassock. It came down to the priest's own ankles, but only just reached below the Prince's knees. In all other details it fitted him well enough, for the reverend gentleman had been blessed with corpulence. A large black umbrella and a round hat completed the picture. The Prince now looked the perfect, shall we say caponized cleric, a picture that is not all that rare in Bavaria.

By nightfall, the Royal party arrived at Tegernsee Castle, owned by cousins of the ducal line. Duke Ludwig Wilhelm of

Bavaria was happy to entertain the completely exhausted Queen and the younger prince, while Crown Prince Otto and Count Seybothenreuth were rowed across the lake by two apprentices from the ducal brewery, who took them to Wiessee, now under American occupation. There the two of them — the Crown Prince still dressed in his cassock — handed a letter of introduction to one Baron Singenfried, a hunting companion of the Duke's. The Baron immediately provided a servant, and had them taken to Tölz in his charcoal-burning three-wheeler. They told an American patrol outside Waakirchen that they were doing their clerical rounds; the Prince even blessed the astonished Americans. In Tölz, Monsignor Zach's car stood waiting for them at the appointed place, and during the afternoon of 2 May, King Rupprecht was able to present his successor to the US commander.

The US General found the Prince likeable, if slightly on the fat side. (He had no idea, of course, that the giant was only a small boy.)

'He'll grow out of it,' said the King.

The dynasty had been saved once again.

As we already knew, for years that near-dumb Hercules Xaver Bohrlein had been looking after his young ward Hermanfried in Bogenhausen without any outside help. (To his honour, let it be said, he had done so with never a thought for himself.) He had, so to speak, stood up to the enemy bombers by waving his bare fists at them. The approaching American ground forces, by contrast (Bohrlein conscientiously followed Wehrmacht communiqués on the radio), filled him with deep foreboding.

On 29 April — it was a Sunday — Bohrlein and Hermanfried had attended 10 o'clock Mass at the George Chapel in Bogenhaus cemetery, one of the few churches in Munich to have survived the raids. At 11 a.m., they were back home, and Bohrlein at once switched on his 'People's Receiver'. Although the top floor was quite uninhabited and Bohrlein could easily have extended his domain to the entire house, he had preferred to stay in his dingy bed-sitting room below the stairs. Hermanfried's room and the large kitchen were next door. Upstairs, Bohrlein had dusted religiously throughout the years, and had also given all the rooms a good airing once a month. Now the old man was sitting in his threadbare armchair once again, his ear pressed close to the loud-speaker, nodding his bald head reflectively from time to time. The only sign of agitation Hermanfried could notice was a convulsive grinding of his 'uncle's' tremendous, misshapen jaws. The Americans, said the Wehrmacht com-muniqué, had just advanced on Landsberg. The German withdrawal had, as ever, proceeded according to plan and the enemy had suffered tremendous losses. Munich, the com-muniqué continued, was being turned into a fortress, and the defenders were throwing in everything they could.

Bohrlein, behaving quite out of character, did not wait for the end of the news. Without warning, he jumped up and switched off the radio. Jerking his head even more violently than usual, he muttered — his sounds are difficult to reproduce — 'Gt yelf ray moy, woff' — Get ready my boy, we're off.

The villa, Bohrlein realized, was as good as lost now, and the sooner he got the boy out of 'Fortress Munich' the better. Few preparations were needed. Bohrlein aired the upstairs rooms for the last time, and in so doing came across a signed Hitler photograph which the Chancellor had reluctantly presented to Prince Moritz on the occasion of the latter's sixtieth birthday, and which the latter had no less reluctantly shoved into a fly-blown old frame and stowed away behind a mass of unused china in a glass showcase — flinging the thing into the dustbin would have been far too dangerous. Bohrlein looked at it now, and realized that he ought to clear the house of all its Nazi relics. During the hour before lunch, he managed to amass a fair collection — including one swastika banner (of the kind almost every German household kept to mark the Führer's birthdays and against the great day of the final victory); twenty-four carefully measured cloth-covered black-out frames for the windows; a signed

75

proof copy of the *Myth of the Twentieth Century* presented by Alfred Rosenberg to Prince Moritz on the latter's sixty-fifth birthday in 1939; a volume entitled *Speeches and Essays* by the Duke of Rosenheim, printed on hand-made paper and bearing an over-familiar dedication ('. . . to my dear Cousin, Moritz . . .'); and a presentation copy of Paul Schultze-Naumburg's *Nordic Beauty*, a book the Prince could not possibly have read owing to the fact that the author had brought it along on the memorable afternoon of his visit, since when it had lain unopened on the console next to the umbrella stand. Bohrlein gathered this motley collection into a pile, and before continuing with his airing of the upstairs rooms, lit a fire in the boiler and threw the whole lot in, piece by piece, with obvious satisfaction. Then he closed all the windows, drew all the blinds and curtains, rolled up the carpets, and locked all the doors. He paid another visit to the boiler and pulled the embers apart with a long rake. Finally he stuffed a few odds and ends into a bag, picked up a chunk of bread, a piece of hard cheese and a large portion of — terribly expensive — salami, plus a Thermos flask filled with tea brewed by Schneemoser, and packed the lot, together with some linen for the boy and a few personal belongings, into a rucksack. Then, after a last cursory glance of farewell, he switched off all the lights, and bolted the front door and garden gate. And there they were outside — Bohrlein with the bag slung over his shoulder, and Schneemoser with the rucksack on his back. Not a soul was stirring. The trees in the garden made a fine show of fresh greenery, but the rest of Munich looked like a rubble heap. Columns of smoke rose up from the stone inferno. A distant rumbling proclaimed the continuous — but doubtless perfectly orderly and planned — withdrawal of German troops (with terrible losses to the enemy).

A blackbird could be heard singing in one of the trees on Hompeschstrasse. Bohrlein looked irresolutely up and down the street. Then he smelled the air and decided: that way. And off they went.

To what heights the German spirit can rise! The 1918–19

revolution had admittedly overthrown the government, but it had been quite unable to shake the civil services. Quite unperturbed, German registrars pulled on their black sleeve protectors on 10 November 1918, before sharpening their pencils on behalf of the German Republic, the self-same pencils that they had sharpened just one day earlier* on behalf of the Kaiser. The storming of Chamnitz Railway Station was called off because the revolutionaries had no platform tickets. Quite unperturbed, German judges pronounced sentence 'in the name of the people' on Monday 30 January 1933, just as they had done on Saturday 28 January (which was then still a full working day). The last civilian aircraft of the Lufthansa line left Berlin on 17 April 1945 — for Spain and on schedule. And when Xaver Bohrlein and his 'nephew' Hermanfried reached the remains of Holzkirchen station during the early afternoon of 29 April, the Munich-Holzkirchen-Schliersee-Bayrischzell passenger train too left punctually at 14.02 hours. Some of the carriage windows could no longer be shut because the leather straps had gone (they made excellent shoe leather); the station loudspeaker likewise seemed out of order, and several sidings were filled with carriages rendered more or less unserviceable by enemy air raids. Through the cracks in their torn flanks you could see burst suitcases and boxes, together with the mortal remains of many a passenger. But for the rest, the clerk was still selling quite ordinary tickets (though from the auxiliary signal box), the conductor still punched them with his normal clippers, and the train still blew its normal whistle before it pulled out. The clacking and rattling of its wheels drowned the roar of the approaching American guns. And that, too, was the work of the great German spirit!

In the present case, however, it worked no further than

*This is not quite correct: 9 November 1918, the day on which Chancellor Prince Max of Baden proclaimed the 'de facto' abdication of the Kaiser, was a Saturday. The German registrars thus sharpened their now republican pencils not one day, but two days after the abdication.

Miesbach, for when the train tried to pull out of Miesbach station it found itself without current. For a time, the passengers waited for the electricity to come back on again, but in vain. The conductor felt no need to stand on great ceremony for so few people — he simply walked along the train, shouting: 'That's it! Terminus! All out! Collect your refunds at Bay I!'

Bohrlein and Schneemoser got out.

'What now, Uncle Xaver?'

Bohrlein ground his jaws and looked round vacantly. Then he went up to the conductor and spluttered amidst convulsive jerks: 'Zthere . . . notrn . . . Barishzlll?'

'No damn trains at all. Are you deaf?' said the conductor.

'Mnbs?' asked Bohrlein.

'Eh?' said the conductor.

'A bus,' Schneemoser translated.

'Where the hell do you think we can get a bus? Not a hope in hell. Maybe tomorrow. If you want to get a refund, go to Bay I.'

And Bohrlein duly cashed in the tickets. The clerk — and this shows once again to what great heights the German spirit can rise — calculated the refund exactly, counted out the correct sum, and sullenly slammed the window shut — but no harder or more sullenly than he would have done under more normal conditions.

It was now 4 p.m. Bohrlein and Schneemoser walked about the little town in search of transport until their feet ached. There was one lift they refused: on a dung-cart, which moreover was going to Agatharied. By 5.30 p.m., by which time they had collapsed on a bench outside the church, they had come to regret that refusal — even the dung-cart would have been better than nothing. At the station, to which they returned as soon as they had recovered, their train still stood as they had left it. Tomorrow, some people said, the current might well be back on again. Bohrlein decided to spend the night in Miesbach.

The 'Waitzinger', the large inn on the square, was closed. Outside the 'Baderwirt', a hunchbacked bootboy was sweeping the steps. 'Fact is,' he said, 'you're out of season. For all I know it's out of season for good now.' But perhaps Bohrlein might like to have a word with the landlord. As luck would have it, the latter agreed to put them up for the night, and even served them a passable supper (roast potatoes and steamed kohlrabi with a scrambled egg each). Bohrlein drank a half of *ersatz* beer and joined the landlord in listening to the latest Wehrmacht communiqué. American spearheads had (with tremendous losses) reached the outskirts of Munich. German troops were falling back according to plan into the centre of the capital, which was still seemingly being turned into a fortress with feverish zeal. Grand Admiral Dönitz felt absolutely confident of final victory.

The innkeeper, who did not know what to make of Bohrlein, switched off the radio without a word.

That night Bohrlein and Schneemoser, who had survived bombs and raids without a scratch, only just escaped the fate of a hero's death. Because the air had turned chill, their host had decided to warm up the guest room. Since there was no coal, the hunchbacked bootboy was ordered to sweep up the coal dust in the cellar and to bring it up in a bucket.

'That'll never burn,' the innkeeper's wife muttered.

'But the Party directive was quite plain,' protested her husband. 'Weren't we told to speed the final victory by heating our houses with anything we can burn?'

By the time the bootboy brought the bucket in, the landlord had kindled some wood in the large yellow stove. The bootboy poured on the coal dust, the landlord slammed the stove shut and rubbed his hands in gleeful anticipation.

He was still rubbing away when the stove exploded with a fairly soft thud (like an air bubble escaping from boiling porridge). Not a single tile broke; the stove simply doubled its size for a moment, before releasing a cloud of black smoke and soot between the tiles, and then, outwardly undamaged, subsided into the correct proportions. The whole place stank of sulphur and tar. The hunchback, who had stood closest to the stove, looked the very picture of a

79

chimney sweep, and the innkeeper too was as black as pitch on the side he had turned to the stove. The more remote parts of the room — including Bohrlein and Schneemoser — were dusted with a blackish sort of powder. The door had been burst open by the force of the explosion, and the innkeeper's wife came in cursing and yelling: 'Bugger your final victory!'

She took Bohrlein and Schneemoser outside and brushed them down, while her husband and the servant changed into fresh clothes. No one had been hurt, but the fun had gone out of the company. Bohrlein and Schneemoser retired to bed.

Next morning at dawn — it was by now Monday 30 April — Bohrlein woke his protégé (as we may surely call the boy, after all that Bohrlein had done for him over the years). The innkeeper's wife was already up, and served them fig coffee (the 'Franck' brand — the other available blend was 'Andreas Hofer'). It came in chocolate-like squares, from which the required portions could be broken off and crumbled, and tasted — reputedly — of pulverized cockchafer.

In Miesbach, which was close to the sources of nature, Bohrlein and his protégé were served their cockchafer liquid with real milk; and though there was no sugar, they were helped liberally to saccharin — minute white pills that dissolved in the 'coffee' with tiny explosions of foam. (Many, many years later, the wretched saccharin came back into favour with people anxious to fine down their waistlines.) As if to make up for all these substitutes, the innkeeper's wife, after a few minutes' reflection, fetched a lump of butter from one of the back rooms — a lump of real, yellow, pearly, honest-to-goodness butter — and a loaf of freshly baked bread to spread it on. Bohrlein showed his appreciation and gratitude by violent jerks of his head, which the innkeeper's wife was unfortunately unable to interpret.

After breakfast, Bohrlein paid the bill and took Hermanfried back to the station. Their train had not moved, and the station-master thought the chances of having the current restored very slender indeed. Out on the station square, Bohrlein began cursing the war, Hitler, and all Nazis. He kept cursing for all he was worth — but ran no risks at all, for no one could understand a single word. Even so, a passer-by realized that Bohrlein was protesting at something or other and asked Hermanfried what the matter was.

Hermanfried explained the situation. The man then offered to take them to Schliersee in a horse-cart, if they were prepared to wait for two hours or so. Bohrlein accepted with alacrity. And so, after taking another cup of Franck coffee in the 'Baderwirt' and having watched the innkeeper set fire, not to the final-victory-enhancing coal dust, but to all the Hitler portraits from the various guest-rooms, they were taken to Schliersee in an open hay-wagon. (Bohrlein paid the driver in salami.) When they arrived in Schliersee, towards noon, the place looked like a graveyard. Not an inn was open, and the peasants had barricaded all their houses. No one would give them even one word of information — either the people of Schliersee were more frightened than those in Miesbach had been, or else they had just received some terrible news. (Bohrlein grew nervous: he had failed to listen to the latest Wehrmacht bulletin.) Just outside the last house in the village, they came upon a deaf old peasant sitting on a bench smoking his long-stemmed pipe.

'Gdy,' jerked Bohrlein.

'What?' said the peasant.

'Schzll?' asked Bohrlein, and pointed to the valley.

'Yes,' said the peasant, 'it's chicory I'm smoking.'

'Nth gng Schzll?'

'Nothing but chicory, these past two years,' said the peasant.

'Ha, hng,' said Bohrlein.

'Been wondering if there'll ever be anything else to put in my pipe but chicory.'

At this point, a woman of uncertain age shot out of the house and swore at the old man. Before Bohrlein could put another question, she had dragged him indoors and slammed the door shut.

Since there was obviously no means of getting a ride to Bayrischzell, Bohrlein and Schneemoser had to walk. It took them two and a half hours. They met no one on the way, and no vehicle of any kind overtook them.

Bayrischzell was a little more alive, but when they asked about transport to Kufstein, people shook their heads gravely. The Nazis, they explained, had been kicked out from the Tyrol. The best way across the border was at night. And so Bohrlein and Schneemoser waited until long after midnight before setting off towards Bäckeralm.

'It's snowing across in the Tyrol,' people had told them in Bayrischzell. Bohrlein accordingly took out their waterproofs from the tightly packed rucksack, and they put them on there and then. This, if anything, showed that Hermanfried was no normal child — what fourteen-year-old boy likes to put on a German waterproof? The article in question could only have resulted from an unremitting research for the absolute in unbecoming ugliness. Not only that: a German waterproof is a purely practical affair, and makes its wearer look ridiculous, disfigured, almost insect-like. He takes on the appearance of a beetle, or perhaps a woodlouse. Children are extremely sensitive to this sort of thing. Thousands of them had to be tortured and forced by their coarse-grained parents before donning the awful things. Hermanfried Schneemoser, by contrast, put up no resistance at all, not even when Bohrlein — whose bull-like figure could not, aesthetically speaking, be made any less appealing even by a German waterproof — passed him, not only that abhorrent object, but also a beret-shaped rubberized hat to go with it. Hermanfried said not a word, which ought to have made even Bohrlein sit up.

They walked for one and a half hours without meeting a soul. Now and then, Bohrlein would shine his pocket torch on a signpost; otherwise everything was totally dark and silent. Schneemoser was tired, and though he was now steaming under his waterproof, kept a stiff upper lip, following quietly one pace behind Bohrlein, with a bowed head. Just before they had reached the end of their long climb, Bohrlein stopped abruptly so that Schneemoser ran into him.

'Psst,' said Bohrlein (one of the few sounds he could utter correctly), and pointed forward. Four shadows had stepped out of the woods, and were making for a signpost at the crossroads just in front of them. Bohrlein froze in his tracks, and Hermanfried held his breath. The four figures stopped beneath the signpost, and then walked on to a bench under a tree. Bohrlein looked for some way of avoiding the bench — but there was none — a brook, hedges and bushes saw to that. And so he rushed out like a bull, or rather like a tank, pulling Hermanfried behind him, and made noisily for the bench. Bohrlein flashed his torch at what he thought was a slightly-built man, and fell upon him. Another figure moved up, Bohrlein took a swing at him, and the stranger crumpled. Now the shadow of a giant rose up before him. Bohrlein dragged Hermanfried away; they ran a hundred yards up the road and disappeared into the forest.

'I say, Uncle Xaver,' said Hermanfried, 'I think the one you knocked down was a woman.'

Bohrlein mumbled something that even Hermanfried could not understand, and kept stomping through the under-growth — which, thick though it was, was quite unable to slow down his tremendous momentum. Hermanfried was hard put to it to keep close enough behind Bohrlein for the path to remain open for him.

When at long last they emerged from the forest below Thiersee, it was broad daylight. They reached Kufstein about 8 a.m. Here the Nazis were still in charge, and the good old State Railways were still busily sending off goods trains to Innsbruck. The guard was kind enough to allow them on as far as Wörgl. They travelled on the engine. But not even the fact that it was Hermanfried's first (and last) journey on a locomotive, was enough to keep him awake. Many years later, when he had climbed to giddying heights, he was invited to travel in the same way. He was close to accepting the offer — but although he had attained a great deal in his life, this was something he never again achieved. Still, the fact that he fell asleep on his only journey on an engine was far from unnatural. Every other boy, no matter how great a railway enthusiast, would have fallen fast asleep at the very first chance he had to rest after so long a march.

Towards evening Bohrlein and Schneemoser (they had

continued on a post-office bus, two peasant carts and the charcoal-driven three-wheeler of the *Tschurtschen Valley Daily Messenger*) stood before the Queen Mother in Hunger-bichl Farm. The Queen Mother was outraged.

'What an absolutely idiotic idea, Bohrlein. What on earth brought you here of all places?' she asked.

Bohrlein was used to the proverbial ingratitude of the great. And since the Queen Mother could not very well leave the two of them outside, she assigned them an attic room, formerly occupied by the stableboy.

Sarabande

Baron von Speckh closed the *Süddeutsche Zeitung* and laughed. Or rather, he did not so much laugh as utter a series of bleating sounds, his mouth pulled open into a thin slit.

'You may return the paper,' the Baron said to the maid, who was clearing the coffee table on the veranda. 'I'll just keep this page. Sondermeier won't be particularly interested in it, I'm sure. The rest will keep him busy enough.' The maid placed the paper on the coffee tray. 'Tell him he'll get the missing page in the evening.'

The maid curtsied and left. By resorting to all sorts of complicated manoeuvres (not excluding bribery), Baron von Speckh had not only been able to hang on to the Jewish properties which his friend, the late Duke Hermann von Rosenheim, had kindly put his way, but had also exploited the agrarian reforms — the 'equalization of burdens' decree and the fiscal reforms — to round off his estates. This, in spite of the fact that all these measures had been passed for the express purpose of taking a little from the rich and handing it to the poor. ('The devil does not give a damn for the masses,' Suffragan-Bishop Theodorich Zach used to say, though only when von Speckh was not within earshot.) The Baron, moreover, always refused to subscribe to a newspaper in the ordinary sense of the word. He simply borrowed the *Süddeutsche Zeitung* from his chauffeur, Sondermeier, whom the reader may remember from the hunt for the missing galoshes at the grave of General Ludendorff.

Fräulein Dr Gerch, who when dressed in her hand-knitted grey cardigan looked no older and no younger than she had twelve years earlier when she had presented the Führer with her son Rudolf Sigurd, was gazing across the lake. It was a mild, not too warm, late afternoon in mid-August. Quite a few citizens of the Federal Republic had already exploited the economic miracle to acquire expensive sailing boats, which were now tacking to and fro in the gentle breeze. The Baron's villa was situated above Prien and had cost him a pretty penny. Everyone who knew the Baron had been astounded by this purchase. It was generally believed that he had bought the property to please his new wife — in a fit of love-sickness, against which not even the most case-hardened banker is proof. The Baron himself explained — to those who had been bold enough to ask him outright — that he had bought the place because the hairdresser in Graben-stätt charged a mere sixty pfennigs for a haircut, so that the house would pay for itself in time.

Baroness von Speckh (nee Schnürl; formerly Frau Klette), was something of an enigma to all the Baron's acquaintances. The mere fact that after the death of his first wife he should have engaged in so costly a business as a second marriage was incomprehensible enough. Worse still, the Baroness was a redhead. There was nothing — including the spending of good money — to which the Baron was more averse than to red, in whatever shape or form. And, as if that were not bad enough, the Baroness dressed almost exclusively in that colour . . . Only blind passion could have forced the Baron's hand. And since nothing seemed more out of the Baron's character than passion, his marriage remained shrouded in mystery.

The Baroness had many admirers, especially among the short and the corpulent, who seem particularly susceptible to the aura of redhaired ladies. On the afternoon in question, even Dr (*honoris causa*) Anton Joseph Kofler was well on the way to joining their ranks. The Baron took it all in his stride, provided only that the admiration did not go too far, and was accompanied by adequate presents to the Baroness — thus saving him the trouble of having to pay for such trifles out of his own pocket. He also prized the bad conscience the Baroness evinced on such occasions, because it would often persuade her to don a yellow or blue dress instead of the offending red.

Anton Joseph Kofler, the former Nazi boss from Landl, had been kept locked up in the mortuary for two days; but when the Americans had failed to materialize and a heavily armed SS unit was known to be advancing on Kufstein, the Landlers had second thoughts, wiped out every trace of their recent conversion to democracy, and set him free. A few peasants even came up to him and assured him that they had not been present during the riotous proceedings. But Kofler was wise enough not to waste this brief respite on petty revenge, and took to his heels instead. He was, in any case, not a Landler by birth but came from Fischbachau, in the Schliersee district. Needless to say he made for a place where nobody knew him. (His wife, incidentally, when the banner of free Tyrol finally fluttered over Landl for good, was dipped in the cesspool with redoubled fury, locked up in the mortuary and finally carted off to Innsbruck prison, where she starved to death.) Anton Joseph Kofler made straight for Munich, and here he chanced upon — what you might call — discreet Nazi circles, who with the help of several myopic ex-members of the Centre and People's Parties, gave birth to that hybrid, the Christian Social Union. Soon afterwards, Kofler was making his voice heard at countless executive meetings, and blowing up his own importance. He was a deputy in the first post-war Bavarian Parliament, and by 1949 he had taken his place in the new Federal Assembly. It was only after he had been appointed to several important Party offices, had been made an honorary doctor of Würzburg University and Chairman of Mühldorf District Council, that the CSU got wind of his Nazi past. Kofler at first issued a string of categorical denials, but had to give way under the pressure of the documents placed before him, whereupon he denied that he had ever denied anything. There were terrible scenes amongst the CSU top brass. Quite a few former Sturmbannführers, Ambassadors, Deputy-Gauleiters, Reich Commissars and the like were heard to protest that they could not possibly serve under one who had never risen above the rank of cell leader in remote little Landl. From this internecine struggle, Dr (*honoris causa*) A. J. Kofler MP emerged as one of the most promising candidates for a senior ministerial post. Baron von Speckh, who knew better than most what advantages could accrue to anyone abstaining from direct political activity, first met Kofler in 1952 — in fact, during that very afternoon on which he had read his chauffeur's *Süddeutsche Zeitung* with so much amusement.

It was Fräulein Dr Gerch who had brought Kofler to the Baron's house.

Fräulein Dr Gerch had been thrown out of the Ferdinand-Maria gymnasium after the collapse of the Third Reich. She took legal action — as soon as that could be done again — and was granted a small pension, on the grounds that she had at no time been an official Party member. She would even have been taken back into the educational service, had she not hit upon something much more rewarding in the meantime.

Here it is necessary to introduce the writer — Kurt Zusel by name — who before 1945 had written such great novels as *Konradin's Sword*, *The Jew of Torgau*, such inspiring volumes of poetry as *Baptism of Fire* and *War Hymns*, and such fine plays as *The King Never Sleeps*. During the night of 7 May 1945 Kurt Zusel had quite suddenly seen the democratic light — whereupon he had come out directly with such fine writings as *The Palm Ship* and *Eternal Aphrodite* (of which the blurb said that it was an extremely sensitive piece of autobiography, with a light erotic touch) — and had also founded a literary and artistic circle, the 'Klüterblatt', a meeting place for all sorts of Nazi scribblers. Not that the Klüterblatt meetings, held behind locked doors in a spare room of the 'Neuner' wine-bar in Munich, did nothing but drum up old Nazi ideas. On the contrary, at the gatherings, the old Party faithfuls made it a point *not* to talk of their embarrassing past. For the rest, all of them had the unforeseen and inestimable advantage that though they had been sponsored by the rulers of the Third Reich and been showered with all sorts of honours and material goods, no one else had taken the least notice of their literary outpourings. The fact that Will Vesper's *The Tough Race*, Hanns Johst's *Schlageter* and Heinrich Anacker's *Call to the Reich* had run to such large editions was solely due to the existence of innumerable Hitler Youth, Hitler Girl, People's and Party District libraries in which these writings had attracted nothing but dust. Their patriotic authors were as good as unknown to the public at large. Few of them, according to extant reports at any rate, had actually been Party members. (It sometimes seemed as if no one at all had joined the Nazi Party, with the possible exception of Hitler, who had resigned in 1944.) And since even the denazification-obsessed Americans, surprisingly ill-informed about the whereabouts of the real Nazis, treated these scribblers as harmless fools, most of them were allowed to drift aimlessly on. It was in order to remedy their general lack of purpose that Kurt Zusel had founded his poetic circle. Fräulein Dr Gerch, who as was only to be expected took a keen interest in nationally-inspired *belles-lettres*, soon found herself among the very few who regularly attended the poetry readings of the 'Klüterblatt' group. One day that exalted body had reached the point where it needed a business manager, and there was no one better fitted to fill that post than Fräulein Dr Gerch. It is probably of small historic interest whether or not Fräulein Dr Gerch's special relationship with Kurt Zusel was a causal factor in her appointment as business manager of the 'Klüterblatt' or vice versa, or, indeed what the nature of that relationship really was. Suffice it to say that in 1950 Zusel dedicated his extraordinarily long and dull poem *Fugue and Counterfugue* (subtitled 'Frederick the Great and Johann Sebastian Bach' — Zusel's special contribution to the Bach Year) to none other than Ingrid Gerch.

Many 'Klüterblatt' poets found their way to embracing not

only the cause of democracy, but also the Christian faith (generally Catholicism). This may partly have been their way of escaping into more unimpeachable spiritual spheres, but it also reflected their appreciation of the fact that the greatest bastions of their new-found faith were also the only semi-fascist regimes to have survived the war: Franco's Spain and Salazar's Portugal. Both were extremely loyal to Mother Church. Clerical Fascism alone seemed to have kept the much-maligned and fading flame of true patriotism burning bright. As a tangible expression of this complex intellectual development, the 'Klüterblatt' had begun sending a delegation to the Corpus Christi Day procession as early as 1946. In 1947, Fräulein Dr Gerch became a regular part of that delegation, leading her swarthy young Rudi, who was un-usually small and bow-legged even for a primary school pupil, by the hand. It was during one of these Corpus Christi Day processions that Fräulein Dr Gerch had made the acquaintance of Anton Joseph Kofler who, holding a large candle, was marching directly behind the canopy of the CSU, his head bowed in prayerful worship.

History is not concerned with aesthetics. In particular, history has no sense of smell. Anton Joseph Kofler had a rather poor digestion — he suffered alternately from con-stipation and the runs. Two days before the procession, an explosive discharge had caused that now famous politician a measure of embarrassment. It had all started during an important and strenuous meeting of the CSU local branch, which had continued deep into the night. Kofler and two or three colleagues had then proceeded to a certain house in Hohenzollernstrasse. The girl was undressed, and Kofler had already taken off his trousers when he suddenly lost control.

Kofler had nevertheless been forced to pay the full fee. The pimp came in, held his nose with one hand, and with the other shook the politician by the collar until he parted, not only with the regular fee, but also with a decent surcharge for cleaning up the mess. The Federal deputy was as brown as he had been during the incident in Landl several years earlier.

Normally Kofler would have stayed at home next day, but

as his presence at the Corpus Christi procession (shortly before a Cabinet reshuffle) was essential to his career, he could not possibly absent himself. And so he ate nothing but charcoal and grated apples. The result was not wholly satisfactory. Anton Joseph Kofler was caught short at the corner of Theatiner and Perusa Streets, at a spot a long way from the nearest public convenience. His pitted and pasty face turned scarlet, he threw the candle away and was just about to throw all caution to the winds in the pillared entrance to the Central Land Mortgage Bank, when Fräulein Dr Gerch passed by in the 'Klüterblatt' contingent. She at once grasped the gravity of the problem. She also, and quite literally, carried the key to its solution — for the offices of the 'Klüterblatt' were right across the road, on the first floor above the 'Café Feldhernhalle', which was closed for the holiday. Fräulein Dr Gerch quickly showed the Bundestag deputy to the lavatory upstairs. Even the candle was saved: Rudi Gerch had seen to its rescue.

There may have been flaws in Anton Joseph Kofler's character, but ingratitude was not one of them. When Rudi Gerch was confirmed in 1953, Dr (*honoris causa*) A. J. Kofler was his sponsor and presented the boy with an — admittedly inexpensive — wrist-watch of the Kienzle brand. We shall have occasion to refer to this present again later on in our story.

Christa Schnürl, who had been Frau Christa Klette for a few years, had been reunited with her old school-friend Ingrid Gerch after a long break, soon after Frau Klette's husband had run off. Frau Klette found that Fräulein Dr Gerch was someone who at long last (and without showing the least sign of boredom) was prepared to listen to her unending accounts of Herr Klette's character faults. Better still, and this might throw some light on the far from unequivocal events that preceded Fräulein Dr Gerch's presentation of her son to the Führer, Fräulein Dr Gerch joined fulsomely in her friend's railings — not so much against Herr Klette (whom after all she had never met) but against the male sex in general.

When Frau Klette married Baron von Speckh a year later,

the ties between the two women were, if anything, strength-ened further. Fräulein Dr Gerch paid frequent calls on the new Baroness in Chiemsee (the Baron liked her; she did not smoke, spoke considerably less than his wife, and never did more than sip at her liqueur). She was generally accompanied by her bow-legged Rudi, and on this occasion also by her new acquaintance, Anton Joseph Kofler, CDU deputy in the Bundestag.

'The paper says that Hitler has just been spotted in Uruguay. And that he now goes by the name of . . .' the Baron raised his pince-nez to his eyes and looked at the page he had kept back, '. . . Carlos Mulden Mendoza, and works in a general store. They even have a picture of him . . .'

Dr (*honoris causa*) Kofler picked up the page. 'I have only seen the Führer, I mean Hitler, at really close quarters on one occasion. That was in the autumn of 1942 . . .' — during a reception for younger Austrian NS officials in Berchtesgaden, a fact Kofler thought it best not to mention — '. . . he even shook me by the hand . . . well, you know, at the time one simply couldn't help that sort of thing . . .'

'Really? Shook you by the hand?' said Fräulein Dr Gerch.

'People can say what they like,' Kofler continued, 'but he did have a way with him, at least when he was at his greatest. There is no doubt that this Mendoza looks a bit like him, particularly if you add a moustache . . .'

'Stuff and nonsense,' said the Baron.

'Is it your view, then,' said Fräulein Dr Gerch, picking up her liqueur glass with the tips of her fingers and taking a genteel sip, 'that the Führer has not survived the war?'

'All who knew him were completely blinded by the Hitler legend. Did nobody ever wonder why he let so few of his old cronies come anywhere near him? He either liquidated them like Röhm, or else kicked them upstairs like Göring. Those few men Hitler kept near him were all of the newer Nazi breed. And only a handful of these were fully in the secret.'

'What secret?' asked Fräulein Dr Gerch.

'I was probably the only one to see him from time to time during the war, and even after 20 July 1944, who was not completely taken in. I for one knew, or at least suspected, the truth, all along.'

'The truth?' said Fräulein Dr Gerch, holding her breath.

'And yet there were so many pointers. To begin with, there was that affair with his niece, Geli Raubal. She was not the first girl to whom Hitler had — apparently — paid court. Even before 1933, he had had a whole string of them. But when you asked any of these girls what actually went on, they would tell you a different story altogether. Apparently he just had little chats with them, or occasionally took them to the pictures. He liked straight horror films, and is known to have seen his favourite, *King Kong*, more than thirty times —more times, that is, even than 'Parsival'. And even in the cinema he'd only share a box of sweets with them, nothing else. If more indiscreet questions were put to them, the girls would at once pout and shut up like clams. Geli Raubal stuck it longer than most. She even let Hitler paint her, in the buff, but not in the way that artists normally paint their models. He just made large drawings in great detail of what she had between her legs . . .'

'That can't possibly be true,' said Fräulein Dr Gerch.

'My dear Fräulein Gerch,' said the Baron. 'I myself had to buy those damn pictures back from a blackmailer in Geneva for 250,000 gold marks. God alone knows how they ever fell into the wrong hands. In any case, the crook threatened to publish the drawings, and by that time Hitler was Chancellor. We only just managed to avoid an international scandal.'

'How perfectly awful,' said Fräulein Dr Gerch.

'One night, when Geli was no longer content with playing the model, she made for Hitler's bedroom. What she saw left her no choice. She shot herself there and then.'

'What on earth did she see? Was he covered with hair, or running sores, or what?'

'He was neither hairy nor covered with sores, nor even with scales. In his way, he was perfectly normal. Unity Mitford found that out to her cost as well. You will remember that scatterbrained Englishwoman, with her head stuffed full with Nazi ideas and with Hitler in particular. When Hitler declared war on Poland, and thus risked a clash with England, Unity Mitford tried to avert the worst at the last moment. She stormed into the Chancellery, refusing to be put off by all the adjutants and attendants, rushed on like one possessed and forced her way into Hitler's private suite. Hitler was splashing about in his bath, but not even that stopped Miss Mitford. She made straight for the bathroom — and when she came out again, she too reached for a revolver.'

'What on earth was wrong with him?' asked Fräulein Dr Gerch, now in obvious anguish.

'Was?' said the Baron, 'Not was, but is!'

'So the Führer is still alive?'

'Yes, but not in Uruguay, and not as Señor Carlos Mulden Mendoza.' The Baron rose and waved the page from the *Süddeutsche Zeitung* in the air. Frau Marx, a woman in her sixties who acted as a superior housekeeper *cum* lady companion in Baron von Speckh's establishment, came out onto the veranda. Baron von Speckh handed her the page with instructions to return it to Sondermeier, and also asked her to have his suitcases packed. He intended to go to Bayreuth next day, he explained. 'Tristan and Isolde, you know.'

Fräulein Dr Gerch let a reverent sigh escape from her lips, and hugged her grey hand-knitted cardigan closer with deep emotion. The eyes of Frau Marx, too, lit up visibly — though only for the briefest of moments.

The Baron went indoors, followed by Frau Marx. The Baroness, Fräulein Dr Gerch and Anton Jospeh Kofler stayed behind on the veranda.

'Have you any idea what your dear husband was trying to say?'

The Baroness shook her head.

That summer afternoon Baron von Speckh's veranda overlooking Lake Chiem was both the starting point, and also the junction, of two distinct threads of activity. One of these threads later became the fuse of a violent explosive charge, but even the other was not, so to speak, without a momentum of its own. Let us anticipate by saying that the Baron — as ever, or nearly so — at no time lost control of the situation.

The Baron had known a great deal about Dr (*honoris causa*) Anton Jospeh Kofler's past, even before that afternoon. As soon as Kofler's impending visit was mooted, the Baron, disregarding its purely social nature, had instituted a further series of investigations. Hence when Dr (*honoris causa*) Kofler eventually joined him on the veranda, the Baron knew all there was to know about the man, and had already decided — subject to the personal impression Kofler would make, and that impression was wholly positive in the event — to send Dr (*honoris causa*) Kofler a second invitation to Prien just a few days after their first meeting. We shall have further occasion to speak of that second meeting. That it was in fact their third meeting, was something the Baron may possibly have failed to appreciate.

But first the Baron repaired to Bayreuth. We should have given the reader a completely false impression of Baron von Speckh had we led him to think that it was love of opera which was responsible for his presence at the opening night of 'Tristan and Isolde'. The venue had been chosen on purely geographical grounds (Bayreuth was some thirty miles from the borders of the German Democratic Republic, or from the 'zone' as it used to be called) and also because, from the resumption of the Wagner circus until the middle of the sixties, the Bayreuth Festival held a kind of monopoly in inter-German cultural interchanges. Since time immemorial, the core of the Festival orchestra and the choir had been recruited from Saxony, or more precisely from the Dresden Opera. Even during the most glacial phases of the Cold War, the 'Zone bosses' considered the opening night of the Wagnerian season of such obvious importance that the bassoonists and viola-players and all the brilliant musicians of the hallowed Court Opera were allowed to cover the thirty or so miles to the West without the least impediment.

The visiting group invariably comprised the odd traveller with an oboe in his luggage who could not have produced a single note on that instrument. One of these, who went by the name of Lurz (which suggests that his real name must have been anything but that), had signed in at the rather shabby Hotel Wolffenzacher the day before Herbert von Karajan conducted the 1952 performance of 'Tristan and Isolde' (this now forgotten and, as far as Karajan was concerned, purely ephemeral episode in the history of modern music). It was expressly for the purpose of meeting Herr Lurz that Baron von Speckh had repaired to Bayreuth.

Herr Lurz and Baron von Speckh did not know each other, had never seen each other, and never saw each other again. When two people who do not know what the other looks like, arrange a meeting, they usually wear a red carnation in their buttonhole, or carry, say, a copy of *Der Spiegel* in their right overcoat pocket. But this method of identification may lead to embarrassing misunderstandings if some outsider should, by pure chance, also wear a carnation in his buttonhole or have a copy of *Der Spiegel* stuffed in his right coat pocket. The subject the Baron wished to discuss with Herr Lurz was important enough, and at the same time confidential enough, to call for less equivocal methods — in the event, two tickets for the opening of 'Tristan and Isolde', one marked with a discreetly pencilled 'Left', and the other with an equally discreet 'Right'. One of the tickets ('Right') had been posted to Baron von Speckh, and the other had been handed to Herr Lurz. Once the fanfares from the Festival Hall balcony had died down, this clever arrangement was bound to bring the two of them together in an audience of thousands and inexorably so, as if joined by fate.

How and at what precise hour Herr Lurz arrived in Bayreuth has not been recorded. He probably travelled quite inconspicuously in the 'Inter-Zone Train' during the previous afternoon, possibly in a third-class compartment.

Baron von Speckh did not leave Prien until 8 a.m. on the appointed day. The Baroness was still asleep, for she was always a late riser. The Baron made a brief stop in Munich for the express purpose of terrifying the manager of his bank by his unexpected arrival. At about one in the afternoon, back on the old Munich-Nuremberg autobahn, the Baron ordered Sondermeier to pull up in a lay-by just outside Ingolstadt and ate two hot Spam sandwiches, which he washed down with lukewarm camomile tea from a beer bottle. He refused absolutely to acquire so fragile a luxury as a Thermos flask.

As he chewed at the rubberlike Spam, he read Sondermeier's *Süddeutsche Zeitung*. After a careful study of the latest stock exchange prices and the business section, he flicked briefly through the remaining pages, for further news of Carlos Mulden Mendoza. There was none, and he flung the paper irately on to the back seat, munched some more, took another sip of tea, and fell into a reverie. Suddenly he had what can only be described as a brainwave.

'Sondermeier,' he said.

'Herr Baron?'

'I've had an idea. You subscribe to the *Süddeutsche Zeitung*, don't you?'

'I do, Herr Baron.'

'You pay your subscription monthly?'

'Yes, Herr Baron.'

'And they send you receipts?'

'Yes, Herr Baron.'

'Would it make any difference to you if you changed your subscription to my name? The paper, I can assure you, will remain your personal property as always. All I want is the receipts. That won't cost you anything extra.'

'Indeed not, Herr Baron.'

'Well, you'd greatly oblige me if you saw to that. Perhaps the whole thing might be made retrospective.'

'By all means, Herr Baron. But whatever for, if I may make so bold as to ask?'

'I've just had a thought. After all, I do read the stock exchange section most carefully, and that counts as work. As such I ought to be able to declare the subscription as an expense in my income tax returns.'

Just outside Bayreuth, the Baron ordered another stop, this time in a wooded lay-by, and put on his dinner suit behind a bush. He had not the least intention of using, let alone paying for, the hotel room that had been booked for him, though he was equally determined to put it down as a tax-deductible expense.

The Baron was driven straight from the autobahn to the Festival Theatre on Grüner Hügel. During the interval, he complained bitterly to Herr Lurz that 'Tristan and Isolde' of all things had been chosen. 'I quite realize,' he said, 'that this business with the two tickets is as safe as houses, but why did it have to be this damn opera? What a waste of time! Couldn't they have picked something shorter?'

'To my reckoning,' Herr Lurz stammered in broad Saxon, 'there's nowt shorter to be had, not by Wagner, any road.'

The Baron took his leave of Herr Lurz rather curtly, picked up a grey file and an envelope stuffed with money (fee and expenses), sold the ticket for the remaining two acts of the opera, whistled for Sondermeier, and drove off. At first he had asked the full price for his ticket — 'You've missed absolutely nothing,' he assured the prospective buyer, an Englishman, who strange to tell was wearing a red shirt, a red handkerchief, red socks and carried a red umbrella with his dinner jacket. 'Nothing at all has happened so far. It's only just starting in earnest,' persisted the Baron. But the Englishman obviously knew his Wagner, and hence realized that nothing at all would happen during Acts II and III either. He offered half the full price. The Baron then proposed two thirds. 'It's only fair,' he said, 'one third per act.' Whereupon they struck a bargain.

The Baron added the banknotes the Englishman had handed him to Herr Lurz's envelope. Then he gave a big smile: 'The whole damn lot is tax-free!'

While Martha Mödl and Ramon Viney sang at each other in the late Wagner's completely darkened 'Garden outside Isolde's Chamber', the Baron was rushing south on the autobahn. As the hunting horns proclaimed the approach of Hans Hotter, his car was just crossing the Danube at Ingolstadt.

The Baron clung to the grey file throughout the drive home. The reader may gather how important it was when we tell

him that the Baron clutched it to him even more tightly than
the envelope with the banknotes.

That night turned out to be one of the stormiest in post-war
Bavarian history — politically rather than meteorologically
speaking, that is. (The weather itself was anything but
stormy: it was a mild July evening, though later a frontal
system did move across from the West and hid the moon.
And during the next few days there was even the odd spot of
rain.) The storm also had no direct connection with the
Baron's mission to Bayreuth, though no one can tell what
would have happened without that expedition.

'Take my word for it,' the Baroness had said, 'if he's been
given a ticket, he will sit it out to the bitter end.'

Cardinal Faulhaber, Archbishop of Munich and Freising,
who had played a not too glorious role during the Nazi heyday
(the reader may remember his 'Jewry, Christianity and
Germanism' of 1934) and who could not really stomach the
restoration of more liberal ideas after the war, had died on
12 June 1952. With surprising alacrity, the Pope had seen fit
to name his successor — Johannes Baron von Hauberisser —
even before the month was out. Hauberisser was fifty-one and
his appointment to one of the most important German sees
caused several raised eyebrows. The newspapers (it was
summer and there was the usual dearth of real news) looked
deeply into the past of the new pastor-in-chief, and found it
singularly devoid of incident. The fact that his late grandfather, Joseph Georg, Baron of Hauberisser, had built the
new Town Hall and St Paul's Church could hardly be put to
the grandson's personal credit. Nuncio Pacelli — later Pope
Pius XII — had been a friend of the Hauberissers and had
paid frequent visits to their home during his stay in Munich
(from 1917 to 1924). It was said that the Nuncio himself had
persuaded young Johannes to enter the priesthood. In any
case, it had been Pacelli who had ordained young Hauberisser

in 1922. In 1924, when Pacelli was made Nuncio in Berlin, the Bishop of Berlin had summoned young Hauberisser to the capital — no doubt as a personal favour to Pacelli — and made him his chaplain. In 1928, Hauberisser had become Professor of O.T. Exegesis at the University of Breslau; in 1936 he had been transferred to Munich University, and in 1939, by which time Pacelli was Pope, he had been called to the Papal Academy of Science and also to the Secretariat of State, that is to the Papal Foreign Office. Hauberisser had remained in Rome until 1949. In 1940 he had been made a Cardinal, his highest office until he became Archbishop of Munich-Freising. The newspapers were unable to establish what precisely he had done during his ten years' stay in Rome but there was some reason to think that he had played an important backstage role in framing Vatican policy during the war.

In 1949, Hauberisser had had a vision of the Blessed Virgin. Since Pope Pius XII was to have a similar vision in 1950 — the precise details of either event were unknown — it seems reasonable to assume that Hauberisser's vision had been of a premonitory kind, so to speak, a kind of a preparation for the Pope's. For not even the Blessed Mother of God would have dared to appear unannounced before the Holy Father.

Shortly after his vision, Monsignor Hauberisser had been granted leave of absence by the Pope — for reasons of health, it was rumoured. Hauberisser had retired to Andechs Monastery — the abbot was an old schoolfriend — and had written an edifying book entitled *The Sword of Truth*. It had appeared in 1951, but was certainly not the cause of his elevation in July 1952.

What every paper failed to comment upon, oddly enough, was the exceedingly strange fact that Johannes Baron von Hauberisser was not only the same age as ex-King Luitpold of Bavaria (who, as the reader may remember, reigned from 1938 to 1945 when he was deposed by his previously deposed father) but also that he was one of the seven noble boys who had been chosen as the then Crown Prince's school companions. Hauberisser had also served with him in the Cadet Corps, and their paths had only parted when Hauberisser had been called to the priesthood. During Luitpold's reign, that is during the war, Hauberisser was seen in Munich with astonishing frequency, obviously on special Papal missions to the Bavarian king.

In 1945, ex-King Luitpold, the Nazi or pseudo-Nazi, was banished to South America, where the House of Wittelsbach had had extensive economic interests for a century. In 1948, he was given tacit permission to return to Leutstetten Castle. Now Leutstetten is just a few miles from Andechs Monastery . . .

Another circumstance in the life of the new archbishop would not have attracted attention even had it been generally known. Before the First World War one Anna Mansegger from Fischbachau had served as cook in the Hauberisser household. Even her marriage in 1909 to the valet Kofler would probably have caused little of a stir; at most people might have noticed that, after the early death of her husband (he fell in the 'tank battle' of Cambrai in November, 1917), Anna Kofler returned to service with the Haubersissers. With her she brought a son, Anton Joseph by name.

The plan for a coup d'état was first mooted during an 'informal discussion' in Leutstetten, attended by ex-King Luitpold, Monsignor Baron von Hauberisser and Dr (*honoris causa*) Anton Joseph Kofler. It was Kofler who adumbrated the dream of a Pan-Bavarian empire: Bavaria, united to Austria plus the South Tyrol and Trentino, together with the old 'Bavarian Province of Verona', Treviso, Friuli, Carniola and Bavarian Istria — a solid chunk of country round the Eastern Alpine massif, firmly set between the Adriatic and the Danube, joined together under one crown and safe in the lap of the only true church.

'It is not enough just to unify,' Anton Joseph Kofler explained in a loud, rather hoarse voice, his face earnestly wrinkled. 'Protestants, Franconians and Swabians must be encouraged to leave.' The new empire, based on the solid rock of historical tradition would act as a bulwark against communism and the so-called Enlightenment, and become a stronghold of Catholicism. It would be a constitutional monarchy on a permanent footing (i.e. without political parties). Since the Catholic Church would enjoy a dominant position, there was little doubt that God's blessing would rest squarely on the new state. Kofler also added that such persons as had resided outside the new Bavarian Empire before 1 September 1939 would not be granted the privilege of Bavarian citizenship; they would have to depart within a fixed period of time. This would solve the refugee problem at one stroke. Needless to say, allowances would be made for cases of special hardship — for instance, those married to Bavarians, provided of course that they had consummated their marriage by joining the Church, and also those of clear Bavarian descent whom chance had caused to be born or to reside in foreign parts before 1 September 1939, etc.

The Plan received the wholehearted support of both the ex-King and the Cardinal. During subsequent meetings of the three founding fathers, soon augmented by other sympathizers, the plan was fined down, further details put on paper, and new problems resolved. For instance, what to do with Arch-Duke Otto, the pretender to the Austrian throne; how to cope with American reactions or with the inevitable protests by Italian monarchists; what to do about the Tyrol, which according to Kofler was a dubious addition, in view of the financial collapse it had suffered as recently as 1809. Compromises were agreed; new links forged; optimists even started to design new postage stamps, and to distribute bishoprics and licences. In the summer of 1951, when Monsignor Hauberisser returned from a visit to Rome, even the financial aspects posed by the coup d'état seemed to have been as good as solved. For the rest, the Holy Father had conveyed his blessings. All that remained was to deal with a number of purely technical problems.

Needless to say, no one was foolish enough to think of building the empire overnight. The first step was to seize power in Bavaria, to depose old King Rupprecht, to restore King Luitpold to the throne, and to proclaim a new constitution. Parliament and all political parties would be dissolved, and Dr (*honoris causa*) Anton Joseph Kofler would become Prime Minister with comprehensive powers. When Hauberisser succeeded Cardinal Faulhaber as Archbishop of Munich, Kofler thought there was no need to wait any longer.

'X-Day' had been planned as follows: a Berchtesgaden rifle club (three-quarters of which consisted of illegitimate descendants of the House of Wittelsbach — the illustrious gentlemen had always sought their sport in Berchtesgaden) would assemble on the Theresienwiese, march on the Royal Palace and take it. Reliable squads of the Catholic Youth Movement would seize all the ministries and the most important administrative centres, while special commandos of the Catholic Men's Union and the Catholic Trade Unions would capture the radio station. King Luitpold would be carried in triumph from Leutstetten and installed in the Palace. In the Church of Our Lady, the Archbishop would then intone a solemn Te Deum, which would be broadcast to all the most important squares in the city. The new King would read a Proclamation and call upon Dr (*honoris causa*) Kofler, who intended to lie low until that moment, and ask him to form a government. Since the Chancellery was in remote Prinzregentenstrasse, Kofler would deliver his inaugural address from the balcony of the Town Hall. For a whole week, there would be free beer and an amnesty for anyone guilty of manslaughter, provided that his victims had been adult Prussian Protestants or members of the Social Democratic Party.

It was left to the 'Huosigau Alpine Costume Preservation Society' to tackle the delicate task of seizing the person of the Crown Prince, who lived in Nymphenburg Castle, and to restore the legal guardianship of his father. The people had to be shown not only that the continued existence of the dynasty was assured, but also that the insurgents did not think in terms of momentary advantages, and had their sights firmly fixed on the centuries to come.

The Huosigauers were to be led by their fugleman, one

Herr Pointner, ably assisted by a reliable adjutant: the twenty-one year old law student Hermanfried Schneemoser, who had recently joined the movement.

In order not to draw attention to himself, Dr (*honoris causa*) Kofler decided to withdraw, as he put it, to the mountains a few days before 'X-Day'. Up there he worked at the speech he intended to deliver from the Town Hall balcony. Twenty-four hours before 'X-Day' — the speech had been written — he had a final meeting with Schneemoser, and gave him last-minute instructions. Next, he paid a secret and again totally inconspicuous visit to a villa in Prien. In the evening, he proceeded to his friend's house in Berlach where the King's call was to reach him.

'X-Day' dawned at last. It was, as we have said, a glorious July day. It goes without saying that Dr (*honoris causa*) Anton Joseph Kofler — temporarily condemned to in-activity — was on tenterhooks, and he decided to while the time away with another visit to Prien. The King's call was not expected until about 10 p.m. by which time — as he confided to his friend — he would have returned long since. By noon he had reached Lake Chiem.

Baroness von Speckh had looked at Dr (*honoris causa*) Kofler with what he thought were admiring eyes throughout the previous afternoon. Kofler did not realize that the Baroness was short-sighted: contact lenses had not yet come into fashion and the Baroness was much too vain to wear ordinary glasses. With iron discipline she suppressed the slightest inclination to squeeze her eyes together by opening them much wider than was necessary. If there was a stranger about, like for instance Dr (*honoris causa*) A. J. Kofler, she could gaze at him wide-eyed for hours on end, possibly because she saw more slowly, so to speak, than people with normal vision or spectacles.

Quite naturally, Dr (*honoris causa*) A. J. Kofler, who knew nothing about the Baroness's affliction, took a more personal view of her steady gaze. It is only fair to add that any halfway self-assured man would have interpreted that gaze in much the same way as Kofler did. But not everyone would have taken it as no more than his due.

The Baroness, for her part, seeing Kofler loom before her next day with such unmistakable intentions, was certain that the fire of her charm had flung him to her feet with irresistible force, and felt extremely flattered.

Kofler would never have dared simply to ring her front door bell — he had rightly assumed that the door would not be opened by the Baroness herself but by a servant. However, he had noticed the Baroness's hair: a head full of artistically diverging, enticing red locks, carefully touched up and clearly the result of an expert's daily attentions. Kofler accordingly stationed himself at the corner of the road leading from the villa to Prien, and waited for the Baroness to come out on her way to the hairdresser.

And, indeed, the Baroness did visit one every day, not the expensive one in Grabenstätt, but the fair-to-middling hairdresser in Prien. The Baron had lodged a number of heart-rending protests, but all to no avail; the Baroness was adamant when it came to her personal appearance. In the end, the Baron had been forced to pay a secret visit to the man for the express purpose of negotiating a monthly rebate. The hairdresser readily agreed to forward the latter by post, unbeknown to anyone in general and to the Baroness in particular.

Dr (*honoris causa*) Kofler had thought the Baroness would drive to her hairdresser in the Baron's second car, but since her eyesight was too poor for that, she always went on foot. When Kofler, having waited for about an hour, saw her walking out of the garden gate, he felt Providence beckoning him on. He leapt out of his car, gathered up an orchid wrapped in transparent foil, and ran towards her, a dashing cavalier if ever there was one.

To his dismay, the Baroness refused to give her hairdresser a miss. Kofler had to wait for another hour. He had to admit the truth of her argument: that the Baron would have been quick to notice the omission. Later, the Baroness was only too happy to smuggle Dr (*honoris causa*) Kofler into her house. To Kofler's delight, she had rejected his suggestion of a joint visit to a local café as being much too dangerous. 'Everyone in Prien knows me,' she said.

They had a long chat in her 'boudoir'. As hour after hour went by, and the Baroness kept chatting for all she was worth, Kofler grew increasingly agitated. True, she had taken off her red shoes and allowed Kofler to stroke her rather squat toes, but for the rest all she did was to give him a comprehensive account of the repulsive nature and unequalled ingratitude of her first husband. Dr Kofler was quite unable to make any further erotic progress, for the Baron returned unexpectedly at 7 p.m.

Just before, the Baroness had still said: 'Take my word for it, if he's been given a ticket, he will sit it out to the bitter end.'

The 1952 Bavarian Revolution began to go sour when the King — that is, old Rupprecht I — could not found be in his Palace.

The Berchtesgaden Rifle Club Volunteers, to whom the one policeman on guard at the Palace gate had offered no resistance, blundered about the various corridors, frightened the odd valet here and there, and finally discovered a member of the Royal Family in a small room giving on to the herb garden.

He was Prince Garibald, King Rupprecht's nephew and the husband of Princess Laetitia Annunziata.

The Prince, a tall slender man with an impressive forehead and a strong chin (in profile his head looked very much like the Turkish crescent), was dressed in *lederhosen* and a leather jerkin and was standing at the window with his back to the door. His lips were moving almost imperceptibly: 'Forty-nine million, nine hundred and eighty-four thousand, two hundred and three.'

Prince Garibald was counting. He was not counting flies, windows, cars or anything like that; he was counting in the abstract. At the age of eighteen he had made counting his life's task. That had been back in 1922. Sometimes he would count aloud, but just as often he would count quietly to himself; mostly he would count very softly, just moving his lips a tiny fraction. But whichever method he employed, he would always count conscientiously, and whenever he stopped, jot down the last number in a special notebook. Next day — or more precisely the next working day — he would continue with the next highest number. He had no other interests or hobbies, as he would have been the first to admit. He felt not the least call to the military or clerical professions. Scientific and artistic activities bored him totally. Hunting was uncomfortable. Counting filled his entire life.

He would count nine hours a day, from 8 a.m. to 1 p.m., and after an hour's break for lunch, from 2 p.m. to 6 p.m. On Saturdays, Sundays, holidays and during his annual five weeks' leave he would take a break. His only regret was that neither of his sons — the Princes Ignaz and Hezilo — showed the least interest in counting; there would be no one to carry on the good work after he had gone. Prince Garibald often had moving visions — which he confided to no one — of what might have been. On his death bed, he would hand on the last number to one of his sons, and then expire in the happy knowledge that after a due period of mourning his son would carry on where he had left off. Well, it was not to be. His life's work would perish with him.

That day in July, Prince Garibald was standing by the window and had just reached forty-nine million nine hundred and eighty-four thousand two hundred and four, when he was cut short by the Berchtesgaden Volunteers.

'He ain't the King,' said their leader. All the same they pointed their rifles at his chest.

'I beg your pardon,' said Prince Garibald, 'is there anything I can do for you?'

'Where's the bleeding King?'

'His Majesty? I really have no idea.'

The volunteers looked at one another and muttered. (King Rupprecht, let it be noted, had taken Frau Schumata, his morganatic wife, to the hunt in Fall. Baron Wiemer, a friend of the King's, had rung up that very morning to tell His Majesty that a certain stag, which the King had been chasing for two years, had been sighted on his estate.)

'Hands up!' said the leader of the volunteers after some time, when he could think of nothing else.

'No,' said the Prince.

'You won't?'

'No,' repeated the Prince.

That was something the volunteers had not reckoned on. Once again they were at a complete loss. The leader conferred with his men. 'Take him away,' he ordered in the end. 'Let him keep his damn hands down if he wants to.'

Two volunteers, their rifles at the ready, led the way. Next came Prince Garibald. Behind him, their guns pointing at the Prince's back, came another two volunteers — followed by their leader, sword in hand, and the rest of the contingent. Down the stairs they all went. The policeman on guard had been locked in the gatehouse, and the telephone cable had been torn out. As the volunteers marched past him now with the captured Prince, he glared at them through the small barred window like a poisonous blue fish in an aquarium.

The volunteers veered left just as the little clock tower above the well struck four. (What a different world! In Bayreuth, the cellists under von Karajan's inspired baton were just striking up that unfathomably deep minor sixth at the start of 'Tristan'). The traffic was not too dense. With a mighty gesture, one of the volunteers ordered the astonished drivers to pull up on Residenzstrasse while the rest of the contingent crossed the road. They probably did not realize that it was at this very spot that another putsch — that of 9 November 1923, and Hitler's first — had collapsed temporarily under the bullets of policemen whose aim, alas, was not all it might have been. After another brief conference the volunteers decided to await further orders in the 'Café Feldhernhalle'. How these orders were to reach them was something to which they preferred to give no thought. They rushed into the establishment, held their rifles under the proprietor's nose, flung the other guests out, and ordered liver dumplings and mixed stew all round. Prince Garibald was locked in the lavatory, or more precisely, since no female guests were present, in the Ladies. He sat down on the lavatory seat and counted.

If the action of the Berchtesgaden Volunteers did not rebound on them, it was only because the fish-like policeman — eventually managing to attract the attention of a passer-by who released him and thus made it possible for him to notify Police Headquarters — informed his immediate superiors that the revolutionaries had marched off again, so that Police HQ deemed it unnecessary to do anything further about the Palace. In the meantime, the Catholic Youth contingent had occupied the radio station and kept transmitting a mixture of timely and completely idiotic messages. Soon total confusion reigned all round. The Americans, misinformed as always, considered the whole affair a sort of combined Oktober Fest and Corpus Christi Day Procession. They, too, did nothing at all. The locked-up policeman had also reported that the revolutionaries had carried off His Royal Highness, Prince Garibald. By the time this news had filtered through to the Catholic Youth it had been completely distorted; it now read that the Berchtesgaden volunteers had captured King Rupprecht and had shot him in front of the Feldhernhalle. Travelling along other channels, the message was twisted into the rumour that King Rupprecht was marching on Munich at the head of a contingent of riflemen from Tölz.

The technically knowledgeable Young Catholic, Leo Malferteiner, a youth of eighteen, had seized Radio Bavaria, and now used his practical knowledge to pose witty conundrums to the listeners at large. (For instance: What hangs on the wall, is green and barks? Answer: A dachshund in a rucksack). He also transmitted his favourite tune, 'Granada', sung by Mario Lanza, at frequent intervals. Malferteiner had almost to be forced at gunpoint to fit two sets of false messages from the palace between two successive 'Granada' transmissions.

More than any complete news blackout, or any large-scale action planned by some general staff, the resulting bedlam served to paralyse the entire state machine and the army in particular. Thus the Bavarian insurgents might well have succeeded, and not even the behaviour of ex-King Luitpold, who having heard the news of his father's assassination immediately changed sides and disowned the whole movement in disgust, could have stopped their ultimate victory. What finally did for them was a totally unforeseen development in Nymphenburg Castle.

The Castle is at some distance from the City centre. To reach it, the detachment of the 'Huosigau Alpine Costume Preservation Society' (to which we shall be referring as the Huosigauers in brief) under the leadership of Fugleman Pointner from Uffing on Lake Staffel, ably assisted by Schneemoser, took a No. 3 tram at the Main Railway Station and asked the conductor to put them off at the Castle, which he did in due course. Now the tram stop is at the Canal and not directly in front of the Castle, and once there, the unsuspecting conductor went out of his way to point out the rest of the way.

As the tram rattled on to the 'Botanical Gardens', Pointner ordered his Huosigauers to line up in a wedge-shaped formation. The Huosigauer flag was unfurled. Pointner drew his sword, and the company marched off in step. Walking beside these ranks of dashing Huosigauers, Hermanfried Schneemoser struck a slightly incongruous note, dressed as he was in a black suit, which appeared to be at least two sizes too small for him, and a large fur-lined anorak bemedalled with zip-fasteners.

The Huosigauers had better — or worse — luck than the Berchtesgaden Volunteers in the Royal Palace. Prince Otto was in residence — he was not allowed out, for reasons with which the reader must by now be familiar. But Nymphenburg Castle is not only a royal residence; the rococo rooms of the central block, the state rooms, Ludwig I's 'Gallery of

Beauties' and the equestrian museum are open to the public except during state occasions. The Royal Family — ex-Queen Emilie and her sons Otto and Max Arnulph — occupied the northern wing. Since there was an admission fee of 50 pfennigs (or of DM 2.00 for collective tickets) all gates except one were kept permanently locked. Outside the one that served as the public entrance stood a wooden hut from which a guard sold tickets, postcards and sweets.

Herr Pointner's company marched up to the hut, and ground to a halt. The guard counted them with a practised look, and said: 'You'd be better off with a collective ticket.' He had already pulled one from the roll, when Pointner roared out a command and waved his sabre. A moment later, the hut had splintered and toppled over under the impact of a dozen Huosigauer fists. The guard, abandoning tickets, money, postcards and sweets, only just managed to leap to safety, whereupon he ran away screaming. (He was found next day, still groaning, squatting in a tree in the furthermost reaches of the park.)

Having surmounted this obstacle, the Huosigauers wheeled into the Castle in close formation. Once inside, they marched all over the place, their heavy hobnailed boots resounding on the mirror-bright rococo parquet floors. In the 'Gallery of Beauties', the knowledgeable Herr Pointner stopped before a female likeness, pointed to her nostrils with his sabre, and said:

'That one is Lola Montez, the ol' hoor.'

Half an hour later — the small clock over the castle chapel had just struck four — they discovered, by pure chance rather than sound judgment, the passage from the state rooms to the administrative block, and hence to the Royal suite.

Prince Otto, who had been brought to Munich from Eichkatzlried to be re-united with his grandfather King Rupprecht as a guarantee and living witness to the dynasty's future, was by now eighteen years old. Everyone's worst fears had come true: he had never stopped growing. True, there had been no more of the four-inch bursts of growth he had suffered on the way to Bäckeralm; instead there had been regular bursts of just one-and-a-half inches. Even the Prince's wolf-like appetite during such bursts had fallen off. Prince Otto had been placed under permanent medical supervision. A suitable diet had been prescribed and he had been ordered to avoid all forms of excitement. For all that, he now measured seven foot ten inches, and weighed close on 360 pounds. His underwear was laundered by a special corps of Royal washerwomen, who were sworn to silence.

Special, and needless to say extremely discreet, private tutors saw to the Prince's high-school education, and though the Prince shone in no one subject, he did not do too badly at his lessons.

To provide him with a school companion, it had been decided to have his brother, Max Arnulph — though of perfectly normal size — share all his lessons. Poor Prince Max Arnulph had the feeling — which incidentally he could not have articulated — that he lived constantly under an over-hang of some Mt Everest, never reached by the sun.

Otto had been Crown Prince from 1938 to 1945. Upon his father's abdication, he too had been demoted, though it had been decided to placate the boy's father by appointing no one in Otto's place.

Around 1948, by which time Prince Otto had passed the six-foot mark, his grandmother at last had her way: Otto was dressed in billowing togas and similar garments. He quickly became used to them, and in due course even grew to like them. And apart from the fact that occasionally his clumsy movements would cause him to sweep the coffee service from the table with his billowing sleeves, his immediate entourage, which in truth was very small, soon became used to his strange apparel.

As had been her wont for fifteen years, Queen (now ex-Queen) Emilie sat down to coffee at three o'clock in the 'guinea-fowl-coloured salon'. For fifteen years, the Queen had resented the presence at this ritual of her cousin-by-marriage, the Princess Laetitia Annunziata, but though she had given the matter considerable thought, she had never hit upon a good reason for excluding the Princess. Hildegard, the

Queen-Mother, was always present as well, and these ladies were generally joined — as on the day in question — by Suffragan-Bishop Theodorich Zach. As soon as Prince Otto and Prince Max Arnulph were old enough, they too were allowed (or rather expected) to attend these three o'clock coffee get-togethers.

Suffragan-Bishop Zach had arrived late that day. Over the years his love of heraldry had made way for a passionate interest in public transport — he rarely missed an opportunity of blessing a new engine or tram. The St Christopher's branch of Catholic Railwaymen had long since made him an honorary conductor. But his deepest affection was reserved for time tables and ticket lore. All tram and train inspectors went in fear and trembling of him because he always knew everything better than anyone else. Thus when he travelled to Rome one day with the late Cardinal Faulhaber and their official carriage was attached to the wrong section of the train in Bologna (it was during the night) Suffragan-Bishop Zach rose from his bed in the *wagon lit*, put on a waterproof over his pyjamas, stormed on to the platform and delivered a flaming sermon to both the engine driver and the shunter-in-chief. The Bishop spoke Italian in an extremely cultivated style, reminiscent of Church Latin, and the Italian railwaymen were duly impressed. The train was reshunted, and as a result ran some twenty minutes late. That fact incensed the good Suffragan once more, so much so in fact that he nearly resigned his office of honorary conductor. He reported the whole affair to His Holiness, whom he belaboured so long and so obstinately with his accounts of railway mismanagement, that Pius XII promised to use his personal influence with the appropriate authorities.

This new interest of Monsignor Zach's appeared soon after he had passed the motor-cycling age. Cats' skins and warm leggings no longer helped, nor the fact that he had his waterproof lined with a fur collar: he regularly caught cold. And since he was not licensed to drive a motor car, he was forced to frequent trams, and thus embarked upon his new obsession, which soon blossomed to include public transport in general.

At the time — it was 1952 — he was busily drafting new plans for the Federal Railways, which involved — quite apart from panoramic cars, buffet cars, office and conference cars — the addition of rolling chapels to every long-distance train so that masses could be read while the train was in motion. He also sent an appeal to the Federal Government (and Adenauer heard of it with pleasure) to appoint a Federal Railway Bishop. He was, of course, the only eligible candidate, and hoped that his appointment would also entitle him to a permanent free pass extending to all European railways.

In Munich, the Suffragan had already been issued with a free tram warrant. His new method of travel unfortunately proved a great handicap on the day in question, when there was yet another traffic jam outside the Central Railway Station, caused this time not by snow, rain, an accident or some mysterious electricity cut, but by the revolution. The Suffragan did not realize what was going on, and was doubly incensed at the half hour's delay. It so happened that the Huosigauers were also travelling on the same tram. But when Suffragan-Bishop Zach jumped off with them at the Castle Canal stop, and made quickly for the Castle in his billowing waterproof (which he insisted on wearing in all weathers), he failed to notice the volunteers lining up in wedge-shaped formation to his rear.

When Suffragan-Bishop Zach was finally seated at the coffee table after many a breathless apology, he was the only male present — the Princes had been dismissed by their mother and had returned to their own rooms. By the time the Huosigauers had completed their noisy march from the tram stop, stormed the ticket hut, and at last accidentally stumbled upon the passage leading to the Royal suite, the Suffragan-Bishop had been able to take two cups of mocca and eat a slice of fruit cake with cream. He was just scraping up the crumbs from his plate, when a valet burst in.

The valet had given the Huosigauers considerably more trouble than the ticket seller. But then he had been, strategically speaking, in a far more advantageous position. Much like Alexander at Issos, he was guarding a narrow access (a door, in this case), an obstacle the enemy could only confront one at a time. When the valet insisted on keeping up the ceremonial appearances, Schneemoser felt it was best to avoid an unnecessary show of force, and asked the valet to announce them.

'Whom shall I announce?' asked the valet.

'Tell them,' said Schneemoser, 'that the Revolution wishes to speak to Her Majesty. Not a hair on her head will be harmed, nor for that matter on the head of any one else. Far from it, we have come to convey His Royal Highness, the Crown Prince . . .'

'You mean, His Highness the Prince-Royal,' the valet interrupted.

'His Royal Highness, the Crown Prince,' Schneemoser repeated with emphasis, 'to his . . .'

'To his what?' asked the valet, when Schneemoser hesitated.

'To his rightful place.'

'And get on with it,' said Fugleman Pointner impatiently, 'or else you'd wish you was never born.'

The valet brushed this threat away with an imperious wave of his hand, a motion of such cold dignity that it would have frozen a bombshell in flight. He turned on his heels and disappeared through a door. By then the Huosigauers were filling the entire antechamber.

'Your Majesty,' the valet explained once he had closed the door behind him, 'some Revolutionaries have come to ask for an audience. They wish to take His Royal Highness, the Prince, with them.'

'Well, I never,' said Suffragan-Bishop Zach, who was notorious for his unexpected reactions to unusual situations. 'Are we having a Revolution today?' he went on to ask, in roughly the same tone of voice another might have used to ask 'Is it full moon tonight?'

'Revolutionaries?' said the Queen.

'Yes, Your Majesty!'

'With rifles?' asked the Queen.

'Yes, with rifles, Your Majesty.'

Princess Laetitia Annunziata had hysterics. Princess Hildegard slid, almost as silently as her late husband had done from the sofa (though this time it was only a faint.) Suffragan-Bishop Zach picked up the mocca cup (his third) and retired to the window. The Queen turned pale and said 'No, no, no . . .', ten times in quick succession. 'Tell them I refuse to receive them. Tell them to go back where they came from.'

Then everything happened very quickly. The Huosigauers had heard Princess Laetitia Annunziata's hysterics and had mistaken the noise for a siren. Whether intentionally or otherwise, a shot went off and tore the nose off the Count-Palatine Gustav Samuel Leopold of Kleeburg-Landsberg-Zweibrücken (1670-1731), whose portrait was hanging on the wall. The siren was immediately pitched a whole note higher. The Queen jumped on to a chair, as if the Revolution were a mouse, and fell over backwards, chair and all, with an almighty crash. The revolutionaries at the back had begun to push at those in front, and the door was suddenly forced open by their combined weight. In the process of thus entering the Royal chamber, the leader of the revolutionaries succeeded in cutting his left thumb on his drawn sabre. Schneemoser pushed his way forward and shouted: 'Not a hair on your heads will be harmed . . .'

Then another door opened. Prince Otto, measuring seven foot ten inches in his stockinged feet and wobbling like a jelly with excitement, loomed up before the assembled company. He had heard the shot and the crash.

'I'm hungry,' he roared.

And at once had a fresh burst of growth.

The revolutionaries froze in their tracks.

The Prince swelled up like a noodle, like a balloon, and it appeared as if the room might burst with him.

'Jesus Christ Almighty,' whispered Herr Pointner.

The Prince threw himself on the remains of the cake (a good half of it was left) and swallowed it in one go. Then he cast a gluttonous glance at the fat thighs that protruded from Herr Pointner's taut *lederhosen*, and continued to grow.

'Let's get the hell out of here,' screamed Herr Pointner, and beat a hasty retreat over his fallen Huosigauers. A kind of suction wave now seized the revolutionaries and flung them down the stairs with irresistible force. The valet quickly threw a coffee pot at the retreating enemy. From the Castle windows it was possible to see the Huosigauers in full flight across the lawn.

A doctor was called in, and the Prince was taken to his eight-foot-long bed, which was by now once again too short for him. Princess Laetitia Annunziata stopped screaming. The Queen Mother recovered consciousness. Only Suffragan-Bishop Zach had disappeared. When everything had quietened down, a strange sound could be heard in the room. The sound seemed to come from the window, and here the Suffragan was eventually found wrapped in the long curtains, the mocca cup in his hand rattling against the saucer.

Bishop Hauberisser was due to intone the Te Deum at 8 p.m. The confusion of news had been confounded even further by the events in Nymphenburg. The Huosigauers, who thought the end of the world had come, had returned to the city centre muttering prayers, even while smashing and looting the odd window and raping the occasional passing Prussian woman. Traditions that most people thought had been buried with the Thirty Years' War had been resurrected overnight. The bells were tolling. Here and there a house stood in flames. The unhappy director of the Bogenhausen Observatory was strung up by members of the Legio Mariae who found that his great telescope refused to fire shells.

Young Schneemoser had parted company with the rest of the Huosigauers outside the Castle. No taxis were plying for hire, and so he went on foot. At the Neuwittelsbach roundabout he came upon an unlocked tricycle with a delivery box in front. It bore the legend 'PIPPINGER'S BAKERY AND CONFECTIONERY, 19 ROMANSTRASSE, MUNICH'. As Schneemoser jumped into the saddle, the baker's apprentice came out of a customer's house. The boy gave a yell and threw himself at Schneemoser, stumbled and nearly pulled the tricycle over with him. Schneemoser was able to right it again in the nick of time, and before the apprentice could rise to his feet, began pedalling away for all he was worth. The apprentice cursed loudly after him and then hobbled off sadly in the direction of Romanstrasse, convinced his employer would not believe a word of his story.

Schneemoser made for the Archiepiscopal Court. He was immediately admitted to His Grace, to whom he made a full report of what had happened in Nymphenburg.

He could only surmise, Schneemoser explained, that the House of Wittelsbach had been deploying inflatable robots against the Revolution. The Archbishop was visibly shaken. He had not been in office very long, and hence had not yet been made privy to the Prince's peculiar habits.

The Pastor-in-Chief of all Bavaria walked up and down in complete silence. There was no mistaking the fact that he found the whole affair uncanny in the extreme.

'Did you learn anything about the King?' he asked after a long pause.

'Which one?' said Schneemoser.

'Rupprecht.'

'No,' said Schneemoser.

'They say he was killed,' whispered the Bishop.

'God Almighty!' said Schneemoser.

'There's nothing for it now,' said the Bishop. 'We have to stake everything on a single card. There is no going back. We'd best send for Kofler.'

'I thought he was meant to wait for King Luitpold's call.'

'We need a strong man right now,' said the Bishop dully. 'Fetch him here. Do you know where he is?'

'Yes, of course . . .'

'Then go and fetch him. In God's name . . .'

'Your Excellency . . .' said Schneemoser.

'What is it now?'

'I only have a tricycle, just a . . .'

'Then, for God's sake, take your tricycle and be off. You wouldn't get through with a car in any case.'

And so Hermanfried Schneemoser rode straight through the Bavarian Revolution on the tricycle owned by the Pippinger Bakery and Confectionery, 19 Romanstrasse, and made for Perlach. The tricycle was inordinately heavy, and Schneemoser had to push it up Giesinger Hill, However, while crossing Martinsplatz, Schneemoser happened to open the box on the front of the tricycle. Inside, he discovered eight undelivered cream buns. By now, he felt, he had certainly earned himself a rest, and so he sat down on a bench and at once consumed all eight of the buns. Then he cycled on with a slight feeling of indigestion. Towards eight o'clock, just as the Bishop began to intone the Te Deum, he pulled up outside the house in Perlach where he expected to find Kofler. But little did he realize what had become of Kofler.

'Dear God — my husband!' said the Baroness when she heard a car draw up.

Anton Joseph Kofler, who had just been reaching out for the Baroness's toes once again, hurtled out of the room like one possessed and made straight for what turned out to be the Baroness's bedchamber. The Baroness ran after him.

'You can't possibly stay here . . .'

'I . . . I . . . I . . .,' said Anton Joseph.

'What happened between us . . .' The Baroness hesitated. 'What happened between us was nothing at all.'

'I must not be found here. I'm only thinking of . . . I'm only thinking . . . I'm only thinking of . . .'

'Of what?'

Two tears were running across the fatty bags under Dr (*honoris causa*) Kofler's eyes. 'I'm only thinking of the Fatherland.'

'I don't follow that,' said the Baroness.

'What are you talking about? Your husband may come in at any moment and you're just talking. How on earth do I get out of here?'

'We're on the top floor — there's no way out at all.'

'I'm finished,' wailed Kofler. 'Please don't think I'm

concerned about my own person; I'm only thinking of the Fatherland. I simply have to get out. One way or another.'

'I can't see how. If only you pulled yourself together . . .'

'Why ever did you tell me he was bound to sit it out to the bitter end?'

'Is it my fault that he's decided not to?'

'I am ruined. Let me into your wardrobe!'

'But there isn't any room.'

'I've simply got to get out! I must — for the Fatherland. Can't you get it into your head? The Fatherland may call for me at any moment . . .'

The Baroness squinted through the curtains at the garden path.

'It's a fact. My husband is back.'

'What time is it?'

'Half past seven.'

'Dear God in Heaven,' moaned Anton Joseph Kofler, climbing out of the window and crawling on all fours along a ledge that gave on to the garage roof.

'I'm liable to vertigo,' he still managed to whisper, 'you might have thought of that.'

The Baroness began to close the window.

'No, no! Leave it open!' hissed Kofler.

'Do you want to climb back in?'

'No,' said Kofler. 'Can I be seen from anywhere?' He clambered to the corner of the garage roof, where he was screened behind a large tree.

The Baroness went downstairs to greet her husband. She had — after all what harm can come of caressed toes! — a perfectly clear conscience. Still, a man on a garage roof who seems capable of all sorts of foolishness is enough to upset even the clearest of consciences. Deep within her, the Baroness was burning with rage: rage against Kofler and rage against herself. The two feelings rose and fell inside her like two hostile, dark liquids in a retort. The Baroness grew so irritable that even the Baron was struck by the change.

'For God's sake, can't you put your idiotic share quotations to one side for even a moment?' she hissed.

'Whatever is the matter with you?' said the Baron, who unlike his wife was filled with contentment.

'How was Tristan?'

'Well, you know,' said the Baron, 'just what you would expect of Tristan.'

'That's a perfectly silly answer. How many acts did you see?'

'One!'

'No doubt the first.'

'Probably,' said the Baron. 'A woman swallowed some kind of a drink. And a man as well.'

'That was the first act, all right.'

'Just what I've been saying.'

'Didn't you see anything at all of the rest?'

'No,' said the Baron. 'I sold the ticket.'

'It's a good thing, that's all I can say, a good thing you didn't see the second act.'

'How so?'

'What happens in the second act is something that can happen to any one of us. Anyone at all who keeps reading the stock-exchange quotations.' The Baroness jumped up. 'I'm going to bed.'

'Do you mean to say the second act takes place in the stock exchange?'

The Baroness walked out without a further word. Her husband shook his head and returned to his quotations.

The Baroness looked out of the window. It had meanwhile grown dark outside, but Anton Joseph Kofler was still sitting on the garage roof. Time passed, and with it the hour of the King's call. Several times Kofler tried to pull himself together. He would crawl to the edge of the roof — intending to jump off, to race to his car and make for the scene of conflict, to where the old régime must now be tottering on its feet, while the nation was waiting expectantly for the man of the hour . . .

He might have made it, too, if he had not been seized by that stupid vertigo time and again. Each time he would grasp the roof convulsively, only to retreat with his tail between his legs.

121

Now there could no longer be the least doubt: it was too late. For an hour, a cat had been looking down at Kofler, perfectly relaxed, from a wooden shed across the road. As if to mock him, the cat was lying on the very edge of the roof, one paw hanging down, as peacefully as if it were lying on a sofa. With mild disdain and mild interest — no mouse was stirring — the cat kept watching Kofler's every move. No stone, no piece of iron, nothing he could have flung at the animal was within Kofler's reach. And even if there had been, he would never have dared to throw anything lest the noise betray his presence.

At about midnight — her husband was by then safely ensconced in his bed — the Baroness went down into the garden and placed a ladder against the garage. Crawling on his stomach and holding one hand before his eyes, Kofler negotiated the edge of the garage roof and groped for the ladder.

'Too late,' he hissed at the Baroness, as soon as he touched ground. All the same, he hared off like one possessed. The cat blinked after him. When he had disappeared, it stood up, arched its back and gave a huge yawn that almost turned it inside out. Then it lay down on its other side and hearkened into the night. To human ears, the night was perfectly still. But even the stillness of the stillest of nights is full of crackles and rustles, of creaks and little squeals that come from God knows where and then scuttle off: a hedgehog, two branches rubbing together, a wooden fence cooling off. Even the silence must breathe. Its quiet sounds fill the air with magical arabesques that few cats can resist, the less so when no mouse is in sight.

Gavotte

As might have been expected, things grew even more con-
fused after the abortive coup d'état of July 1952 than they
had been during the insurrection.

Those actively involved proved exceedingly nimble and
managed to change sides even during the attempted over-
throw, though needless to say some were more nimble than
others. Archbishop Hauberisser began his Te Deum in
celebration of the inauguration of the new Pan-Bavarian
Empire, and ended it — unnoticed by his congregation —
as a prayer of thanks for the salvation of King Rupprecht
and democracy. Free beer was liberally dispensed in any case.
Beer is very tolerant — it foams no matter what the occasion.
The Huosigauers and the Berchtesgaden riflemen continued
to march through the town, now cheering King Rupprecht
and Adenauer. Catholic Youth contingents released prisoners
taken by the Legio Mariae, and *vice versa*. Let it be said
in their favour, that few if any of the active rank and file had
known what they were fighting for in the first place. As for
the dangling director of the observatory, the Public Prosecutor's office readily admitted that it might have been a case
of suicide: 'the man had debts, kept a mistress and was
suffering from cancer.'

Prince Garibald was released by the manager of the
'Feldhernhalle' just as soon as the Berchtesgaden riflemen,
their stew duly consumed, had marched off again. Ex-

King Luitpold, as we have already said, had discovered the movement in good time. That this had been due to a misunderstanding, was something no one was ungenerous enough to dwell upon.

Dr (*honoris causa*) Anton Joseph Kofler reported to a parliamentary committee the very next day and declared under oath that he had had nothing — literally nothing — to do with the whole affair. At the time in question, he had been in a friend's house: the home of Baron von Speckh in Prien on Lake Chiem. And that was, in fact, the undiluted truth.

Only young Schneemoser had some awkward moments. Confectioner Pippinger had given his poor apprentice a good wallop and had then rung for the police. Those who think that during a coup d'état the German police cannot be bothered to look for stolen bicycles had better think again. After waiting for over an hour at the appointed place for Kofler, Schneemoser had belatedly set off back on his purloined tricycle. However, on his return through Ohlmüller Strasse, a radio patrol car spotted him just as he was passing Nitzinger's Stationery.

'Where did you get that tricycle?' one of them asked.

Schneemoser said nothing at all.

'Is it your property?'

'N . . . no,' said Schneemoser.

Then the radio patrolman, putting on a Sherlock Holmes expression, looked at the box and read out firmly and loudly: 'Pippinger's Bakery and Confectionery, 19 Romanstrasse, Munich'.

'That's right,' said Schneemoser, 'I know.'

'You don't happen to be from Pippinger's Bakery and Confectionery, do you, by any chance?'

'No.'

'Are you coming along quietly, or do you need a hand up?'

Schneemoser dismounted and pushed the tricycle towards the policeman.

'That's better,' said the officer. 'What is your name?'

'Hermanfried Schneemoser.'

Had it been eight years later, the policeman would have turned to stone at the sound of that name.

Schneemoser climbed into the patrol car. One policeman sat down next to him, the other took the wheel.

'What do we do with that damn machine?' asked the third policeman.

'Take it along, of course,' said the first policeman.

As there was no room for it inside, the third policeman had to pedal the tricycle back to the station. This proved particularly embarrassing when the convoy passed through the notorious environs of the Viktualienmarket.

'I thought so,' a pimp shouted after them. 'Them buggers get so little pay they have to deliver rolls in their spare time.'

'Two tarts and an Angel's Delight, Constable,' said a whore.

'Go to hell, the lot of you,' the hard-pressed constable yelled at them. And he summoned up what little strength he had left to keep up with the patrol car.

'How could you involve my name in that affair?' said Baron von Speckh.

'I don't rightly know. It was just that your name flitted through my head when they asked where I was that day . . .'

'You ought to keep some control over what flits through your head. But what's done is done. Nothing we can do about it now.'

The Baron's conciliatory tone would have been enough to make lesser men flinch, but not Kofler, who had been a politician for far too long to bother about anyone other than himself.

'And exactly what were you supposed to have been doing here?' said the Baron, still perfectly calm and friendly.

'No one is likely to ask.'

'Who can tell? A lie must have some basis in fact. If they do ask you, you had better come out with a good story.'

'I shall say that I came to consult you financially. For a good tip.'

'I'm no tout. I give tips to no one. Also I was in Bayreuth that day as anyone who cares to can easily find out.'

'Well, then . . .' said Kofler.

'I can see that you're a rank amateur when it comes to lying,' said the Baron. 'Let's say you called on my wife.'

Kofler paled.

'That makes you think, doesn't it?' said the Baron with a laugh, while Kofler stammered out something or other.

'That's the only natural explanation,' said the Baron. 'The husband is away, and so Dr (*honoris causa*) Kofler pays his respects to the charming Baroness. That's something everyone will believe. In any case, it would be quite in your line, as far as I can gather.'

Kofler felt a constriction in his chest. 'But what will the Baroness say?'

'Who cares? Needless to say she will deny the whole thing. But she'd only be expected to, wouldn't she?'

'I don't much like the idea,' said Kofler, and he was speaking the plain truth.

'I can well believe it,' said the Baron. 'But then I didn't start it all. It was you who involved me with the Parliamentary Committee, not I who got you into that mess. No, no, believe me, no one will accept your silly story. People much prefer the most far-fetched lies. But every cloud has a silver lining; this time it's brought you back here. In fact, if you hadn't called I should have had to send for you. I had even drafted the letter. Now I can save myself the stamp.'

Then Dr (*honoris causa*) Kofler — who was so immersed in his own thoughts that he had not even heard the Baron's last remark — came out with what was probably the silliest remark he could have made in the circumstances.

'But you yourself, Herr Baron,' he said. 'Surely you don't believe that I spent the afternoon with your wife?'

'Why? Did you, by God?'

'No,' said Kofler. 'Of course I didn't.'

'Here is a sheet of paper,' said the Baron. 'Just write down that you were in this house on such and such a day for the express purpose of engaging in extramarital relations, etc. etc. with the Baroness.'

'Engaging in . . .?' said Kofler, but nevertheless wrote as he was told.

'I don't mind if you use a more suitable expression,' said the Baron.

'Let's say, "stroking her toes".'

'Stroking her toes? However did you get that idiotic idea?'

'Oh, very well, I shall write whatever you want.'

Dr (*honoris causa*) Kofler handed the sheet to the Baron, after first putting his signature to it. The latter was more in the nature of a signatorial printing than the usual affair: the 'Anton' flew across the sheet like an arrow; the 'Joseph' had the jagged elegance of the lightning symbol; and the 'Kofler' towered with a tremendous baroque flourish over the relatively modest 'MP' which the uninitiated might have mistaken for the artist's initials. The 'Dr h.c.' at the beginning resembled three powerful strokes, their points so many blows of the fist. The whole signature had been specially devised by a famous designer from New York.

'Well, now we can get down to the real business,' said the Baron. 'I am quite certain, of course, that you will accept my offer. But just in case you don't, I shall keep this thing here' — he waved the sheet of paper — 'as a guarantee of your silence. I myself was in Bayreuth, of course. Tristan was terribly boring. I don't understand why anyone should want to listen to that sort of stuff. There's obviously no accounting for tastes. Some people actually like roast hedgehog. But that's not what I wanted to talk to you about. To put things in a nutshell: I am thinking of founding a new political party.'

'Very interesting, Herr Baron. But don't we have a surfeit of political parties as it is?'

'Don't interrupt. My party is just what the country needs. A strictly conservative party . . .'

'But we've got one of those as well; quite apart from the fact that the CSU . . .'

127

'Why do you keep butting in? Of course we have — or rather we used to have — conservative parties. But all of them were so much baloney. All of them were lacking in . . .'

'A Führer,' said Kofler.

'Tommy rot. In funds. They were all of them short of money.'

'You don't mean to say that *you* propose to back it?'

'It will be known as the NPD: the National Democratic Party. Needless to say, I myself shan't be contributing a single penny. All the money will come from abroad.'

'From abroad? From America, you mean.'

'No, from the Soviet Zone.'

'But that's as good as impossible.'

'You may remember that about eighteen months ago the President of the People's Assembly in the GDR, Herr Dieckmann, wrote a letter to the President of the Federal Republic. In that letter, he put forward certain proposals for the reunification of Germany. They had to swallow a lot of their pride over there, believe me, before they came out with these proposals. Which, incidentally, were far from silly — quite the contrary, in fact. They were obviously prepared to sacrifice quite a bit of their precious socialism . . . Of course, I don't for a moment suggest that they were contemplating political suicide. No one could have expected that of them. No one that is, except our own blundering Federal Government. In January 1951, Ehlers replied with a blank refusal, and those across the border felt quite rightly that their message of good will had gone for shit paper. Not a nice feeling, that.'

'But we couldn't possibly have . . .'

'I know all that idle chatter. Just keep quiet for a moment, will you please? To those in charge of the Soviet zone, Ehlers' reply was as good as a declaration of war. And that is precisely why I propose to found the NPD.'

'I get you at last — as a kind of counterweight.'

'Rubbish. I am founding the NPD on the orders of the GDR, and with funds provided from that quarter. I myself shall keep well out of the public eye, of course. Though, needless to say, I shall keep a tight rein on the finances.'

'On the orders of the GD . . . I mean the bosses of the Zone? A national party?'

'Right enough. Nowadays no one is stupid enough to be taken in by straight communist propaganda. Even that bunch of idiots running the German Communist Party on this side has dropped that sort of thing long ago. And even so they're about to be prosecuted. Much to the delight of the GDR, I might add. It means they won't have to go on giving *pro forma* support to that bunch of idiots, and can use their money for much better purposes: for supporting the NPD . . .'

'I am completely at sea. I must confess . . .'

'But it's all perfectly simple. A strong party of the Right, one that sets up the proper nationalist clamour, if possible with military undertones, must willy-nilly produce a strong reaction from the Left. That follows almost like an amen follows a prayer. Not among the workers, of course, but among the intellectuals. That's much cheaper than having to buy them outright, and much less dangerous as well. If you buy three influential journalists, you can bet your bottom dollar that one of them will turn tail in no time at all, if only because all intellectuals are so miserably stupid. And something like that does more damage to the cause than all the good their scribblings were supposed to do. But no one will ever believe that the NPD is backed by the Zone. And it can't possibly collapse because all the purse strings are in my hands, and in my hands alone. And I don't give up that easily. You just wait and see — all the intellectuals will automatically veer left just as soon as our Party starts marching about to the rousing tune of "Unbeaten in the Field" and the like.'

'But that's a perfectly devilish plan . . .'

'You're exaggerating again. But it isn't half bad, though I say so myself.'

'And you, Herr Baron, are you really prepared to soil your hands with this kind of filthy intrigue.?'

'Don't come with all that pathos. The GDR is making

an initial down payment of eight million dollars. I get six per cent. They offered four, and it took me the whole of Act I to get them to raise their offer. A lady behind us was getting terribly annoyed.'

'And for six per cent you are prepared to sell your Fatherland?'

'Just wait and see if I deliver!'

'You mean you are proposing to double-cross them?'

'The Leftist rubbish that keeps pouring at us from the papers, the radio stations and the German television — which is bound, sooner or later, to become the most important of all our media — will get on people's nerves sooner or later. If we play our cards carefully, we shall have a Civil War on our hands. Those Leftist dreamers will drive themselves into an ever greater frenzy, and we shall help them along. They'll start shooting in the end, and then the hour of the strong man will have struck. And believe me, he won't be a Leftist.'

'A Führer!' said Dr (*honoris causa*) Anton Joseph Kofler. 'The penny has dropped at last!'

'And you want me to assume the leadership of your new Party ...'

'Don't you even think of it! You just stay meekly in the CSU. No doubt you'll go a long way with that lot. And of course, you'll get some of that Zone money from time to time. No, what I want from you is the odd sceptical remark about the NPD though not too sceptical, mind. In *refracta dosi*, if you follow me. For the rest you will keep us, that is the Party, informed of all the government's plans. And when we are good and ready, when the hour of the strong man has struck, who can tell? — fate might even stretch a hand out in your direction, dear Kofler. What you tried to grasp a few days ago, in so irresponsible and diletantish a manner, may easily fall to you then,'

'I had nothing to do with that business!'

'Oh, I see. You were really paying court to my wife.'

'Of course not,' said Kofler quickly.

'Well, then?'

'May I have a day to think it over?'

Kofler, who was perspiring now, pulled out a handker-chief and wiped the sweat from the folds of his neck.

'Stroking her toes, my foot,' laughed the Baron.

'Very well, then,' groaned Kofler, suddenly quite hoarse. 'Very well then. My answer is "Yes".'

In 1948, Princess Hildegard decided to sell Hungerbichl Farm. When her lawyer, Dr Peter von Scheuchenzuber (nephew of the Counsellor-at-Law) drove to Eichkatzlried to show the place to a Dutch industrialist by the name of Cuypers, he discovered to his surprise that the farmhouse was inhabited. Everyone had forgotten Xaver Bohrlein and Schneemoser.

In the autumn of 1945, just as soon as the noise of the German collapse had begun to die down, the Princess had joined her daughter in Munich. At the time, even members of the Illustrious House found crossing the border a difficult business; in fact, they found it more difficult than most, because the new Austria was as strenuously Republican as few other countries — at least for a time. This also explains why they refused to issue an exit permit to Bohrlein and Schneemoser, with the result that poor Bohrlein was once again left with the thankless task of watching over an empty house and an unloved bastard.

During the first few months, the Princess sent them money, but then her memory slipped and she left Bohrlein to his own devices. Luckily, the larder was well-stocked and Bohrlein had his savings. Now and then, his noble employers had paid his wages, and by living carefully he had managed to save a good proportion of this. In the spring of 1946, Schneemoser sprained his wrist. Bohrlein did not send him to the doctor. He remembered what his mother had told him about the healing powers of certain yellow flowers, and it happened that these plants grew in abundance in the meadow behind the farmhouse. Bohrlein picked them, boiled them, steeped a muslin gauze in the concoction and bandaged

Schneemoser's wrist. The skin came off, but the wrist healed with amazing speed.

The news spread quickly. Within a few days, the owner of the next-door farm appeared, driving a limping cow before him. Bohrlein produced his concoction and bandaged the cow's leg. The cow recovered, and the peasant recompensed him with thirty eggs and a lump of butter. It did not take very long before people from Eichkatzlried turned up in droves with lame, sickly and otherwise decrepit dogs, cats and canaries, all of which — with the odd fatal exception — Bohrlein was able to cure with his elixir of flowers. Townsmen usually paid him in cloth and once — at Bohrlein's special request — with a few lengths of guttering. By the autumn of 1946, Bohrlein had been forced to introduce regular consulting hours: he officiated on Monday, Wednesday and Friday mornings. He never took money from any of his clients.

Since peasants firmly believe that anything good for cattle can do no harm to man, the ranks of pet owners in Bohrlein's consulting rooms were soon swelled with ailing people. He used his yellow flowers to brew herbal teas, to roll pills, and soon afterwards expanded his repertoire with other herbs that he and Schneemoser went out to gather, often in the highest Alpine meadows. Several devastating setbacks frightened neither him nor his by then blindly credulous patients, the less so as the perfectly harmless yellow flowers from the meadow behind the house remained his chief stock-in-trade. And though some voices in Eichkatzlried argued about whether or not Bohrlein's juice was the best means of curing cancer, pulmonary tuberculosis and stomach ulcers, everyone was agreed that when it came to the feet (by which the locals, following High German usage, meant the legs) there was no one quite like the 'Chinese doctor'. Bohrlein was generally known by that name, because Hungerbichl Farm had been called the 'Chinese place' ever since it had been inhabited by the Japanese Ambassador. As time went by, Bohrlein's fame spread ever further afield — in the end, people queued up outside the house till they dropped with fatigue. Many arrived on the first train, at six in the morning. Those suffering with bad legs would get off the train at the Birkensee stop and hobble the one and a half miles to Hungerbichl Farm at such a trot that their crutches and artificial limbs flailed through the air like so many birds' wings. Many sceptics attributed the Chinaman's success to these very curative movements.

The doctors, needless to say, soon got wind of the competition. More than one inquiry was held, but dropped again because no one could swear that Bohrlein was taking money for his services, let alone asking for it. When a special committee of the Health Department came over from Innsbruck at the beginning of 1947, they were so impressed by Bohrlein's successes and testimonials that they even offered him a — restricted — licence to practice as a naturopath. From then on, Bohrlein would have been legally entitled to charge regular fees, but he refused to do so. He contented himself with an enamel plate on his front door, and with the happy knowledge that the district doctor could no longer make trouble for him. He did, however, earn some money by selling the excess produce the peasants kept bringing him from a stall in Eichkatzlried market (on Tuesdays, Thursdays and Saturdays). After a while, he found that his time was better occupied with his patients, and had his stall run by Mother Stecher, an old woman who lived in a hut on the fen and normally sold peat and fish.

Another problem — even before Bohrlein's medical fame had spread — was his nationality. Bohrlein and Schneemoser were foreigners, of course, and one day a gendarme turned up to investigate. Bohrlein told him at length, in great excitement and with many a sideways jerk of the head, what the situation was. The gendarme understood not a word, and so Bohrlein was summoned to the police station. Here too, no one could make the least sense of him. They did their best of course, and kept asking questions; but these only served to increase Bohrlein's obvious agitation, which rendered him less comprehensible still. Schneemoser shammed total ignorance. In the end, there seemed nothing for it but to grant residence permits to them both.

In May 1948, when the farm went up for sale, Schneemoser was attending the Eichkatzlried Gymnasium. In winter, he would go to school on a sledge (which he would pull behind him on the journey home); in summer he made the way down on roller skates. In 1947, a grateful peasant presented him with an old bicycle, and ever since Schneemoser had been cycling to school.

Dr von Scheuchenzuber had warned Mynheer Cuypers the house had been empty for three years and was no doubt in a state of utter disrepair. Hence he and the prospective buyer were even more surprised by the well-kempt look of the place than by the presence of Bohrlein and Schneemoser. Bohrlein had kept everything in perfect order, repairing the roof whenever necessary, and even replacing the broken old staircase with a new one. Moreover a grateful plumber, whom he had cured of gout, had helped him to install a water closet. Dr von Scheuchenzuber at once raised the asking price.

'Oh, it's only old Bohrlein,' said Princess Hildegard, when the lawyer explained the position. 'I had completely forgotten about him and his nephew. I don't think I need him any longer.'

And so Bohrlein was dismissed. Whereupon he tried to continue his practice from old Mother Stecher's hut. For the sake of appearances, he was even prepared to marry the old woman, who was as ugly as night. But once Mynheer Cuypers had bought Hungerbichl Farm and refused Bohrlein access to the meadow with the yellow flowers, Bohrlein's career was finished. The patients simply melted away. Incidentally, Mynheer Cuypers had little joy of the place — he died a ridiculous death while hunting the Tazzel Worm, a fabulous creature that is said to appear during weather changes — but that, as they say, is quite another story.

Schneemoser was sent to a monastery school in Switzerland in preparation for taking the cloth. This sudden change proved a most painful, though portentous, break in his seventeen-year-old life.

Another decisive and even — to employ a misused but in this case fully appropriate term — existential turning point had already left its mark on his life, though he himself had failed to notice it. It had happened in 1944, when Bohrlein and Schneemoser still lived in the late Prince Moritz's villa in Bogenhausen. One day while Bohrlein was listening intently to his 'People's Receiver' and hearing yet another optimistic Wehrmacht report about the planned evacuation of Northern France, he looked reflectively at the then thirteen-year-old boy immersed in his homework. Bohrlein stared at the boy hard and long. The Wehrmacht report was over, and now it was the turn of the 'From the North Sea to the Alps' programme, with songs by the People's Choir of the Reich Labour Service. Bohrlein was still staring.

'What is the matter, Uncle Xaver?' Schneemoser asked when he eventually took notice.

Bohrlein muttered something quite incomprehensible even to Schneemoser's practised ears.

Next day, Bohrlein shaved the boy. It was perhaps a little too soon, but not very much so. The boy had a slight down on his upper lip, but in addition a few straggly hairs had begun to sprout on his chin; they grew thin and straight, as on an unkempt mandarin.

Bohrlein brushed soap on Schneemoser's face and then — deliberately controlling his tremendous strength and working with the gentlest of touches — applied the razor and scraped off the offending hairs. Not a cut marred the boy's face — that did not happen until later, when Bohrlein had taught Schneemoser to shave himself. During their second year in Eichkatzlried, Schneemoser was given his own shaving tackle. And when Hermanfried eventually entered the Upper Sixth of St Hilarius Monastery School in Rabenbrunn he was forced — to the envy of his room mates — to shave twice daily.

The hair on his head, too, grew rather quickly. Even in Bogenhausen, Hermanfried had been forced to visit the barber's more often than other boys — not conspicuously so, but more often nevertheless. In Eichkatzlried, it was

Bohrlein (himself quite bald and hence in no need of a barber) who at first cut the boy's hair. He produced no better, but also no worse, results than the official Eichkatzlried barber, Herr Cerka. Herr Cerka was an extraordinarily weedy man who felt threatened by epidemics, bankruptcies, murder, arson and other private and public disasters. He expected the end of the world by the hour. In good weather he invariably prophesied a change for the worse. In bad weather, by contrast, he always predicted that it had come to stay. He read all news of bad harvests, insolvencies, railway disasters, floods and earthquakes, with groans but undiminished avidity. On the first of January and during the next few days, he would greet all his clients with: 'Let's just hope the coming year will turn out better for you than it's likely to turn out for me.' He never forgot to add that he had some private information from which he could only conclude that the — relatively — good times were over and that the world was racing downhill.

For all that, Cerka was doing extraordinarily well. His business flourished, and he bought up one house after the next. All that was really wrong with him was his knee, which, moreover, enabled him to predict bad weather with regular if reliable monotony. Soon after Bohrlein had begun to cure human beings as well as animals, Cerka had presented himself for treatment. Needless to say, his ailing knee did not improve. But Cerka was extremely correct, and when Bohrlein refused payment he offered him free haircuts instead. Bohrlein accepted and transferred the privilege to his adopted son, Hermanfried. In 1948, Hermanfried went once a week to Master Cerka, and that was by no means too often. Master Cerka suffered visibly. He had long since begun to regret his generous offer — an act, he now realized, that was bound to bring financial ruin upon his head, the more so as a comet had recently appeared and the Holy Virgin had been sighted amidst a forest, in a sea of flames, proclaiming the end of the world.

In Rabenbrunn, the task of cutting the boy's hair fell to a lay brother.

One of the long, echoing, whitewashed corridors of the gigantic and rambling seventeenth-century monastery led to Brother Maurus's 'tonsorium'.* Behind a heavily carved oak door, which was set off to great advantage by the plain walls, a glittering hairdressing salon with all the trappings of modernity had been fitted up. The only difference from the more usual establishment was that the various salves and hair lotions were not set out on gaudy shelves, but kept in old — though perfectly hygienic — cherrywood cabinets. For the rest, the place was equipped with a chair, which at the merest touch of a pedal rose and fell to just the desired height, and also mirrors, a washbasin, and all the other required paraphernalia. Fr Maurus wore a white hairdresser's coat over his soutane. It was not for the sake of the pupils that the tonsorium had been fitted up so elegantly; even the Abbot ('Reverendissimus Pater ac Dominus Romualdus IV (Oscar) Zumtobel, Doctor Juris Canonioi, Abbatiscellanus ex Appencell, Abbas LIV Ordinarius, etc. etc.') had his hair cut by Brother Maurus, and the venerable Pater and *professor musicae* Ansgarius Feusisberger was also said to get his impressive white beard trimmed in that very place. Father Feusisberger had made his name as a moderately progressive composer with his 'Missa Rabenbrunnensis', 'Appencell People's Mass', 'Brief Appencell People's Mass', and various organ works, including a 'Fantasia and Fugue on an Alpine Theme', Opus 28a, dedicated to Pope Pius XI.

Young Schneemoser, whose great diligence and good behaviour quickly made him the pride and joy of all the fathers, wended his way to Brother Maurus's tonsorium so frequently that the good tonsor felt obliged to report the matter to the Abbot.

*The *Catalogus Religiosorum Monasterii Rabenbrunnensis* bears the following entry: Fr. Maurus (Carolus) Bächtiger, Sangallensis ex Joaschwil, *coques et tonsor*, nat. 8 mai 1921, prof. 31 mart. 1947.

In translation: Carl Bächtiger from Joaschwill, in Saint Gallen, born on 8 May, 1921, took holy orders on 31 March 1947, adopted the name of Maurus and worked as cook and hairdresser. (Later – in 1957 – Fr Stephanus Rüttiman – 'Suitensis ex Galgenen' – was to join him as supplementary *tonsor*, but this happened long after Schneemoser had left the school.')

137

The Abbot then summoned Schneemoser's form master. He learned that Schneemoser was a model pupil in all respects, with first-class marks even in such subsidiary subjects as biology and PT.

'Well, well,' said the Abbot, and called Brother Maurus back. 'Does he grow his hair on purpose?'

'No, Father, it's just that his hair seems to grow with unnatural speed.'

'Well, well,' said the Abbot, and decided to drop the matter.

In the summer of 1949 Schneemoser matriculated, needless to say with brilliant marks — or, as his report put it, with 'excellent and partly astonishing success in all subjects; average mark A+'. He was given a special medal of honour blessed by His Holiness the Pope. Cardinal Blutscher, titular Archbishop of Artaxata, 'Rabenbrunn's great son', who had taught here and had been Abbot Zumtobel's predecessor before becoming Cardinal and 'Praefectus S. Congregationibus pro cultu divino', was present during the end-of-term ceremony. He handed the medal to the prize pupil in person, and kissed him on the forehead while looking long and deep into his eyes.

Schneemoser, who of course had been given an A+ for music as well, delighted the assembled company with a rendering of the 'Hymn to the Virgin' (Opus 143c, I) for solo voice, choir and organ, specially composed for the occasion by Father Feusisberger. (The organ was played by a not quite so brilliant fellow matriculant, Daniel Keel, whose future career proved a great disappointment to the Reverend Fathers, but that again is quite another story.) Schneemoser, who was singing in public for the first and last time, was extremely nervous. All in all, the examinations had utterly drained him. He was the typical model pupil: the more he knew, the more certain his knowledge was; and the more his teachers assured him that there was nothing, absolutely nothing that could go wrong, the more nervous he grew, and the more afraid he became that something might nevertheless upset the applecart. Not that Schneemoser was the kind of scholastic pusher who would have considered a B a shattering defeat; he was simply afraid of flunking.

Barely was the examination behind him, than his nerves were tried almost more severely by the rehearsals for the Hymn to the Virgin (Opus 143c, I). This may explain why, from May 1949 until the final ceremony in July, Schneemoser's face was a constant purple. It was with a sigh of tremendous relief that he at long last took possession of his medal, sang his solo and sat down again. One of his teachers delivered a farewell speech.

Let us depict the scene: on the decorated stage there now stood the lone teacher delivering his address. In the hall sat the younger pupils, behind several rows of their teachers; these in turn sat behind the guests of honour who were ranged on either side of the Abbot and the Cardinal. In front of the first row, the school-leavers had been placed on special seats, the prize-winner right in their centre. Whenever the Abbot was not looking at the speaker, his glance rested squarely on the back of Schneemoser's head. And as he watched, he could see Schneemoser's hair growing visibly.

'As true as I hope to consign my soul into the Saviour's hand,' he confided to Schneemoser's form master that very afternoon, and also to the Cardinal and to Brother Maurus, 'I actually watched his hair sprouting out of his head.'

'Motht interethting,' said the Cardinal, who lisped — unless he took particular care his sibilants were rather watery affairs. 'Why did you not draw my attenthion to it?'

Had he been forced to speak the truth, Abbot Romuald IV would have had to say: 'Because I did not wish to waken Your Eminence.' But that is not, of course, what he did say.

'I took the liberty some time ago . . .,' said Brother Maurus.

'I've never seen the likes of it,' the Abbot continued.

'It was gruesome. He stepped down from the stage, purple in the face . . .'

'He's always been terribly nervous,' said the form master.

' . . . So I noticed. But then he calmed down and assumed a more normal complexion . . . Quite suddenly the beastly stuff started to grow.'

'What thtarted to grow?' asked the Cardinal.

'His hair, that's what. Like noodles squeezing through a colander. Black noodles.'

'But surely it's no longer our problem, now that he has passed out,' said the form master.

'Of course it still is. And *a fortiori* so. Schneemoser is . . . shall we say . . . a special case. I am not allowed to tell you more than that' — not that he in fact knew any more — 'but according to the express wishes of those who have sent him here, he is intended for Holy Orders.'

'Has he no parents?'

'The whole thing is terribly confusing. I am beginning to wonder, and I make bold to ask Your Eminence, whether we dare run the risk of preparing someone like that for the priesthood?'

The Cardinal wagged his head from side to side. It might equally well have been a shake or a nod.

'He is the best and most talented pupil our school has ever produced . . .' said the form master.

'That's the rub,' said the Abbot. 'If only we could be sure that he would remain a village priest, or a missionary where the pepper trees grow. But with his talents the boy is bound to press on much further than that.'

'Like noodlth out of a colander?' lisped the Cardinal.

'Who knows but that his hair will not fall out in time,' said Brother Maurus.

'Hath he ever been douthed in Holy Water? Really douthed and rubbed hard?' asked the Cardinal.

'No,' said the Abbot.

'Try it,' said the Cardinal. 'I shall menthion hith cathe to the Holy Father. In nomine Patrith et Filii et Thpiritu thanctu. Amen.' The Cardinal blessed those present, rose, offered Brother Maurus his hand to kiss and left.

Schneemoser's head was rubbed with holy water. His hair grew no more slowly but no faster either.

A year later, when Schneemoser was in his second year at the Rabenbrunn Priests' Seminary, and was about to be made a deacon before moving on to the theological faculty in the University of Fribourg, a message was received from Rome: Schneemoser's unnatural hair-growth must be considered a gross irregularity. Since, moreover, it prevented the application of the tonsure, an essential part of the consecration ceremony, this irregularity could only be the work of Satan, and hence not subject to dispensation. The boy could never become a priest.

Schneemoser, who naturally had long since outstripped all the other pupils in the seminary, was for a while disconsolate. The Abbot, who dismissed him personally and shook his hand several times, tried to cheer him up.

'After all, you can also serve Mother Church as a layman. Times being what they are, you could well be more use that way than as a priest.'

'How do you know,' Schneemoser said, though only to himself, 'that I still want to serve the Church?'

The day before Schneemoser was due to leave he was handed a sealed envelope. It contained a banknote of a large denomination, a ticket to Munich, and a short message requesting him to call at the Munich offices of the lawyer, Dr von Scheuchenzuber.

In Munich, Schneemoser walked with his small suitcase straight from the station to Briener Strasse, where the lawyer's office was located. He was received by the younger Scheuchenzuber (the old Counsellor-at-Law was by then no more than the nominal head of the firm) who delivered himself of the following set speech:

'In November, you will be nineteen. By a decision of the Munich District Court of 4 July 1950 (Ref. No. Xb 242/50) — I am handing you a certified copy — I have been appointed your legal guardian. The whole thing is little more than a formality. I shall not be interfering with you in any way. You are old enough, in any case. I have been entrusted with a sum of money from which I shall let you have 250 DM per month. You had best fetch your cheque on the first of every month from this office. Or do you intend to move from Munich?'

'I haven't decided yet,' said Schneemoser.

'If you intend to study, I am authorized to pay your

university fees, your expenses for books and other essentials, against the production of the requisite receipts. All this is over and above your monthly remittance. Do you intend to go to university?'

'I haven't decided yet,' said Schneemoser. 'But I think I probably shall.'

'You have no legal right to these remittances. But I can assure you . . .'

'Where does the money come from, Herr von Scheuchenzuber?'

'I am not allowed to say. If you have not completed your professional training on your twenty-first birthday, which is only to be expected if you decide to study, the monthly remittance will be increased to 350 DM. On your twenty-fourth birthday, you will receive twelve times that amount, that is DM 4,200. If you decide not to study . . .'

'I think I shall study all the same, if you don't mind.'

'It would be a downright sin if you did not, what with your school reports. May I formally offer you my congratulations? If you . . .'

'Herr von Scheuchenzuber, may I ask you one thing?'

'I'd rather you didn't.'

'Could you please tell me what's happened to Bohrlein?'

'Who is he?'

Schneemoser explained.

'Oh, that fellow. I can't tell you. I'm very sorry, but I honestly don't know.'

'That's a great pity,' said Schneemoser.

'If ever you are in need of advice, please don't hesitate to come to me. After all, I am your legal guardian. Do you perhaps need anything else straightaway? Here is your first cheque.'

Schneemoser thanked him and left. He decided to read law, a choice that took him no longer than a day. He was talented enough for anything, and had done extraordinarily well in every conceivable subject — from mechanical engineering to egyptology. Such highly talented people are invariably thrown together with less talented dunces. Both alike are tortured by subconscious guilt feelings, the latter because their inferiority is such as to make them bungle every science so that they are good enough for nothing but the law, the former because, by choosing any one of the sciences they are doing a grave injustice to all the rest — a kind of Don Juan complex on a purely intellectual plane: they remain single, as it were, and choose the law as well.

During the summer term of 1952 — his third at law school — Schneemoser had already collected all the necessary course credits, laid down the law to the civil law class, though in a purely factual and modest way, was feared by several professors and had pointed out to various lecturers that there were serious gaps in their understanding of this problem or that. Even earlier, by the end of the second term, he had been exempted from all but selected lectures (e.g. 'Special Problems in International Exchange' or 'Babylonian Corporative Law with Practical Exercises'); all the rest was too paltry for him. He was reputed to work for sixteen hours a day, and to go through all the major textbooks systematically and without any assistance. When asked point blank, he would not deny it. 'I simply cannot let N.N.' — he mentioned a famous jurist — 'get away with his cavalier treatment of multiple causality.' Did he then take no time off from his studies at all, he was asked. 'Indeed, I do,' said Schneemoser. 'At night, when I'm tired, I often retire to bed and leaf through the *Pandects* for light relief.'

That was, of course, an exaggeration. In fact, young Schneemoser devoted much of his spare time to politics. Abbot Romuald had handed the young man a letter of introduction to the Abbot of Andechs Monastery, a fellow Benedictine. Schneemoser, who knew nobody in Munich other than Scheuchenzuber, had presented the letter in due course, and was invited to Andechs several times. It was here that he made the acquaintance of Monsignor Hauberisser. Anyone who had penetrated as deeply into the precincts of the Catholic hierarchy as Schneemoser had done, never again sheds his clerical style. It sticks to him like the smell of garlic. It takes the form, not simply of a somewhat unctuous

143

manner, but also of a rather choice and celibatory aura. Schneemoser, who at the time was still very close to his clerical past, fitted almost organically into the clerical evenings at Andechs Monastery, so much so that the reverend company had more than once to remind themselves that the brilliant young man in their midst was a mere layman.

Despite this obvious handicap, Monsignor Hauberisser confided all his political plans to young Schneemoser, introduced him to Dr (*honoris causa*) Kofler, and was thus ultimately responsible for Schneemoser's stay in a cell at Police Headquarters in July 1952, after he had been charged with the theft of a tricycle.

During his preliminary interrogation, Schneemoser readily admitted that he had taken the machine, and also that he had consumed several buns, but for the rest he refused to admit anything whatever. Since there were no other charges, and since the whole case against him was trifling, Schneemoser was released with a caution.

He made straight for the Archbishop's Palace, but was not admitted. Then he rang Kofler, only to be told that this gentleman knew no one by the name of Schneemoser, and moreover had had nothing — literally nothing — to do with the whole affair, as he could easily prove.

'But I mentioned no affair with which you may or may not have had anything to do . . .'

Dr (*honoris causa*) had hung up.

Schneemoser was on the point of blurting out the whole truth to the newspapers or to the Public Prosecutor. He could even have produced some, albeit sparse, evidence . . . but in the end he thought better of it. It would have been only fair had he given the game away, but no tangible advantage would have accrued to Schneemoser himself. And Schneemoser was always loath to do anything purely altruistic. The rights and wrongs of the matter were something on which he preferred not to dwell — he had a rare gift of turning his back on the past, casting it off like an old suit, or an old brief. In other words, having filed every last detail for future use,

144

he put the whole business *ad acta*, in the astonishing archives that constituted his memory.

In this connection, one may wonder whether it was by pure chance, or as a reward for his discretion, that the dossier in which the tricycle theft was recorded disappeared from Police HQ without a trace. In any case, Hermanfried Schneemoser did a political somersault. He joined the Social Democratic Party.

Minuet I

Once the truth about Prince Otto had leaked out, the Illustrious House met in council and decided to brazen the whole thing out. The Prince's abnormal stature was played down, but otherwise freely admitted. After all the situation had changed, or if you like, grown more acute. King Rupprecht was eighty-three years old. He was still spry, no doubt, but with all the love and reverence in the world, you had to agree with Counsellor-at-Law von Scheuchenzuber that 'we must sadly count on his demise in the foreseeable future'. And what would happen then? It is possible to hide a Crown Prince, but not a King, and after the abortive coup d'état it was unthinkable that ex-King Luitpold should ever be restored to the throne.

The Prince made his first public appearance on Wie-sensonntag 1952, when he represented his indisposed grandfather. He stood at a Palace window on the first floor and waved at the October Procession. He was wearing a *loden* suit with green lapels and cuffs, cut for perspective effect. The ex-Queen and Prince Max Arnulph were standing by the Prince's side, but on special pedestals invisible from below, and smiled with grim determination.

Prince Otto loomed very large, but not frighteningly so. The people were content.

In December — King Rupprecht was indisposed once again — the family were bold enough to allow the Prince to receive the Ministerial Council. This time no perspective effect would have been of the least use, nor was there any point in producing a set of pedestals. Instead Prince Otto was seated behind a desk covered with a white and blue tapestry and decorated for the occasion with giant sprigs of fir, through which he ogled the Ministerial Council like a wild boar at bay.

In February 1953, the family decided to send the Prince on a world tour. He had just turned twenty and measured eight foot six inches.

The decision was taken for several reasons. All Princes had been making the grand tour for centuries, and at a time when the travelling habit was spreading to ever wider strata of society this tradition was anything but outdated. Also, a tour as a reward for covering the thorny path of education is a happy ending to every young man's scholastic career, let alone to that of Prince Otto who had spent most of his life locked up in Nymphenburg Castle.

There was a more delicate reason as well: the dynastic concept. There was no lack of princes in the House of Wittelsbach. The Illustrious House was not threatened by the spectre of extinction. Still, it seemed particularly desirable to ensure the continuance of the oldest line, through the person of its foremost member so to speak.

To that end, the Prince had been examined by several leading physicians. They had all scratched their heads and pulled down the corners of their mouths. Everything, but *everything* about the Prince was outsize. As so often in science, the final answer hinged on an empirical test. Professor Hingerl prescribed a St Bernard bitch, Chief Consultant Dr Franckh a cow.

The Prince's mother consulted the Suffragan-Bishop during the very next coffee hour.

She hummed and ha-ed for a very long time, for she was terribly uncertain how best to put the matter into words.

'The doctors,' she said in the end, 'have suggested that Ottito . . . I should like to have your advice, Your Grace . . . He is, so to speak, an adult now, even though he still keeps

147

growing . . . and that raises certain questions . . .'

'I do not altogether follow you, Your Majesty.'

'We have had him examined. By doctors.'

'Is the poor child ill?'

'No, but . . . You must understand. There are certain things that happen to grown-ups.'

'I see,' said the Bishop, who had no wish to admit that he was still completely at sea.

'Well, there you are. And the doctors have recommended either a St Bernard bitch or a cow.'

'You don't say,' said the Bishop.

'I don't altogether remember,' said the Queen, 'whether it was a St Bernard or a cow.'

'I imagine the whole thing would be terribly uncomfortable for him,' said the Suffragan-Bishop with a measure of directness the Queen had not expected. 'A St Bernard might just about do, but a cow . . .'

The Queen had a rush of blood to her head, and lowered her eyes. 'The question of convenience is something to which I haven't given a thought. All I wanted to know from you is what you think about it all from the spiritual point of view.'

'From the spiritual point of view? There are no objections whatsoever to domestic animals.'

'In all seriousness?'

'But of course. I keep canaries myself, and when times were hard, I even kept chickens.'

'You? . . . You yourself have . . . canaries . . . isn't that against . . . I grant you that I know nothing at all about such matters . . . but isn't it . . . isn't it a betrayal of your vows?'

'Canaries? Of course not. Why do you ask?'

'You . . .' the Queen drew herself up with an almost superhuman effort. 'Do you mean to say you sleep with canaries?'

'No I keep them in a cage in the living room.'

'In a cage? Is there enough space?'

'Of course there is space. There are four of them all told.'

'I'm thinking of you, Your Grace, how can you possibly fit into their cage?'

The Suffragan-Bishop dropped his coffee spoon. He looked at the Queen in utter bewilderment. 'The Archbishop,' he said uncertainly, hoping to change the subject, 'keeps a red setter.'

'The Archbishop, *too*?'

'Indeed he does,' said the Suffragan. 'Believe me. And I know quite a number of priests who keep all sorts of domestic animals . . .'

'Quite a number of priests?'

'The Dean keeps goldfish . . .'

'How perfectly awful! I never realized to what depths . . .'

'Depths? Why? They are perfectly friendly and harmless . . .'

'By comparison, a St Bernard or a cow strike me as being positively normal.'

'Well, I must say, a cow is a bit much, I don't think that's the right kind of pet for a prince.'

'Pet!' The Queen had never before heard such a frivolous expression from the Suffragan's lips. Was he a fit person to have in for coffee?

'A cow is a smelly animal. It stinks. And are you proposing to put straw into his room?'

'If the Dean can engage in unnatural practices with a goldfish,' said the Queen, now visibly moved, 'why should there be spiritual objections to a cow?'

'The Dean engages in unnatural practices with his goldfish?' asked the Suffragan-Bishop. 'Is that physically possible?'

'But that's what you've just been telling me.'

'I?'

'Yes, you. And you yourself . . . with your chickens, when you were younger . . . and that it had nothing to do with your vow of celibacy.'

'Now, I'm completely lost. Of course, my chickens had nothing to do with my celibacy. I wasn't married to them, was I?'

'That's all we are short of!' said the Queen huffily.

The Suffragan-Bishop was contrite. 'I really don't know why Your Majesty is so upset. If you insist, I am quite prepared to let my canaries fly away, my little . . .'

'Your little darlings, why don't you say it?'

'That's just what I was about to say, Your Majesty.'

'For all I care, you can keep them. All I wanted to know was whether a St Bernard or a cow . . . By all means keep coupling with your canaries.'

'Coupling?'

'Yes, what other word should I use?'

Both fell into an embarrassed silence.

'At last, I realize why it had to be a St Bernard *bitch*,' said the unhappy Bishop.

'I do apologize, Your Grace,' said the Queen. 'But I feel tremendously relieved that you have grasped my meaning at last.'

'I must assure you that I kept chickens solely for their eggs . . .'

'But of course. Let's forget all about them, shall we? But is it a sin, if Ottito should, as it were, consort with a cow, seeing the special circumstances . . . ?'

The Suffragan reflected. He poured himself another cup of coffee, added cream and sugar, stirred the mixture, and reflected some more. At last he looked up.

'Seen in this new light, I should imagine that it's even more awkward with a cow than I first made bold to say.'

'But is it sinful? Is there some dispensation, seeing that the doctors have prescribed it?'

'I remember the time when one of my respected colleagues,' said Suffragan-Bishop Zach after further reflection, 'I'd rather not mention his name at this point, came home from Hong Kong . . . The place was called the "Red Junk", I believe. The ladies in that establishment . . . to be brief, Your Majesty, why don't you send His Royal Highness to Hong Kong? It's far enough away from home, no one will recognize him, and all the girls are heathens in any case. A slight lapse like that, and absolution would cause no problem at all. What's more you avoid bestiality. And, when all is said and done, a cow does rather stink.'

And that was how the Prince's world tour came about.

Because Prince Max Arnulph seemed much too young to go along too, let alone visit the 'Red Junk', Prince Otto was accompanied by Prince Ignaz, the son of Garibald the Counter, and also by the Royal Steward, Eugen Leodegar, Count of Durach.

The Princes and the Count set out on 1 February 1953. Rome — with a Papal audience — Athens and Cairo, were their first ports of call, followed by Teheran, Delhi, Bangkok and Hong Kong. They stayed in Tokyo for close on a month, and in Hawaii for another three weeks. Then the tour continued to San Francisco and New York, with a slight detour to South America, where Prince Otto was allowed to call on his exiled father. Then back to New York, London, Paris, and on the Suffragan's special advice, to Lourdes. From Lourdes the Royal party returned to Munich via Geneva and Zurich.

In July — while Prince Otto and his companions were being bored by New York, which was deserted for the summer — Baron von Speckh summoned Dr (*honoris causa*) Kofler to Prien. It was almost a year since the failure of the Bavarian coup d'état, and Anton Joseph Kofler had tied a large metaphorical rock to that embarrassing interlude before consigning it to the depths of his subconscious. By July 1953, he had firmly convinced himself that he had had nothing, literally nothing, to do with the whole affair.

Baron von Speckh had maintained close contact with Kofler ever since their 'pact' of 1952. Kofler came to Prien quite often, and it did not take him long to realize that every piece of advice the Baron kept proffering was, in fact, an order, and that there was nothing he could do about it. In any case, he was not in the least surprised to receive his summons in July 1953; the only thing he *was* surprised at was its form.

Normally, the Baron would ring up or have someone else do it with: 'The Baron would like to see you at 4 p.m. tomorrow.' But this time the Baron had sent a special invitation on the best writing paper. It said: 'Baron and

Baroness von Speckh request the pleasure of your company at a private supper . . .'

'Is it the Baron's birthday?' Kofler asked Sondermeier who opened the door to him.

'No,' said the chauffeur. Good servants have an almost seismographic feeling for class distinctions — they know the distance they must keep to within a millimetre. And ever since Sondermeier had come to appreciate — unconsciously — that Dr (*honoris causa*) Kofler, too, was just another of the Baron's lackeys, he had been adopting a familiar tone towards him. 'No,' he said. 'The Baron's birthday is, if anything, in December. I should think that he misses every second one for reasons of economy.'

'Then what is the great occasion?'

'No idea, Herr Doktor. The table is laid for six. Rudi Gerch is eating in the kitchen, with the staff.'

The meal proceeded without incident, though the fact that the Baron was entertaining guests for dinner was remarkable in itself. The six places had been set for the Baron, the Baroness, Fräulein Dr Gerch, Frau Marx, Kofler and one of the Baron's sons by his first wife, a gawky twenty-year-old boy who bore no resemblance to his father, called Othmar. He had been educated at a boarding school, and his manners suggested that the Baron had not chosen the most expensive.

Kofler was shown to a seat next to the Baroness. The relationship between these two was strained, to say the least. Kofler did not know whether the Baroness knew that he had made a sham — though was it really a sham? — confession to the Baron; the Baroness, for her part, vacillated between feeling insulted at the fact that Kofler had taken liberties with her, and the equally insulting realization that he had never repeated the offence, though God knows he had had plenty of chances to do so.

After the meal, when the Baron asked his guests, in another unaccustomed burst of formal politeness, to join him in the drawing room, Kofler seated himself as far away from the Baroness as he possibly could. The maid served liqueurs to the ladies (Fräulein Dr Gerch sipped hers with the little finger extended as far as it would go) and whisky to Kofler, who had recently acquired a taste for this fashionable beverage. Frau Marx and Baron von Speckh drank soda-water.

For a while, everyone sat about in some embarrassment; they were all waiting for something to happen after the unaccustomed treat, though no one could have said precisely what. In the end, the Baron rose, walked to a cupboard, opened it and said after an obvious inner struggle: 'Kofler, would you like a cigar?'

The cigar was fat, though any cigar-smoker could have told you that the Baron was no connoisseur. It looked like an expensive import, but cost a mere thirty pfennigs and smelled of seaweed. 'That's why it bears the "Navigador" band,' Sondermeier used to say when the Baron handed him one on his birthday or at Christmas. In general, the Baron preferred to employ staff whose birthdays fell on the 23rd, 24th or 25th of December, thus letting him off with one set of gifts instead of two.

Then there were a few more embarrassed moments. At long last, the Baron said: 'Well, Frau Marx, it's your party, after all.'

What happened next took everyone completely by surprise. Frau Marx rose, raised her right arm, laid the left across her stomach, turned her face slightly downward, and screwed up her eyes. Then she roared 'Heil!' A lock of hair fell across her forehead.

'The resemblance!' screamed the Baroness.

'Resemblance, indeed!' said Frau Marx. 'It's me !'

'It's unbelievable,' shrieked the Baroness.

'Say what you like,' said Fräulein Dr Gerch, 'but it's not right to play fast and loose with his memory.'

Frau Marx's eyes brightened suddenly, and then she went up to Fräulein Dr Gerch, stroked her ash-blonde bun and said: 'You're a wonderful, dear little girl!'

'Are we supposed to be having fun?' asked young Baron Othmar.

'Heil!' roared Frau Marx once again, turned on her heels

and walked out of the room with firm steps.

'Call a doctor, quickly!' shouted the Baroness.

'She's out of her mind,' said Fräulein Dr Gerch.

'It's the liqueur,' said Baron Othmar.

'But all she had was soda-water!'

'The resemblance!'

'I always took her for such a sensible person . . .' said Dr (*honoris causa*) Anton Joseph Kofler.

'Just calm yourselves,' said the Baron. 'I had best tell you the whole story. A year ago, you may remember, I mentioned the Hitler enigma. I told you about Hitler's attitude to women. But there is another chapter of the same story, namely Hitler's attitude to men.'

'Dear, oh dear,' said Fräulein Dr Gerch.

'Udet, Dietl, Rommel — to mention but a few who caused a stir in their day, though everything possible was done to hush matters up. I myself was made privy to the sad story, or at least the bitter end, of Surgeon-Major von Fuchs, one of the many cases that went completely unnoticed. A Surgeon-Major is a soldier of relatively low rank. Surgeon-Major Dr von Fuchs was assistant to Hitler's personal physician. In general, Hitler would not let anyone except his personal physician, who was sworn to silence, come anywhere near him. But in 1941, or more probably in 1942, Hitler needed an enema urgently, and his personal physician was unfortunately ill in bed. Hitler — I hope you will forgive these unappetizing details, but after all we have finished our meal — had to put off the enema for several days. What with his poor digestion — he kept stuffing himself with puddings and sweets — he was nearly exploding, and still his personal physician kept lying in bed. There was nothing for it, someone had to administer the damn thing. The personal physician sent for Dr von Fuchs, his particularly reliable and national-socialistically minded assistant. Hitler gave orders that Dr Fuchs must touch him no more than was absolutely essential for the purpose of introducing the enema. Hitler, as Dr von Fuchs himself has told me, was lying on his stomach and had dropped his trousers. It was all terribly difficult, Dr

Fuchs said. Hitler carried on like a primadonna; he refused to take his trousers off altogether and kept squeezing his buttocks together for all he was worth. When Dr von Fuchs was finally there, he noticed something which gave him such a shock that he nearly dropped the enema can: the Führer, beyond all doubt, was of the female gender.

'Of course, I'd suspected this all along. It was perfectly obvious: the Polish campaign was only just over and the special problem it posed — our relations with Russia — was still far from solved, when Hitler sent our troops into Denmark and Norway. And barely had they landed there, when he lost interest in the whole business and turned against France. And when we had occupied France, he got bored just as quickly. "Now for England!" he said, and threw himself whole-heartedly into "Operation Sea-Lion". And when the English put up more of a show than he had expected, he lost interest once again, and picked out the Balkans with a pin. That affair hadn't been settled when he said: "Let's quickly take Russia before we finish England off." And when he got stuck in the Russian mud, he turned to Africa . . . Not even an ounce of political, let alone military, strategy — not even a series of accidents. All of it just like the whims of a capricious woman. So when Dr von Fuchs told me, he merely confirmed what I knew already.

'And then Hitler had to fall in love with the dashing young doctor, and Fuchs killed himself. It was just like Udet, Dietl and Rommel all over again . . .'

'Who would have believed it!' said the Baroness.

'No!' whispered Fräulein Dr Gerch.

'That's why,' the Baron continued, 'Hitler could disappear so easily in April 1945. He just shaved off his little moustache and married a Swiss Nazi, the secretary to the Swiss legation in Berlin. Unfortunately, his name was Marx. But Hitler had no choice . . .'

'Frau Marx!' exclaimed Dr (*honoris causa*) Kofler.

And then the door was flung open.

'My Führer!' sighed Fraulein Dr Gerch and sank from her chair.

155

Frau Marx, alias Adolf Hitler, who had grown a little older during the past eight years, stepped into the room dressed in Party uniform, a swastika armband and a false black moustache.

Dr (*honoris causa*) Kofler rose from his chair and raised his arm in the Nazi salute.

Shortly after midnight Baron von Speckh found himself alone with Dr Kofler in the drawing room. The Baroness, Fräulein Dr Gerch and Frau Marx, alias the Führer and Reichs-Chancellor, had retired to their respective bedrooms after the night's excitement. Baron Othmar had stayed on for a little while and had eventually left as well. Kofler lit a cigar of his own.

'What was your reason for giving us this demonstration, Herr Baron?'

'My reason? None at all. I knew Herr Marx pretty well. He helped me during the war, and later on too. We were engaged in a whole series of financial transactions. As a Swiss he had a more or less free hand. Unfortunately he died in 1947. He was no youngster, you know. Some time earlier, while he was still in a convalescent home I agreed to take his wife into my house.'

'Wasn't that rather dangerous?'

'I myself did not think so. Who on earth could possibly know Frau Marx's secret? At most the Israelis. And if they carried her off — well, that was that. Could they have proved that I, too, was in the know? That I ever mistook her for anyone else than the wife of a dear Swiss friend? In any case, I took legal advice. There is no case against Hitler. There are no charges, no warrant has been taken out against him, no investigation is under way. There are no constitutional grounds for handing him over to the Allies. There might have been in 1945, but not today. In all probability, Frau Marx is entitled to draw the pension due to a former Reichs-President and a Reichs-Chancellor, back-dated of course. And don't forget that the King is eighty-four. If he dies, it will be Luitpold's turn once again. And though little love was lost between Hitler, I mean Frau Marx, and Rupprecht, her relationship with Luitpold has always been extremely cordial . . .'

'Did he, I mean she, have an . . . er . . . with Luitpold as well?'

'No,' said the Baron, 'absolutely not.'

'But what will Adenauer say?'

'That's what we've got you for, Dr Kofler.'

'We? You mean the NPD?'

'It is the Führer's, I mean Frau Marx's wish, to change her sex once again. I had no part in that decision.'

'But you haven't tried to stop her either?'

'No.'

'I consider the whole thing somewhat premature. I wonder if she oughtn't to be stopped.'

'Come, come . . .'

'After all, look at your own position, Herr Baron. You'll have to own up now willy nilly. If you keep her here another minute, how can you ever pretend to ignorance . . . ?'

'Why ever not? I am having her taken to a mental home. There are quite a few lunatics who claim they are Hitler, though no female ones have presented themselves so far. She needs me to prove that she is in her right mind.'

Dr (*honoris causa*) Kofler whistled through his teeth. 'I must say I admire you. The whole thing is so complicated . . . aren't you ever afraid of losing your grip? The slightest mistake, and you're for it . . .'

'I think that extremely unlikely,'' said the Baron.

That night was to provide quite a few further surprises. When the clock over Prien Parish Church struck one and Anton Joseph Kofler, dressed only in red checked woollen underpants that reached loosely down to his knees, was wiping the sweat from his neck with a girdle of the same colour and pattern, the door to his room opened softly. Hitler appeared in a long nightdress. He had taken off his moustache.

157

'I've changed my mind,' said Hitler and prepared to pull up his night shirt while uttering a strident: 'Youuuu...'

Anton Joseph Kofler jumped out of the window. He landed on the familiar garage roof, lay down flat on his stomach, and shivered with cold and vertigo.

At that very moment another figure was creeping along the corridor: Fräulein Dr Gerch in a pale-brown hand-knitted nightshirt. She wanted to hear the full story. 'What luck,' she said when she found Frau Marx's door ajar. But all she discovered in that lady's bed was a false moustache, the size of a cockchafer. She waited for an hour and then returned to her own room in great disappointment, shortly before Hitler, tired of waiting for Kofler's re-appearance, returned to hers.

Only Kofler stayed where he was. He dared not move for fear of falling off the roof. He counted the hours and watched the sky growing lighter over the lake. At about six o'clock, Sondermeier shook his head with a thoughtful expression and fetched the ladder. Kofler clambered down, and said: 'Please don't get the wrong idea, Sondermeier. I am a somnambulist. It's a terrible affliction, believe me.' Then he went into the house, shivering all over. The sequel was a very nasty bout of enteritis.

The Princes Otto and Ignaz travelled incognito as the Counts von Scheyern — there was no need to broadcast to all the world how much fat the Royal family could lay down.

Needless to say, they did not keep up this charade during their Papal audience. The Holy Father spoke quite openly of the Prince's strange affliction, offering much solace and adding a special, additional, blessing upon the three feet by which Prince Otto towered over him.

Apart from the vast crowds that collected to look at the giant whenever he went sightseeing or visited a museum, and the keeper's refusal to let the Prince climb the pyramid in Ghizeh, for fear that it might collapse under his weight, the tour proceeded without a hitch as far as Hong Kong.

In Hong Kong, the Princes were met by Professor Hingerl and Chief Consultant Dr Franckh, who had arrived a few days earlier by plane and had already enlisted the help of the German consul and a doctor attached to the German colony. The 'Red Junk', recommended by Suffragan-Bishop Zach, was easily located. But either the Suffragan had misunderstood his informant, or else the place had changed hands. Professor Hingerl, a bald man with a moustache, who from time to time still dressed in a stand-up collar and wore a pince-nez, had amused himself greatly by watching a lady, wearing roller skates on her hands and feet, strip while circling the stage. For the rest, the 'Red Junk' offered no entertainment of the required type.

The Professor threw himself fervently into the search for something more suitable. During the few days before the Prince's arrival, he had completely exhausted himself, but was otherwise in radiant good humour. He had managed to dig up four ladies, one of whom, he hoped, would suit the Prince very well, even in respect of her internal measurements. They were Madame Tang and her daughter Miss Cho, her niece Miss Wu and her daughter's girl friend Miss Ni. All of them were highly experienced and had been declared free of venereal disease. Mme Tang herself, according to Ashot Tigrumiyan, an Armenian night-club owner, had been wonderfully successful with a donkey; Miss Ni (on the reliable evidence of the Japanese night-club owner Tanajoke and his Philippine business manager, Luis B. de Suelvas-Suarez de Mendoza y Irribaja Santos) was a dab hand with a coconut. The ladies insisted at length that their real names were not Tang, Cho, Wu and Ni (meaning 'Dancing Peach-blossom', 'Dreaming Swan in Late Autumn', 'Choice Cloud Formation over the Emerald Mountains' and 'Waning Moon crossed by a Flight of Mandarin Ducks (as expressed by the character "Eternal Sorrow")') but something quite different. Tang, Cho, Wu and Ni were their stage names, specially adopted so as not to offend their relatives.

With the help of an interpreter, Dr Franckh undertook, not so much to explain things to the ladies, which would have

159

been superfluous, but to point out the very special requirements of their prospective client. Professor Hingerl, for his part, was to instruct the Prince.

A suite in the Plaza Hotel had been booked, and the ladies were shown up to one of the back bedrooms, through the servants' entrance. Dr Franckh and the interpreter joined them there. Next door was the master bedroom, and it was here that Professor Hingerl had been lecturing the Prince. What, in the circumstances, do you tell a young man who has lived all his life in complete seclusion? It is hard to say what the right approach ought to have been, but it was certainly not the one used by Professor Hingerl.

'Well, now, Your Royal Highness,' he said with that mixture of earthiness and scientific pedantry that is, alas, far too common in great physicians. 'You have absolutely nothing to fear, I assure you.'

The Prince looked puzzled.

Professor Hingerl stomped up and down and delivered himself of a technical lecture, interspersed with several not very funny jokes, by way of footnotes as it were, on the essence, significance and consequences of sexual intercourse. He unrolled a number of anatomical charts, pointed to a model, and drew freely on the blackboard he had ordered for the occasion. He ended with a not so much scientific as florid and down-to-earth description of the charms of Mesdames Tang, Cho, Wu and Ni.

'And that's that, Your Royal Highness.'

The Prince hunched up his gigantic shoulders and said: 'I'd rather not, if you don't mind.'

The Professor leapt back on to his feet and started his lecture — in compressed form and seasoned with several new jokes — all over again. This happened three or four times. But all the Prince ever said was: 'I'd rather not, if you don't mind.'

Then the Professor lost patience. 'I'm acting on the orders of His Majesty and of your mother as well. You will just have to lump it. Off with your trousers, if Your Royal Highness pleases.'

'Oh, dear, no. I'd much rather not,' said the Prince.

The Professor now pulled out all the stops of his great oratorical organ: he appealed to the Prince's dynastic honour, to his nationalism, to his manhood. But all the Prince did was to keep whining: 'No, please, I don't want to.'

Then the Professor tore open the door to the bedroom, where the four ladies were all sitting stark naked in a row. Dr Franckh and the interpreter had retired by then.

'On your marks,' said the Professor. Since the ladies did not speak German in any case, he did not bother to choose his words. They understood him well enough. Giggling, they all stood up and went across to the master bedroom.

'Please, I'd rather not,' said the Prince and looked away.

'Well, if that's not the giddy limit!' said the Professor. Then, turning to the ladies, he added 'Let's have a bit of the old one-two-three.'

The ladies needed no further urging and straightaway engaged in extremely enticing movements. 'By Christ,' said the Professor appreciatively, 'you don't get to see that sort of thing every day. And four of them, at that!'

'But I won't be able to,' whimpered Otto, though he did risk a glance at the ladies over his shoulder.

'But I've explained it all four times over,' said the Professor pointing to his charts and the model.

'But I didn't understand any of it . . .'

Then Professor-in-Ordinary Dr Hingerl lost his temper completely. 'Just take a good look, then,' he said. He dropped his trousers with lightning speed — the ladies' movements had encouraged him visibly — and completed his theoretical deliberations with a wholly practical demonstration.

'That's how it's done,' he said rather brusquely as he buttoned up his braces. 'And now there is not the slightest excuse . . .'

The Prince sighed. 'Could I at least have the blinds pulled down?'

An hour later, when Professor Hingerl peered cautiously back into the drawing room, the Prince declared roundly that he was desperately sorry he had behaved stupidly earlier

161

on. Now he was determined to take all four ladies back with him to Munich.

It proved more difficult to talk him out of that plan than it had been to coax him before, and Professor Hingerl and Count Durach had to fall back on stealth. When the Royal party boarded the ship in Hong Kong, Tang, Cho, Wu and Ni were fetched into the Prince's cabin and left there for an hour or so. Once Otto was fast asleep, the ladies stole out of the cabin on tiptoe and disembarked. By the time Otto woke up and noticed the deception the ship was well out at sea. He nearly jumped overboard.

The ladies had been subjected to a thorough gynaecological examination by Messrs Hingerl and Franckh immediately after their first encounter with the Prince. None of them had suffered the least damage.

Madame Tang, the 'Dancing Peach-blossom' said — through the interpreter — that she had been tremendously impressed. She had had many memorable experiences — on one occasion a mute had recovered his powers of speech in her arms; an epileptic had swallowed his false teeth during congress with her; and once the wooden leg of a retired RAF Squadron Leader had caught fire (no doubt due to the friction) — but never before had any of her clients grown by four whole inches during the act.

Professor Hingerl and Dr Franckh flew straight back to Munich, leaving the two princes in the care of Count Durach. After a brief period of mourning for Tang, Cho, Wu and Ni, Prince Otto declared that he had no other interests now, and that he would like to be introduced to some of the ladies on board. He came to know most of them intimately. In Tokyo he measured well over nine foot six inches. Luckily he did not grow by four inches on every such happy occasion.

Ex-King Luitpold lived on a hacienda in the mountains of Northern Brazil, close to the Equator. The hacienda was almost the size of the Kingdom of Bavaria, a fact that consoled the Royal Family — territorially speaking Luitpold was no worse off than ever he had been. They liked to say that the ex-King reigned over his hacienda, but that was far from true. During the first few months he had looked at the bailiff's account with unconcealed boredom, and had occasionally cast a tired glance at his herds of cattle from an aeroplane. Half a year later, he gave that up as well. Now, he did nothing but drink, and his only other memorable activity was sweating a great deal.

He would sit, an emaciated old man (though, in fact, he was in his early fifties) on the rear terrace of his manor, from where he could not even look at the river — just at the walls of the gigantic silos — and swill fig brandy, a potent local beverage that tasted like a mixture of honey and methylated spirits.

In August, the Princes and Count Durach made a detour from New York to visit the ex-King's hacienda. There they were introduced to Dr (*honoris causa*) Anton Joseph Kofler, who was also paying his respects to the ex-King — on Baron von Speckh's behalf. The ex-King was sitting as usual in his favourite, worn-out old wicker-chair and was sweating away. He had his back to the terrace door. An Indian servant, who had had the most essential German phrases knocked into his thick head, approached him reverently and announced the visitors. Ex-King Luitpold did not bother to turn round; he merely made a kind of deprecatory gesture, and in so doing knocked over the fig-brandy bottle, quickly catching it in mid-air with the assurance of a somnambulist. He used the extra impetus to pour himself another tumblerful.

The bailiff now tried his luck. And indeed, he succeeded in getting the ex-King to turn round in his chair and to stare at the visitors.

'May I present Your Majesty's son?' said the bailiff, pointing to Prince Otto.

'What of it?' said the ex-King and turned back to gaze at the silo wall.

The Princes and Count Durach stayed for four days, Dr (*honoris causa*) Kofler for only two. Luitpold ignored them all.

The ex-King, Kofler reported to Baron von Speckh on his

return, had been sweating like the proverbial pig. He could sympathize with the ex-King's predilection for fig-brandy. For the rest — and that was the result of his mission — there could be no question of restoring him to the throne after King Rupprecht's demise. There was nothing else for it now — the problem of Frau Marx would have to be discussed with Prince Otto.

Prince Otto had meanwhile (and particularly in Lourdes) made the acquaintance of a host of new ladies. The oppressive regularity of his bursts of growth abated, and his blood was not nearly as hot as it originally had been. Still, he never again lost his affection for the weaker sex. 'God knows,' said Counsellor-at-Law von Scheuchenzuber, 'it's in the family.' And Otto always remembered the four ladies from Hong Kong, Tang the 'Dancing Peach-blossom', Cho the 'Dreaming Swan in Late Autumn', Wu the 'Choice Cloud Formation over the Emerald Mountains', and Ni the 'Waning Moon crossed by a Flight of Mandarin Ducks (as expressed by the character "Eternal Sorrow")'.

Bourée

The shirt-sleeved beer evenings of the new generation of socialists were not Schneemoser's cup of tea, and not simply because the comrades kept making fun of his hair. Luckily they did not keep count of his haircuts, but on Monday one of them was sure to come out with the by now hoary old joke: 'Schneemoser, you ought to draw social security for your barber's bills.' Schneemoser always had his hair cut on a Tuesday; by Friday, no traces of that operation remained, so that another comrade could repeat the same joke. It was a good thing that they all had short memories, and that, in any case, they were not all that interested; even Socialists are mainly concerned with themselves.

Schneemoser's modest budget did not allow for more than two haircuts a month, but it was not purely for financial reasons that he had tried do-it-yourself methods. Alas, hair-cutting was one of the very few experiments in which Hermanfried Schneemoser had failed miserably. Even the best barber, they say, cannot cut his own hair. And so Schneemoser was forced to rely on others when it came to this, his weakest, point. He used three barbers as far away from one another as possible: Barber Grasmugg in Laim, Barber Frühauf in the Central Railway Station, and Barber Winterl in Herzogstrasse. He called on them in rotation: one every six weeks. As a result none of them grew suspicious.

This method had another advantage: Schneemoser who

was averse to mingling with the lower classes (at the time good socialists were still expected to do just that) was able to learn from his barbers what the man in the street really felt. And because Schneemoser had no less than three such reliable sources, he possessed himself of three distinct perspectives. Master Grasmugg in Laim was a Sudeten German. He had deserted during the war — which he had considered sheer folly — and had spent years in South America. He was also in favour of a moderate all-party dictatorship representing all classes, but with a slight Leftist bias (his ideal would have been a cross between Franco and Castro). Master Frühauf was a strict Catholic, and as such he ranted against immorality, communism and permissiveness; every time a girl passed his window with swinging petticoats — then the latest fashion — he would snap his scissors and shout: 'Off with them! That's what I would do, cut them off!' He was blindly loyal to Adenauer and thought that Hitler, too, hadn't been as black as he was painted. Master Winterl was an anarchist. 'Law and order is the scourge of mankind,' he used to say. The look of his shop bore him out. He was annoyed at everything and by everyone, including his wife, whom he often beat up on the grounds that only by destroying the insidious matriarchal rule that was sweeping the country was it possible to attain freedom, or rather disorder. 'The ideal,' he would often say 'is baldness. Total baldness. The void.'

Master Grasmugg was a keen supporter of Bayern Munich Football Club, Master Frühauf a supporter of the '1860 Athletics'. Master Winterl too, took a keen interest in the game: 'I would love to see the day,' he said with much gall, 'when all the clubs of the First Division lose their damn matches.'

Even before taking his law finals, Schneemoser had been forced to add a fourth barber — by then he had to have his hair cut every ten days. In Master Etzel, Tegernsee Landstrasse, Schneemoser discovered a freethinker, who believed that mankind would be as good as gold if only the ideals of true humanity were constantly held up before them. He worshipped Albert Schweitzer and supported the 1st Nuremberg Football Club. 'All we need,' he roundly declared, 'is to keep broadcasting: "Be good! Be peaceful! Be contented!" loud and clear, from amplifiers on every street and square.' If only that were done, mankind would respond magnificently. 'Because they'd keep hearing it all the time, you know.'

And so the barrister-to-be, Hermanfried Schneemoser, learned the views of the people from the mouths of their barbers. In particular, he knew all there was to know about the ups and downs of the three leading Bavarian First Division football clubs, and was thus able to keep up with the comrades over their beer. But there was one problem not even his four barbers could help him to solve: Schneemoser had come to realize that the hair on his body, too, was beginning to grow in a frightening manner.

Schneemoser, as we have said, did not love socialist beer-parties. And the comrades, in turn, did not love Schneemoser, though — for a time at least — he busily helped them to stick up posters. After six months of this menial activity he was made district secretary. By the time he took his written exams in October 1954 (naturally with top marks) he had already advanced to the post of legal adviser to the Royal Bavarian Social Democratic Party. And when he attended the Solemn Act of Homage in the autumn of 1955, he had already risen to further heights.

The Solemn Act of Homage

Ever since 1806, Bavaria had been a kingdom, with a proper monarch and a crown — a masterpiece of classicist craftsmanship, too large to fit the head of any Bavarian king, and hence kept behind plate glass in the Royal Treasury Museum. No Bavarian ruler had ever been crowned, for historical reasons. Who could have crowned the first Bavarian King in 1806? Napoleon? True, Bavaria was a kingdom by his grace, but no one was anxious to acknowledge that fact in public. The Bishop of Freising? Count Montgelas, the then *de facto*

167

ruler of Bavaria, was a freethinker. The King himself? Max I Joseph, a modest, downright bourgeois prince, was much too self-effacing for that. 'The burden of a crown is forced upon us, not assumed,' he roundly declared. And when Montgelas cited the example of the Elector Frederick III of Brandenburg who, 100 years earlier, had seen fit to crown himself King of Prussia by his own hand, Max Joseph retorted: 'Just so, of *Prussia*!' And that was a decisive argument in Munich, then as always.

Hence there had never been a coronation. But since something had to be done — His Majesty could not simply send out cards ('. . . have the honour to inform you that we shall henceforth be known as King of Bavaria and hope that we shall continue to enjoy your esteemed patronage . . .'), Montgelas decided to institute a Solemn Act of Homage. In 1825, when Ludwig I came to the throne, the act was repeated. In 1848, when it was the turn of Maximilian II, the act was omitted '*pro tem*, because of disturbances caused by our ungrateful subjects'. But the omission was not made good under his reign even when the said subjects had grown less disturbed, though never much more grateful. Only when Ludwig II ascended to the throne in 1864, was there another Act of Homage, the last for close on a hundred years. For when Ludwig II was deposed by his uncle, Prince-Regent Luitpold, and drowned a few days later in Lake Starnberg, his *pro forma* successor, Prince Otto, was mentally deranged, and as such not thought fit to receive the homage of his subjects. Ludwig III, the Prince Regent's son, had Otto I dismissed by Parliament in 1913, and since his predecessor was alive, Ludwig — perhaps for superstitious reasons — preferred to do without public homage. When Otto died in 1916, it was the middle of the war. When Rupprecht I ascended to the Bavarian throne in 1921 he took care not to upset the delicate constitutional apple cart, which suited him perfectly, by something as unequivocal as the Act. It was not until 1939 that the performance was revived — for King Luitpold I — by kind permission of the Nazis, who only agreed to it when reliable Bavarian sources pointed out that the ceremony was an ancient Germanic institution: the Goths had always paid homage to their Führer. (On hearing of this, Frau Marx, then still Adolf Hitler, is said to have toyed with the idea of performing the old ceremony on a Pan-Germanic scale.)

When Rupprecht returned to the throne in 1945, he had contented himself with presenting his own person, and that of Prince Otto his successor (as token that the dynasty had a solid future), to the American Military Governor. Since Rupprecht had already been King once before, an act of public homage seemed superfluous. And besides, such a ceremony would hardly have been opportune in the midst of the grinding poverty of his loyal subjects and the smoking rubble of the Royal city.

When Rupprecht died in 1955, he left two wills: one private and the other public. In the latter he appointed Prince Otto his official heir. The will was read out to the Diet, and duly approved. And that is how Ottito became King Otto II of Bavaria, Count Palatine bei Rhein, Duke of Bavaria, Franconia and Swabia, etc. etc.

But there were certain complications.

Though Otto was in full possession of his mental faculties, he now measured just under ten feet tall, and was as fat as a rhinoceros — so bulky, in fact, that he could barely stand on his own two legs, let alone move about. Nor was it at all certain that he had stopped growing for good. In short, Ottito was a monster, and it seemed doubtful if a monster should be allowed to reign over Bavaria.

Quite a few Bavarian and Federal politicians expressed the view that this was a golden opportunity to get rid of what was to their minds an outdated, and in a Federal Republic, rather unorganic form of government.

To spike the guns of these critics, old Counsellor-at-Law von Scheuchenzuber proposed to the family council that they had best drop Otto II, and following the precedent set under the reign of Otto I, appoint a Prince Regent. The term 'Prince Regent', after all, still had an alluring, indeed magical sound in the ears of all good Bavarians, Social Democrats included.

The next in line was the younger brother of the late King Rupprecht, Prince Franz. But Prince Franz was ninety years old, and he declined the honour. The family tree was brought out. The next but one in line was Prince Garibald, Prince Franz's nephew. Prince Garibald had just reached 54,000,000 and declared that he would much rather continue with his life's work than wear the crown.

The matter was delicate in the extreme. At this point, the family consulted Adenauer, who not only loved political suspense but was also a secret monarchist*. As long as Otto did not grow wattles, a verrucose skin or a tail, Adenauer replied, he had best remain King of Bavaria.

And Adenauer duly sent Vice-Chancellor Blücher to represent him at the Public Act of Homage.

At the time, the throne-room was still a heap of rubble, so the ceremony had to be held in Nymphenburg. It all happened on Wiesensonntag, the last Sunday in September, which marks the start of the Oktober Fest and the opening of the Agricultural Show. The date had been chosen by old Counsellor-at-Law von Scheuchenzuber with great imagination. After the Act of Homage, all the loudspeakers, barrel organs and other sources of noise, suddenly fell silent — everything had been organized to perfection and ran according to plan. Then heralds in white-and-blue jerkins marched

---

*More recent studies have shown that the only reason why Adenauer was attracted to the idea of becoming President of the German Federal Republic, on the expiration of Heuss's term of office, was that he looked forward to the Kaisership, that is to founding a brand-new dynasty. Needless to say, he was not thinking of the upstart Prussian crown of the Hohenzollern with their Wilhelms, but of the true crown of the old Holy Roman Empire, rendered immortal by Charlemagne. Following, so to speak, in the footsteps of Conrad IV, of the House of Hohenstaufen (1237-54), he would have been proclaimed Conrad V of the House of Adenauer. When a discreet opinion poll showed that it was impossible to drum up a majority in favour of this plan, even within the ranks of the CDU/CSU, Adenauer at once withdrew his name from the list of candidates for the Presidency. The agitated members of the Bundestag then chose Herr Lübke as a substitute, precisely because he had no children and was hence most unlikely to spin dynastic dreams.

170

across the festive meadow to the foot of the Bavaria Monument, mounted a special platform and blew a fanfare — duly amplified — into a microphone. One of them, dressed in gold, then read out a very brief proclamation to the effect that following the demise of his gracious and exceedingly beloved grandfather, King Otto II had duly ascended to the throne. As much beer as the populace could swallow that day would be paid for out of the royal purse. The herald concluded with a resounding 'Long live King Otto II!'

There was wild jubilation. Brass bands stepped out of the various beer tents and struck up 'God Save Bavaria', and the entire meadow joined in the noise — it could not be called singing, for no Bavarian knows more than the first line of his ancient national anthem. There followed a booze-up of superhuman dimensions. And when Counsellor-at-Law Dr. von Scheuchenzuber died about a year later, he could do so in the happy belief that his genial idea had helped to bind the nation to its dynasty for at least another generation.

All those who could prove they had been completely besotted that Wiesensonntag, were later handed a certificate and a special commemorative medal. Fugleman Pointner, whom the reader may remember from the events of 1952, had also been present at the Oktober Fest. He became so inebriated that the district surgeon readily endorsed his claim to two such medals.

The Act of Homage itself took place in a more dignified atmosphere. King Otto II sat on the throne draped in a coronation robe with a skilful perspective cut. The throne itself had been placed on a dais covered with white-and-blue carpets. (The special robe proved of little help. Ottito was so tall by then that he dwarfed everyone else, much as the Bavaria Monument dwarfed the heralds.) Pages stood on either side of the throne and held up the crown and other insignia. Federal gendarmes and police officers in full-dress uniform (at the time the German Army existed on paper only) formed the guard of honour. Also present were the Bavarian bishops in their robes, delegations of nobles, members of the Royal House, the entire Order of St George and also of St

Hubert, delegations from every Parliamentary Party, the Bavarian Senate, the Diet, leading civil servants, the mayors of all the larger towns, the three loyal subjects of the crown who had passed the venerable age of 100 (Farmer Schellkopf from Chieming who could boast the biggest goitre between Inn and Salzach; a retired head teacher from Nördlingen; and Ambros Fuetterer, a charcoal-burner from Kötzing who could call his the largest beard in the Bavarian Forest and who still consumed a whole tin of 'Lotzbeck No. 2' snuff every day); delegations from the railways, the post office, the various guilds, corporations, student associations, universities, patriotic societies, even a Prussian from Siemens and Co., such leading personalities as Carl Orff, Sigi Sommer, Baron von Speckh, and last but not least Therese Neumann von Konnersreuth who was stigmatized and hence a candidate for canonization.

Prime Minister Hoegner read the Proclamation. King Otto II swore to maintain the Constitution. Emilie, the Queen Mother, cried. Archbishop Baron von Hauberisser delivered an address. Jackie Roider sang a ballad in dialect, specially composed for the occasion. Finally, all those present, representing the entire nation, and repeating a formula pronounced by Prince Franz (the oldest member of the Royal House), swore everlasting loyalty to the new King.

By way of a finale, the Prime Minister (now Baron von Hoegner), Carl Orff, Thomas Wimmer (Chief Burgomaster of Munich) and other deserving personalities, were knighted, and among those who had been so honoured on previous occasions, the Director of Music, von Knappertsbusch, was made a full Baron and Counsellor-at-Law von Scheuchenzuber a Count.

Chief among the guests seated in the gallery, were Vice-Chancellor Blücher, representing the Federal Government, the Papal Nuncio, several ambassadors, and members of allied or related royal families.

Throughout the ceremony, Hermanfried Schneemoser had stood behind the Prime Minister, with the Social Democratic delegation. As everyone streamed out to the banquet (three

172

large tables had been allocated to the three estates; Schneemoser sat at the third, but he was present and that was
something) he could not deny himself the pleasure of running
into Anton Joseph Kofler, as if by pure chance.

'How do you do, Herr Doctor,' said Schneemoser.

'Oh it's you, Schneemoser. Thank you, I'm tolerably well,'
replied Kofler and quickly passed on.

In 1956, Schneemoser took his finals — needless to say,
cum laude, with a thesis on Bavarian electoral law. Bavarian
electoral law was so complicated that it needed a Schneemoser to plough through its thorny problems. The subject
had the added advantage of allowing Schneemoser to
graduate under a Prime Minister who also happened to be
Honorary Professor of Constitutional Law. Baron von
Hoegner, who had personally invented the complicated
electoral system and was, as ever, the perfect gentleman,
confessed quite frankly that young Dr Schneemoser had a
much better grasp of the whole subject than anyone else,
himself included.

During the autumn term of 1958, Dr Schneemoser took the
written, and in April 1959 the oral part of the State Examination, and again received top marks in both. When he stepped
out of the examination room — in which he had not only
outshadowed the other candidates for four and a half hours,
but had also put all the examiners to such shame that afterwards they hung their heads when they confessed their dis-
comfiture — some sixteen ministerial secretaries and heads of
government departments were waiting for him in the corridor
with letters of appointment. Dr Schneemoser chose to serve
in the Royal Bavarian Constitutional Court, in a post of
almost modest proportions, but extremely elegant nevertheless. He remained there for just a few months. In the summer,
he was elected President of the influential 'Association of
Social Democratic Academicians', and in September 1959 he
became legal adviser to the Munich city fathers. In 1960, the
SPD entered the brilliant young lawyer as a candidate for the

173

mayor's office, as successor to the old and revered Baron von Wimmer, who had expressed a wish to retire. Schneemoser was elected Chief Burgomaster of the Bavarian capital with an overwhelming majority. He was twenty-nine, the youngest mayor any large German city had ever known.

Schneemoser's first official act was of rather a private nature: he made confidential enquiries of the official registration office, now in his charge, whether one Xaver Bohrlein was resident in Munich. As far as the records showed, he was not.

Even before contesting the mayoral elections, Dr Schneemoser had dropped his four-barber system. Instead he had taken Master Frühauf's capable assistant, Klaus Knapp, into his confidence, and had asked him to call every five days. (After passing his State Examination, Schneemoser had rented a two-room apartment in Nymphenburg, which incidentally was not very far from Pippinger's Bakery.) The new arrangement had become unavoidable if only because Schneemoser now had to undress entirely so as to let Knapp shave his body. Needless to say he had been extremely careful in his choice of personal barber. Knapp was a lanky, skew-faced Prussian lad from the Siemens Settlement, not only skilled in his trade but also so unambitious as to be perfectly honest. Once he had been taken into Schneemoser's confidence, he nearly burst with pride at his own importance. No known torture would have wrested the secret from his lips. As soon as Schneemoser was elected Chief Burgomaster, he persuaded Klaus Knapp to give up his job with Master Frühauf altogether, and to take private service with him instead. Schneemoser was by then living in a villa in Ferdinand Maria Strasse. Knapp was given a room in the attic and it was not long before he took complete charge of the place — he liked to refer to himself as the butler. He even designed a special white and green uniform for himself. 'Snow,' he said 'and moss.'

Baron von Speckh's NPD never really took off, partly

because the nationalist idea failed to arouse as many sleeping dogs as the Baron had hoped — despite the funds from the GDR — and partly because, in 1953, few people would have dared to entrust the leadership of any party to the surviving top brass of the Nazi movement. Hence Baron von Speckh had to make do with second-and third-grade material, with people who, before 1945, had not got further than 'Deputy Chief Archivist of the NSDAP' or 'Party Delegate to the Alliance of Large Families'. The NPD did miserably in every election, so miserably in fact that the Office for the Protection of the Constitution, as the Baron learned in a roundabout way, considered it much too innocuous to ban.

In time, the bad news filtered through to the GDR bosses. During the summer of 1956, the Baron was again sent a ticket for a Festival. This time it was in Salzburg, and the opera was 'Idomeneo' under the capable baton of Karl Böhm. Ever since the Treaty of 1955, Salzburg had been neutral territory, and the Russians had set up a trade mission there, with an extravagantly large staff. This time, unfortunately, Baron von Speckh was unable to sell the unused part of his ticket — he had to suffer the entire opera (and what was worse in Italian, a language of which he understood not a word). When it was all over, his contact — another Kofler, a fact that quite startled the Baron, though it was a pure coincidence — invited him over to the Russian trade mission. Although the Baron was treated to sparkling Crimea wine, there was no mistaking the fact that his hosts were seriously displeased with him. That a man, who was obviously a senior secret agent and who did not even bother to use a pseudonym, addressed the Baron pointedly as 'Herr Speckh' was not the worst of it by any means, nor was the fact that he also called him a numbskull. The sting came with the announcement that the Baron would not receive another brass pfennig unless the NPD could show some tangible successes. No advances, no expenses — absolutely nothing at all. 'Not even for this visit?' asked the Baron in dismay. 'I say nothing at all,' hissed the secret agent. 'Not a pfennig. You may leave now, Herr Speckh.'

Avarice too has its good side. Another man might not have taken the insult lying down. The Baron, by contrast, looked deep into his heart and asked himself where he had gone wrong and how he might do better.

It was as a direct result of this bit of soul-searching that Frau Marx was received in audience by King Otto II.

The Baron's daring new plan was both deceptively simple and — as always — two-edged. He first approached Herr Globke, Adenauer's Secretary of State. Globke, who had been Counsellor to the Ministry of the Interior and an expert on questions of national status in Hitler's Third Reich (in other words, had been much more than a mere Deputy Chief Archivist) had no objection to Hitler's re-appearance as a private citizen. There would admittedly have to be an enquiry into the whole affair, but the enquiry could be dropped as quickly and discreetly as it would be conducted. It was an established historical fact that Hitler, personally, had not harmed the hair on a single Jew's head — indeed none of the Nazi top brass had had the least inkling of what had gone on in their concentration camps. Globke himself was proof positive of that. But Globke also advised the Baron to consult the Head of the Federal State in which Hitler proposed to reside, namely the King of Bavaria.

If Hitler re-appeared as a private citizen, the NPD would sooner or later have to make him honorary chairman — or so the Baron surmised. By itself that would not give the NPD a fresh impetus, but the resulting confusion was just what was needed. People would at least be forced to sit up and take notice of the NPD, if only to attack it, thus helping to swell its diminished ranks . . .

And if the plan failed, the Baron would at least be rid of Frau Marx, who had become quite a burden to him — the more so as her consumption of sweets and liqueurs kept rising all the time, both qualitatively and quantitatively.

Then there was a ghastly misunderstanding.

Baron von Speckh was acquainted with the King's Steward, Count von Durach (who owed him a fair sum of money). Ever since Ottito had returned from his world tour, it had been Durach's job to dig up ladies in Munich and nearby, and to convey them secretly to the Palace (so as to make Ottito forget the four peach-blossoms from Hong Kong, or perhaps to keep their memory alive — it all depends on one's point of view). The local girls did not, of course, bear such distinguished names as 'Choice Cloud Formation over the Emerald Mountains' — most of them were called Resi, Marie, Anna or, if they came from a more urban background, Helga, Sigrun, Christl, Sonya and Hermine.

'Well, well,' said the King, 'Frau Marx . . . and what might her Christian name be?'

Contritely, the Count had to confess his ignorance. He had been firmly convinced that, in this particular audience, Christian names would not matter.

When Ottito had taken one look at Frau Marx he began to shake with rage. 'Durach,' he roared, 'what the devil do you take me for! The likes of that! Don't ever dare to show your face again!' Then he rolled out of his armchair, squeezed his bulk through the double doors with amazing agility, and made straight for his bedchamber.

'A misunderstanding,' whispered the Steward and ran after the King, hoping to clear the air.

'I refuse to listen to you,' bellowed the King. 'You have been my Steward for far too long.'

In the confusion, no one paid any attention to Frau Marx. It would have been far better if they had. 'I'll teach him,' she declared — though no one was listening just then — 'to call me "the likes of that".' With trembling hands, she — or rather he — tore the black veil from her face, deftly combed a strand of hair — long since turned grey — across her forehead, took the moustache from her bag and stuck it under her nose.

Only one valet had watched Frau Marx's transformation. He went pale, and his eyes became glazed. Then he hugged the wall and wailed: 'No! No! That's him, that's him so help me God! He shook my hand in 1943 . . .'

The other valets looked up at last, but by then Hitler

was stomping through the antechamber. Two guards swooned on the spot, and as they fell their silver cuirasses clanked noisily on the marble floor. It was not surprising that they should have fainted, for the sight of Adolf Hitler dressed in a billowing black gown was enough to make even the boldest of men tremble.

Hitler made straight for a window, tore it open, and screamed into the night:

'Fellow Germans, men and women! We have borne years of sorrow and humiliation. But the day of our resurgence is about to dawn . . .'

He faltered.

Luckily the window gave on to the park, and since it was night, all the gates had been locked. His audience consisted exclusively of marble gods flanked by hedges of yew.

Hitler was not at all used to making impromptu speeches. Hence he repeated: '. . . is about to dawn.' Then he remembered a telling phrase from an earlier address: 'And this time we shall square accounts in the true National Socialist manner.'

By the time Baron von Speckh had rushed back from the King's bedchamber, the guards had recovered consciousness. 'Get a doctor!' bawled the Baron. One of the valets threw a chair at Hitler, but missed. Hitler cut short his speech and vanished.

Yes, he vanished. It is hard to believe that he should have known about the jib door behind the wallpaper, but then he always had a keen eye for architectural anomalies. The jib door gave on to a landing and stairway that led to the park, but though a full search was started immediately, and most systematically at that, the park was very large and the Führer could not be found.

Baron von Speckh had previously decided that, should Frau Marx ever return to Prien, he would have her committed to the Haar Mental Home without delay. Two male nurses with a straitjacket had been waiting in the Baron's house for several weeks. But Frau Marx did not turn up. Two months later, the Baron sent the nurses away. He did not know whether he ought to feel anxious or relieved.

In any case, he had Frau Marx's room turned out. The Baroness thought they would discover some great surprise, for Frau Marx had never allowed anyone into her room. The Baroness was disappointed. A tattered old book lay on Frau Marx's bedside table. It was called 'The Dukhobors. Their History and Doctrine'. It had come from the library of the Baron's late father, and Frau Marx must have taken it up with her quite some time ago. The Dukhobors ('Wrestlers with the Spirit') were a Russian sect with slightly anarchistic, or to say the least anti-clerical, ideas. They considered themselves specially chosen and believed that they were suffused with inner light.

Minuet II

The Baron's next great plan to help the NPD was not born until the winter of 1956, during a conversation with Fräulein Dr Gerch. It so delighted the contact man in Salzburg that he immediately granted the Baron a fresh subsidy, which though relatively modest was much better than nothing.

Fräulein Dr Gerch had arrived in Prien on Christmas Day. Dressed in ankle-length rubber boots, that set off her enormous feet, she had stalked tearfully through the slush from the station. It was the first time she had come without her Rudi.

At first, the Baron was completely unmoved by the sad tale of her unhappy 'Yuletide', but since no stock exchange reports appeared on Christmas Day, he had listened all the same, if only with half an ear.

Rudi Gerch had always been difficult at school. He found it hard to grasp the simplest ideas, and quickly forgot what little he had managed to absorb. He lacked concentration, and as if to compensate for his failure turned viciously against his teachers. He often cut lessons and was inordinately lazy to boot. Only in such practical subjects as gymnastics or handicrafts did he show the least promise. It was by dint of sheer will power that Rudi had passed his High School entrance examination; even so he was always bottom of his class and had been forced to repeat Form IV.

And he was not even a fair Nordic specimen of a boy. As the years went by, his legs tended to grow more and more crooked, his hooked nose more prominent, and his hair even blacker. Now, in the autumn of 1956, he was just on seventeen and back in Form IV for the second time. He was the oldest and at the time the smallest boy in his class, smoked like a chimney and was having an affair with a fifty-year-old, fat and buxom — almost titan — biology teacher.

'If only you knew what expressions he uses about his — what shall I call it? — adventures with that person! Words I have never heard before. Once he even forced her — just imagine! — to parade about naked in the garden, and then locked the back door on her! He looked out of a first-floor window — she has a maisonette in Trudering — and gloated while he hid from the neighbours behind a bush. I only hope he's invented the whole story.'

'Naked in the garden?' said the Baroness. 'I wouldn't do that for a million marks.'

'Don't blaspheme' said the Baron.

'And when he let her in again . . . no, I can't bring myself to repeat it. I would never have credited a biology teacher with such debauchery.'

'In her fifties, did you say?' asked the Baron.

'Yes,' sobbed Fräulein Dr Gerch, 'fifty-two or fifty-three . . .'

'Then they won't have any children. Lucky, that, or he might have to pay maintenance through the nose.'

'But that isn't the worst of it.' Fräulein Dr Gerch went on to explain that Rudi took no interest in things German or Germanic, that he scoffed at manly virtue and racial purity. 'And his teachers, too, do their level best to drag these great ideals into the mud. The least one might expect of them is neutrality, no matter what their personal views. Small wonder Rudi pokes fun at obedience and discipline, and that he is full of destructive ideas. And yet, his piercing black eyes often put me in mind of the Führer's. The whole class is apparently prepared to follow him through thick-and-thin. They have just elected him their representative — despite all the teachers' protests. He has founded a school paper, with himself as editor. And though the paper is regularly confiscated by the staff, it seems to enjoy a large underground circulation. It is called "The Red Fist". The first issue contained a poem by Rudi which began "Come then pupils, let's rally . . .".'

The Baron pricked up his ears.

'He would have been thrown out long ago, if it hadn't been for the biology teacher. And this despite the fact that he made the best art pupil in his class depict the scene of her sitting naked behind a bush, so that he could print it all in his filthy sheet. I really am at the end of my tether.'

'Do you absolutely insist on his taking the school certificate?' asked the Baron.

'I'd like him at least to become a PT teacher, seeing that he's no good for anything else,' howled Fräulein Dr Gerch.

'And where is he at this moment?'

Fräulein Dr Gerch sat up straight. 'He didn't bother to come home on Christmas Eve. He has gone. He hasn't been home once since the end of term . . .'

'He's probably with the biology teacher . . .'

'I rang her place, but no one answered . . .'

'They must have gone to St Moritz then,' said the Baroness coolly.

'But he can't ski.'

'Perhaps he sets her hopping through the snow without any clothes on.'

And, in fact, Rudi had gone away with the biology teacher, though not to St Moritz, but only as far as Lech. There he had made the acquaintance of a rich young American lady, whom he had joined on a trip to the Riviera, after first locking the naked biology teacher in the hotel broom-cupboard and giving all her clothes away to the village needy.

Next, the American lady had persuaded him to join her on a world tour. They went first to Paris and booked a flight to Tokyo. Rudi was touchingly attentive to Sheralee (that was the lady's name), showed her round the French capital (which he had not visited before), escorted her to the most expensive restaurants (she footed all the bills), and took full charge of her traveller's cheques. Two days later, when they were sitting in the plane, seat-belts already fastened, Rudi said he had to go out for a minute. He never returned. Sheralee had cramps all through the long flight, and when she discovered in Tokyo that Rudi had sent all her luggage on to Buenos Aires, she had a nervous breakdown.

Rudi spent Sheralee's money — not very much, only $1000 — in Paris. He returned home in mid-January, and made straight for the biology teacher. Outside her door, he sang the tender melody to which they had danced once upon a time, and then presented her with a paprika-coloured brassière from Paris. When it came to his mother, his physical presence was enough of a gift, or so he believed.

'That's our boy,' the Baron said to Kofler when they were alone.

'Are you out of your mind?'

'Why? I'm not proposing to give him money.'

And in fact it was not the Baron who provided Rudi with money, but the NPD. This was agreed during a secret meeting in February 1957. The NPD would not only subsidize the 'Red Fist' and equip a discussion centre, run by Rudi, but even pay for a Youth Group visit to Cuba.

Dr (*honoris causa*) Kofler, by now a Federal Minister, spoke to the Bavarian Ministry of Education on Rudi's behalf. Rudi flunked no further examinations. And Dr Kofler did not have to press his case too energetically with the headmaster, who was only too happy to see Rudi's back.

Rudi then enrolled in the University. There, he chose to read a subject that not only happened to be the latest fashion but was also in keeping with his rather intangible scientific talents. That subject was sociology.

In 1958, ex-King Luitpold died in far-off Brazil. The priest from the nearest hamlet was unable to land — a flood had submerged the hacienda airstrip — and had to cover the last

183

stretch — some sixty miles — in a jeep. And so the consolation of Mother Church came too late. The King had only just been able to take a last swig from the fig-brandy bottle before changing position in his sweaty bed under the mosquito net, thus turning his back on death at the very moment the great leveller entered the room.

In Munich, King Otto ordered state mourning for a seemly interval. Ex-King Luitpold's remains were brought home and buried solemnly — but without great pomp and circumstance — in the family vault in the Theatine Church. The funeral banquet was a family affair, at which Ottito could safely wear a thin — non-perspective — toga (with black piping as a sign of mourning).

'It's a long time yet, I know,' said Princess Laetitia Annunziata to the bereaved Queen Mother, 'and I don't wish to press the point, but what happens when it's Ottito's turn for the vault? Is there room enough?'

'How very tactless of you,' said the Queen Mother.

No one suspected that this problem would solve itself, quite automatically as it were.

In 1958 there also occurred the sad demise of Princess Hildegard, the widow of Prince Moritz of Hesse-Darmstadt. Court mourning was ordered for her as well — after all she had been a Princess of Bavaria by birth — and she too was buried in the family vault.

It was with mixed feelings that the family learned of Princess Judith's intention to attend the last rites, for though she was the oldest daughter of the deceased her youthful escapades had been far from forgotten. (She had been living in South America for nearly thirty years, and the family had never once mentioned her name during all that time.) Their fears proved completely unfounded. Gicki was now close on fifty, still handsome, wore the most elegant clothes, and was perfectly discreet in everything she did. And when she decided to stay on in Munich there was no one to stop her, now that her mother was dead. The family discovered to their astonishment that the villa in Bogenhausen, which Gicki now claimed as her own, was still standing.

Somewhat nostalgically, Gicki walked through all the rooms with a notary, opened the shutters which Bohrlein had closed in May 1945, and kicked up the dust of a whole decade with every step she took.

'It seems,' Gicki said to the notary, 'as if the clock has gone backwards here.'

'I beg your pardon?'

'Oh, nothing.'

Thoughtfully, she stopped before the 'Arcadian Landscape' with three pianos. Next day she had it taken away. For the rest, she devoted herself to good works and to reptiles. In South America she had developed a great love of lizards and related creatures, and she now kept scores of iguanas, axolotls, cave-dwelling olms, and even snakes. These pets lived in a delicately controlled artificial environment in the basement, last inhabited — though unbeknown to Gicki — by Bohrlein and Schneemoser. It was a wonderfully peaceful world down there. From gigantic terraria — resplendent with horse-tail, sweet flag and a host of venomous green and violet blossoms — motionless alien creatures displayed their glittering scales; occasionally a chameleon would spread its two toes or whip its long tongue at a passing fly. The pale olm described its blind circles in an artificial cave. A monitor sat on a stone, holding a fish in its mouth and chewing once every hour or so; from time to time it would beat the brackish water with its long tail.

'Ugh!' said Gicki's sister, the Queen Mother, when Gicki showed her the terraria one day. 'If I don't get out of here this second, I'm sure to have nightmares.'

'They make no noise,' said Gicki placatingly.

Gicki's zoological adviser was Professor Burr, an eccentric, who since his youth had focussed his passion on lizards. For years he had — without noticing it — been dressing in lizard-coloured suits, and was slowly beginning to assume a greenish complexion. It was Professor Burr who had persuaded Gicki not to waste her charitable efforts on Catholic working men's clubs or on the Third World, and to concentrate on dumb creatures instead. And that is how it came about that on 14 June 1961, the twentieth anniversary of her father's death, Gicki founded the 'Prince Moritz House for Reptiles and Amphibians' in Hellabrunn Zoo.

During the opening ceremony, the director paid tribute to the Princess' generosity, and to his famous colleague Professor Burr. It was with great pleasure that he also welcomed the Chief Burgomaster, who had honoured the occasion with his presence.

When he had been elected Chief Burgomaster, Schneemoser did not for a moment think that he had reached the peak of his career. On the contrary, all who knew him personally — and these were few and far between — thought they detected an increase in his maniacal devotion to work. Schneemoser took personal charge of nearly every department, and fable had it that he could study and memorize by heart four official files at one go. During important discussions he would, like one doodling while deeply immersed in thought, write long letters and memoranda concerning quite other matters) while at the same time not missing a single point of the discussion. He would turn up in his office at 7 a.m., scan the morning papers for anything they might have written about him, rush indefatigably from conferences to meetings, from interviews to committees, listen patiently to the complaints of every last lavatory cleaner from remotest Thalkirchen, and conduct Council meetings with so firm a hand that even the CSU councillors (i.e. the Opposition) dared not utter a sound. He called himself a democrat and did as he pleased. As well, he wrote articles for the press, received delegations of mayors, deputations in national costume and astronauts. He opened nursery schools, regularly tapped the spring beer on Nockherberg Hill, and even found time to honour the opening of the Prince Moritz House in Hellabrunn Zoo with his presence.

His working day never ended before midnight. Then he was driven home, where he put on his slippers, drank the coffee his 'butler' Knapp served him, stirring it with a biscuit,

186

before sinking into a comfortable armchair to open the *New Law Weekly*, in order to familiarize himself with all the most recent constitutional decisions.

Twice every day he retired from public life, usually between 10 and 11 a.m. and again between 6 and 7 p.m. Then Klaus Knapp would enter his office secretly through a back door — for which reason he became known as the *éminence grise* of the Town Hall — to cut the Chief Burgomaster's hair and to shave him. Twice a week Schneemoser would also have to strip and lie down on a sofa covered in special oil cloth, so that Knapp could remove the proliferating hair from the rest of his body.

There was no alternative. Schneemoser had asked Knapp to look for depilatory salves and ointments, but though Knapp studied the relevant trade journals with the greatest zeal he failed to discover the answer. Unfortunately, ours is the age of the bald, and advertisers are all of them anxious to sing the praises of hair restoratives. As a last resort, Knapp began to correspond with various American institutes, and even tried their cures — but all to no avail.

The opening ceremony was followed by a tour of the Zoological Gardens. It was noon by then and very hot. Most of the animals had crept back as far into the shade as they possibly could. The apes were lazing about on their branches. Only a gorilla ambled forward on all fours as the guests of honour filed past his cage. He was a huge animal, old and grey.

'Whatever is wrong with him?' asked Princess Judith, when the gorilla suddenly rose to his full height and bared his teeth at her.

'Nothing at all,' said the Director. 'He is our oldest ape. His name is Lohengrin. His father, Parsival, was also in this zoo. He died during an air raid . . .'

Princess Judith turned away with obvious lack of interest, and then moved on. When Schneemoser looked back at the apes a moment later, he saw the gorilla raise his right hand

and wave at him.

Professor Burr had noticed, as well. 'Very interesting,' he said. 'Was he saluting you, Herr Chief Burgomaster?'

'I don't think so,' said Schneemoser in a tone of voice that took Professor Burr completely aback.

Gigue

The continued efforts by the Murat family — of which Princess Laetitia Annunziata was a distinguished member — to climb to ever higher rungs of the noble ladder by marriage, culminated in the Princess's attempt to marry her daughter off to King Otto.

Prince Garibald the Counter and Princess Laetitia had three children: Prince Ignaz, who had accompanied Ottito on his world tour, Prince Hezilo and Princess Ludaemilia. Ludaemilia, so her mother had decided, must become Queen at all costs. When consulted about the matter, King Otto said point blank that he did not care one way or the other; all he cared about was to keep the memory of his Hong Kong peach blossoms alive. For the rest, his thoughts might well hold a little extra room to accommodate a queen.

'He takes after his grandfather, the late King Rupprecht,' said Princess Laetitia Annunziata with an affected smile. 'And after Rupprecht's grandfather, the Prince Regent, as well.'

The Queen Mother would have liked to slap her face.

But there was one grave impediment to the marriage. Just before his thirtieth birthday, Otto had had another burst of growth — not only in height (the doctors had recorded an increase of thirteen inches) but also in girth. In the fully restored Palace to which the King returned in 1961 — previously he had spent most of his time in Nymphenburg —

the floors of the Royal suite had been reinforced with triple steel girders. And then there had been the accident, hushed up with some difficulty. During the night of 26 September 19—, His Majesty had exploded one Ursula Wildmann, a twenty-six-year-old divorced illustrator.

Paris, Count of Firman, the new Steward — Count Durach had shot himself soon after the Frau Marx affair had dealt so severe a blow to his honour — had employed Frau Wildmann several times in the King's service, and the King no less than Frau Wildmann had always declared themselves perfectly satisfied with the arrangement. And then the explosion had to happen! The King, a wobbling mountain of naked flesh, sat in a corner of his chamber, towering above the canopy bed and looking like the potbellied creation of a Mannerist artist with a hankering after the grotesque. Two valets and a doctor were picking the remains of Frau Wildmann from the sheets.

'He certainly did not do it on purpose,' said the Queen Mother to Suffragan-Bishop Zach. 'But it does make me wonder about his marriage.'

Suffragan-Bishop Zach asked for an audience of Cardinal Hauberisser, who in turn consulted the Pope.

Unchastity is considered a particularly grave sin by the Catholic Church. In its eyes, unchastity comprises most things that unmarried people do to each other, and several things that married people do as well. If the King consorted with girls from the lower classes, that of course was quite a different matter — but when it came to a King and his Queen, things simply had to be in apple-pie church order. The Pope thought of a way out: he granted the Royal couple a special dispensation by which they were allowed just one provisional sin, namely a trial union. Should the result be such that no marriage could be solemnized, then Ludaemilia would remain a pure virgin in the eyes of the Church. The trial union, however, so the Pope decreed, must take place under direct spiritual and medical supervision.

Rudi Gerch had been reading sociology for six terms without any success. True, he had signed in for several lectures, and had occasionally even sat through them, but only in order to interrupt the lecturer almost as soon as he entered the room, and to demand lengthy discussions of quite irrelevant topics. He had joined the Socialist German Student Society (SDS), but refused to paste up SDP posters and caused confusion at every meeting of the SDS he attended. He fired words like bullets from a machine gun. He had a ready supply of radical catchphrases liberally sprinkled with jokes, which he knew how to re-arrange with kaleidoscopic skill and thus dish up time and again. For the rest, he seemed to swim in money — nobody knew why or how.

As a rule, Rudi did not bother to ask for permission to address Leftist meetings. He would generally arrive, as if by pure chance, roughly an hour after the meeting had started, at the precise moment when the official speakers had begun to bore the audience. He was invariably accompanied by a group of acolytes, and as soon as they stormed into the hall, the whisper would go up: 'Rudi is here!' From that moment, the official speaker might as well have been miles away.

Rudi never stepped on to the platform, but stood right in front of it, as if to demonstrate that he had no need of microphones or other artificial aids, and immediately let fly. His strident voice could be heard perfectly in the last row, and even the comrades at the very back of the gallery, who could barely see what was going on, would later declare that Rudi had kept his deep-set black eyes permanently fixed on them throughout. Rudi never spoke for less than two hours. He sweated profusely. A strand of black hair swept across his forehead, though no one deduced from all these indications whose godchild Rudi Gerch had nearly been.

It did not take long before Rudi Gerch was elected President of the SDS. He at once proposed a programme of university reform, which though it sounded extremely complex and sociological, could have been summed up in three words, namely: no more work. For all that, Rudi looked upon himself as the leader of a workers' movement. That movement — thanks to the good offices of Baron von

Speckh — had plenty of cash, was extremely active, and could boast a fine mouthpiece in Rudi's resurrected and greatly expanded 'Red Fist'. All it was short of was a few honest-to-goodness workers, a lack that Rudi was not alone in deploring.

There was no doubt: Baron von Speckh's political calculations were paying off at last. The gentleman in the Russian trade mission had good reason to be satisfied. The Neo-Nazis broke up SDS demonstrations, and the young Leftists broke up NPD meetings. All alike defaced their opponents' posters, had violent clashes, threw bombs, and generally made themselves known to the public. Life had at last been restored to the West German political scene, which previously had been a deserted landscape almost entirely devoid of extremism. There was no army. The Nationalists had been done for; the Communists were mouthing their ineffectual class slogans with about the same effect as the Salvation Army. The churches, whose leading luminaries had but recently been blessing Hitler's Pan-Germanic tanks and munitions, wisely kept their own counsel. Despite Adenauer, Germany might have been well on the way to liberalism and political maturity, had it not been for the intervention of Baron von Speckh. That intervention alone could not, of course, have explained the success of extremism. In all probability the threatened reign of political reason was something so alien to most good Germans, that they were only too happy to be threatened by red or brown hordes all over again.

The Baron often discussed these and similar matters with Rudi Gerch. He was not yet entirely satisfied.

'You are anarchists,' he said, 'and that's just how it should be. But no one needs discipline and order more than you anarchists do. Else you'll never get anywhere. You don't surely want to remain a debating society and talk yourselves into a political grave within two years? Chaos calls for the most rigorous planning.'

Rudi nodded. 'I know it does. But believe me, it's an uphill struggle.'

'Of course, I realize that you are anti-authoritarian. But let me tell you, young friend, undisputed authority alone can guarantee the victory of the anti-authoritarian principle.'

'But all these fellows are so happy-go-lucky. "Demos before lessons", is all they believe in.'

Still, the real thorn in the flesh of the Left was the persistently negative attitude of the working class, an attitude that — as any fair person will grant — all genuine labour movements must find extremely distressing.

'I'll bet that you've never had a single worker at any of your meetings,' said the Baron.

'That's not so,' said Rudi, but without much conviction.

In the middle of Our Lady of Succour Square, Munich, stands the Church of Our Lady of Succour. The square is the centre of the Au district, inhabited by labourers and other underprivileged members of the affluent society. On the left corner of the square, a commune had recently been established and its members served more or less as Rudi Gerch's general staff. We have said the left corner of the square, but that, of course, depends on where you stand. If you look out from the church, Rudi's is indeed the left corner, but from another angle it is, in fact, the right.

The commune had chosen the Au district because of its 'sociological structure'. This may explain why they raised no protest when they discovered that the locals had abbreviated their official name of 'Commune in the Left Corner of Our Lady of Succour Square' to the 'Suckers' Commune'.

Rudi Gerch was not an official member of the Suckers, though he spent most of his time with them. More precisely, while he pretended to be a member, he in fact lived in a two-room penthouse in elegant Schwabing.

Besides Rudi Gerch (who may be considered as so to speak a corresponding member) the commune consisted of seven adults and two children, namely:

1. Horst Luther, student of sociology and part-time playwright. When the dishwasher broke down Horst immediately warned the comrades not to let him anywhere near the damn thing because he was all thumbs on both hands.

2. Walter Dietrich, student of sociology, whose hair was rather sparse, for which reason he inveighed vitriolically against long hair in general and beards in particular as clear signs of a petty-bourgeois and pro-capitalist attitude, but failed to stem the rising tide. (He subsequently acquired a wig.) Walter was quite prepared to have a closer look at the dishwasher, but when he had done so, merely shrugged his shoulders and returned to the sofa to encourage the growth of his sparse hair.

3. Bruno Heilmann, nicknamed 'Croco' because he never took off his crocodile-skin cap — not even in bed. 'It's not because it's expensive,' he explained, 'but simply because crocodile skin has something tremendously aggressive about it.' In Croco's view the dishwasher concerned no one but the female members of the commune. Croco, too, was a student of sociology.

4. Marvey D. Johnson, American, and as far as the others could make out, another student of sociology. Either Marvey failed to understand what was wrong with the dishwasher, or else he merely shammed ignorance. In any case, he did nothing at all about it.

5. Hans Kuno, Baron von Freiendorff and Kämpenhausen, known generally as 'Arse', after his favourite expression. Arse, as his original name indicated, came from an enormously feudal family, which may explain why he was so Maoistic as to reject Mao himself as a rank revisionist. Arse readily granted that he was perfectly capable of dealing with any kind of dishwasher, but went on to declare that he was damned if he would. He was a revolutionary, and anyone who thought that was not enough needed his authoritarian arse kicked. Arse himself was not a student of sociology, but had been threatening for two years to enrol in the faculty the very next term.

6. Annemie Runkel, known affectionately as 'Rabbit',

student of sociology, and six foot three inches in her socks. Croco often asked her to undress, so that he could lift up one of her gigantic breasts and let it drop back with a resounding smack. The sound would make him laugh uproariously. 'I sometimes think,' Arse told Rabbit on many such occasions, 'that you are nothing but a goddamn bloody petty-bourgeois.' Croco had tried to pay him back for this insult by throwing Rabbit's breast straight into his face. Rabbit started to mess about with the dishwasher but without any success.

7. Monika Runkel, Annemie's younger and smaller sister, and the mother of the commune's two children: Che-Nasser and Grisha. (Grisha was a girl. Her name had been chosen because it ended in 'a' and had therefore been mistaken for a girl's. When the commune learned that it was a Russian diminutive for Gregor, it was too late to do anything about it. By that time the commune had, moreover, long since disowned the Russian brand of communism.) Monika, a student of sociology, told her sister to stop messing about with the dishwasher before she ruined it completely, and rang up Rudi Gerch instead.

'Is it still under guarantee?' Rudi asked.

'How the hell should I know?'

'Don't you have the receipt?'

'We never bother to keep that sort of muck.'

'Well, have a look at the dishwasher itself. It will say "Miele" or some such name. Then look in the telephone book. The firm is bound to have a service department. Ring them and ask them to send someone along.'

And that is how it came about that a mechanic turned up the very next day. He arrived at about 10 a.m., 'shortly after midnight' as Croco called it. Rabbit opened the front door in her birthday suit, as if that were the most natural thing in the world to do. The mechanic gaped, swallowed a few times, and then set to work.

He was about fifty, well-set and short, wore a dirty blue overall and a greasy grey cap. He smoked a small square pipe with a horn mouthpiece.

Croco, who was the first to get up, came into the kitchen

for his butter-milk — without which, he claimed, he could not wake up properly. ('Butter-milk!' Arse always said contemptuously. 'You are a hopeless goddam' petty bourgeois!') Croco looked at the mechanic reflectively for quite some time, and then went back to join the others. 'We've got one, mates!' he said. 'A real worker at last, in overalls and the lot!'

All of them, including the children, now stepped gingerly into the kitchen to gawp at the mechanic. Monika rang Rudi Gerch and told him the latest news. 'I'm coming over at once,' said Rudi. 'Keep offering him beer, and make sure he doesn't leave.'

There was no shortage of beer. Rabbit — now fully dressed — went out to buy the cheese spread and the rolls the mechanic had asked for. He resolutely refused to have any of Croco's butter-milk.

'That proves it,' said Arse.

'Solidarity!' said Rudi to the worker. 'I am Rudi.'

'Huh?' said the worker.

The whole commune, including Rudi, were now squatting in a semi-circle round the mechanic. (The dishwasher was working again.) He himself was seated on a stool, and after finishing his cheese spread and rolls, asked for another beer, and relit his pipe. Everyone was feeling slightly embarrassed. Croco tried to break the ice.

'Why don't we do something amusing? Rabbit, get undressed!'

'Don't you dare!' hissed Rudi.

'Okay then, don't,' said Croco.

'Are you in a Union?' asked Rudi.

'No, I'm not,' said the worker.

'And why not?'

'The subs are too high.'

'Hm,' said Rudi.

The conversation dried up again.

'Is there any more beer?' said the worker after some time.

Rabbit went to fetch one.

'Don't you keep any chairs round here?' asked the worker.

'Oh, yes, but not enough,' said Walter.

'It's a nice place,' said the worker, 'but a bit too filthy for me, I must say.'

'I see,' said Rudi, 'is your place much cleaner then?'

'You bet it is,' said the worker. 'My Zeni, that's the missus, is not what you might call quite right in the top storey, and if she didn't keep the house clean as well, by Christ I'd show her.'

'Show her what?'

'I'd let her have it, by Christ, I would!'

'You'd hit her?'

'And how! That's just what a woman needs, if you ask me.'

'Well, if that isn't the giddy limit,' said Rabbit. 'And in this day and age, too . . .'

'You'd better dry up,' said the worker. 'Running about in your birthday suit . . .'

'Do as he says.' ordered Rudi. 'We shan't get anywhere like that. Now look, Comrade . . .'

'I'm no bloody comrade, so watch it . . .'

'Well, then: "friend",' said Rudi, 'do you really think it right to hit your own wife?'

'Of course I bloody well do.'

'And I suppose she takes it all lying down?'

'I told you. There has to be some order in the place.'

'But what kind of order? That's the question!'

'Just plain order,' said the worker. 'And if the whole lot of you was to do labour service, as we had to do, you wouldn't have no time left over for all your rubbish.'

'What rubbish?'

'For none of it. All you're good at is smashing things up. That's no bloody good to nobody. For Christ's sake, can't you get it into your thick heads? If all you students and communalists was only to pick up a shovel! But you never do. And you might stop talking all that muck, too. I've slaved away all my bloody life. You young people don't bloody well know what it's all about. You're too damn bored with everything. Yes, bored. And why? Because you've had it too good, that's why.'

'We sha'n't get anywhere like this,' said Rudi.

'You're dead right, you won't, because there's no order. You block up the streets with your bloody demonstrations. So that decent people, who've done a decent day's work can't get their bloody tea in time. As if the roads aren't bad enough as it is. You ought to be paving the damn roads, that's what. You'd be doing a good day's work, better than shooting your mouths off. Adolf would have cut off your bloody hair. For the sake of law and order. And he'd soon have settled your hash, believe me. And not the kind of hash you're thinking of neither.'

'What exactly are your objections to . . .'

'It's full of nits, your hair, and filthy enough to stand on bloody end. I'd give myself the bloody creeps walking around with all that greasy muck on my head, so you can't tell if it's a bloody him or a her underneath. It's just no good, if you ask me.'

'But shouldn't you first . . .'

'I wouldn't even let you open your bloody mouths. Cut the damn stuff off, first, that's what I say. Do you have another beer? Let's have it.'

'So you think,' Rudi said, 'we must take the present state of affairs lying down . . .'

'Not on your nelly, I don't. There's nothing in it for the likes of me. Just for you bloody students. What with grants and the likes, just so that you can score more hash. — Thank you very much, and all the best!' (Rabbit had fetched another beer.) 'If you ask me, they ought to bring down the price of food. The pensioners are all of them starving to death, that's what they are. Perhaps some of you will have to live off your bloody pensions one day as well. Then you'll change your tune quick enough, believe me. Then you'll really have something to demonstrate about . . .'

'That's something altogether different . . .'

'Sex and mini-skirts. I don't go to church, I've got no time for those parasites in black. But when it comes to sex, they're only too right. It's everywhere you bloody well look, you can't get away from the damn thing. Sex, nothing but bloody sex. That's bound to lead to rape and bank robbery, if you get me. Clean the whole mess up, that's what I reckon. Law and order. Off with the long hair. Clean the place up. And if you don't like it, well, the sooner you get out the better. Out, I say. The whole damn lot of you, and the foreign workers, the damn sky pilots and the Jews, as well. Let them fuck off to Israel, and let Nasser send a rocket up their backsides. I hope you don't mind a bit of plain speaking. And many thanks for the beer and the grub. I have to be off now.'

'Well, that's that,' said Rudi after he had left. 'Still you have to admit he's pro-Nasser. That's something to work on.'

'If only I knew what he was talking about,' said Horst.

'Is that supposed to be a worker?' said Arse.

'The system,' Rudi explained, 'has had a hundred generations to corrupt his consciousness. And it will take socialism two or three generations to set it right again. But what is that by comparison?'

And yet even Rudi could not get rid of a flat feeling for several days to come.

'Herr Gerch,' said Baron von Speckh, 'your movement will have to be placed on broader foundations. You have been turning the student movement on its head, and that is how it should be. As you recently told me with justified pride, no German university would nowadays dare to pull such old tricks as a rectorial ceremony. You have as good as paralysed all lectures. But when all is said and done, it doesn't amount to very much. Life outside goes on regardless.'

'It's the system,' Rudi said.

'If you don't give your movement broader foundations, you might as well pack it in.'

'Do you want us to start shooting, Herr Baron?'

'You might have something there!'

The date for the experimental royal union was set for 23

November, the night of the re-opening of the Court National Theatre, which had been destroyed in 1943. That night, Professor Johannes Baron of Knappertsbusch conducted Richard Strauss's 'Die Frau ohne Schatten', with the bridal pair sitting in the royal box. Princess Ludaemilia, who must have felt poorly for more than one reason, was glad that the opera dragged on for hours.

Dr Hermanfried, Baron von Schneemoser since the day before, the Chief Burgomaster of Munich, a city now graced by a new opera house, sat in the royal box too.

Like all great cities the world over, Munich had grown too small. Though people have changed their minds a great deal since, at the time they all firmly believed that the congestion could be overcome by improving the traffic system. Schneemoser devoted most of his superhuman labours to this problem. His favourite schemes were a ring road round the Old City — a plan to which most of the Old City eventually succumbed — and an underground railway. Soon after Schneemoser's triumphal installation in the Town Hall, workmen had started to dig with a vengeance. Gigantic moles drove shafts under the city from all possible directions. Tomorrow, as Schneemoser informed the King, would be a momentous day: the two main tunnels, one running north from Marienplatz and the other south from the Triumphal Arch, would — if everything went according to plan — join up and meet beneath Odeon Square.

The King seemed interested, and when Schneemoser invited him to be present at the great occasion, he graciously accepted. In his turn, he invited Schneemoser to the experimental union that very night. Schneemoser made his apologies; he had not yet finished his preparations for the next day, and the opera was going on for much too long. During the performance, Schneemoser read sixteen documents, some more than twenty pages long, concerning a compulsory purchase order, rejected them all, drafted a much better version, and prepared the speeches he and the underground expert would deliver the next day. And despite it all, when Princess Ludaemilia asked him how he had enjoyed the opera, he was able to reply: 'Very much indeed, Your Highness, except for the 2/4 — 3/4 part in the Third Act, you know, when the nurse sings: "Can you not hear me . . . horribly". The score calls for an *accelerando*, but Knappertsbusch, if anything, played the passage a shade more slowly than the preceding 6/8.'

Rudi Gerch had proposed a public protest demonstration against the opening of the opera house, which he described as a particularly provocative expression of the bourgeois-reactionary mentality, the more so as the opera house had been reconstructed in a classicist style and not in modern concrete. There would be a vast number of policemen so that nothing could be simpler than an exchange of shots . . . and then . . .

The Baron rejected the suggestion out of hand. He himself would be at the opening, and that being the case it would be much better to demonstrate against the opening of the underground next day.

'But this opera nonsense takes place in the evening, while the underground will be opened at ten a.m. At that time, most of the comrades are fast asleep.'

'I've told you: it has to be the underground. The police will probably be out in even greater numbers, and there'll be a lot of workers, as well.'

'Workers?' said Rudi. 'Oh, I see what you mean.'

While the court was proceeding to the experimental union, Baron von Speckh was engaged in a discussion with the retired Federal Minister Dr (*honoris causa*) Kofler. Needless to say, Kofler too had been to the opera. Speckh had ordered an extra room in the 'Walterspiel' and — *incredibile dictu* — had invited Kofler for supper.

'You are inviting me?' asked Kofler.

'And why not?'

'I mean are you proposing to pay the bill?'

'But of course,' said the Baron, ordering lobsters as if it were the most natural thing in the world to do.

They also consumed caviar, trout, snails and oysters, accompanied by port and champagne, followed by Turkish coffee, and a cigar for Kofler that did not merely look expensive but actually cost eight marks.

But mellow though this extravagance had made him, Kofler refused absolutely to have any part of the Baron's latest plan. In the end, the Baron had to produce the piece of paper Kofler had signed in Prien many years ago.

'I know a few things about you, as well,' Kofler said.

'Are you threatening me . . . ?'

Kofler twisted and turned.

'All those who have tried have lived to regret it, as well you know. And what do you think will happen to you, if our chaps do better than they did that last time?' The Baron pointed to the paper.

Kofler gave in once again.

Needless to say, none of Rudi's comrades knew anything about his connection with Baron von Speckh. Rudi himself, who had not been told about the ultimate source of his money, and hence surmised that it all came out of von Speckh's own pocket, would sometimes ask the Baron why he, a leading capitalist, was so anxious to subsidise the Left.

'I have a historical conscience,' said the Baron. 'I firmly believe that the future lies with socialism. And I would like to go to my grave with the feeling that I have done my bit for the future.'

'But you and your friends are surely the first whom a victorious revolution will do away with?'

'I firmly believe,' said the Baron, 'that the socialist future will not dawn until after my death.'

Rudi was highly sceptical of the Baron's historical conscience, and was not afraid to say so.

'Very well, then,' said the Baron. 'To tell you the truth, I have another reason as well. The real explanation is that your lot frightens those whom you call "my friends" out of their wits. At Board meetings, I am always delighted when one of my colleagues messes his pants. Absolutely delighted.'

Rudi was still sceptical, but a little less so. 'But what if we give your colleagues good reason to be terrified of us?' he asked.

'Nothing to it! I just turn off the money taps and the whole business is over.'

'Do you really believe it's as simple as that?'

'No money, no revolution. That's the way I read it.'

There Rudi had to agree.

That evening, Baron von Speckh handed Rudi his strategic plans for 'X-Day'. The uprising had been prepared down to the last detail, with provisions against every possible contingency. Rudi looked at this labour of precision with great astonishment. It was obvious that the Baron himself could not have compiled it during his leisure hours. He was on the point of asking who the author was, but then thought better of it.

'The plan keeps mentioning the "Carnation Murder". Whatever is that?'

'An event,' said the Baron. 'A certain event. The detonating spark. Think of the shot fired by the cruiser *Aurora*. Every revolution needs a detonating spark at just the right moment. Just an event.'

'But what sort of event?'

'You'll see,' said the Baron and smiled.

The trial nuptials were a complete failure, to put it mildly. When Princess Ludaemilia saw the reverend gentlemen and the doctors standing round the steel-girdered bed, she refused point-blank to enter it.

The bride's mother had a sobbing fit. Ottito lost interest.

The nuptials were called off. The Cardinal promised to contact the Pope once again to ask for a dispensation against the presence of the clergy.

The King retired to his own bed in a great huff.

The entrances to the underground tunnels were bedecked with flowers and pine. The VIPs, many of whom had not taken off their tail coats until the early hours of the morning, to don grey suits and striped ties after the briefest of naps, now stood in orderly ranks, smart plastic helmets on their important heads. (Even the Cardinal was wearing one.)

A tramway band struck up. Schneemoser delivered his speech and welcomed the King.

Then a huge drilling machine from the St Mary's Square side started up, and Lo! light shone through the tunnel and the spectators on the other side broke into loud cheers.

Schneemoser took King Otto's hand and stepped into the opening. A thunderous 'Hurrah!' reverberated through the shaft.

Whether this 'Hurrah!' was the cause of it all was something no one could ever discover. Suddenly the roof of the tunnel sent down small drips of water, followed by a downpour, and when clods of earth and paving stones started to come down as well, there was general panic. Everyone rushed to the exits — everyone, that is, except King Otto and Schneemoser who were stuck below. Otto had started to grow again, and Schneemoser's hair was oozing from every opening in his suit. Suddenly, all was darkness, followed moments later by the thunderous roar of a gas explosion. The last to emerge from the rubble later declared that they had heard one final scream, but they were unable to tell whether it had come from the King or the Chief Burgomaster.

The demonstration started off well, if somewhat tamely, despite the early hour. Rudi Gerch was not present, but that was part of the plan. The Baron had told him to keep himself in readiness just outside the city limits.

'In readiness for what?' Rudi asked.

'Just wait and see.'

And so Rudi and two of his comrades hung about a certain street corner in a northern suburb.

The demonstration poured eastwards from Königsplatz. On the way to Odeonplatz, they quickly did some unplanned damage to America House. Elsewhere, too, demonstrators abandoned the prescribed route. The Revolution, one of the comrades declared, was like a haycock, only the igniting spark was missing.

Just as the first barriers were being trampled down outside the Luitpold Block, and the first paving stones were being hurled at the police, a car drew up at a street corner far away on the northern suburbs.

Rudi stepped forward, recognized Kofler, and looked startled. Kofler fired three shots, and Rudi collapsed. Before the two comrades realized what had happened, Kofler had stepped on the accelerator and was gone.

The comrades dragged Rudi to a small hut on Oberwiesfeld. Here a hermit, Father Vassily by name, had been living rough for years. Father Vassily was a Dukhobor, and it was in his arms that Rudi died.

The news of his death spread like wildfire. It proved to be the missing spark. One of the comrades got out a bomb and attached its fuse to the 'Kienzle' wrist-watch Rudi had given him for just that occasion.

Even before the clocks on the churchtowers struck the noon hour, a preliminary government of the 'Fatherland-in-Need' Front, made up exclusively of NPD members, had taken over. Its first act of office was to send a huge contingent of policemen into the streets, with orders to put down the revolution. (The civic leaders who had attended the tunnel opening presented an easier target: they were herded into waiting buses and carted off to Dachau, where the old concentration camp still stood in most of its former splendour.)

The casualties consisted of 4,231 Leftists, twenty-two policemen, and one rough-haired dachshund. The elections, which the NPD government declared soon afterwards, earned it more than eighty per cent of all the votes cast. And this time Dr (*honoris causa*) Anton Joseph Kofler was much more circumspect: he avoided all garage roofs, thus making perfectly sure that the Fatherland's call reached him in time.

'They won't take your reptiles away,' said Professor Burr. 'They're not nearly as bad as they're painted.'

Gicki was quite unperturbed by all that had happened during the past few days. She had gone through quite a lot in her life. She now made for the basement, accompanied by Professor Burr, and watched the silent olm at its mysterious circles.

'A strange beast that,' said Gicki, 'ugly and beautiful all at once. At times, nature certainly delves deep into her secret depths, and comes up with quite a demon or two.'